The Huns

Edward C. Petrovics

The Huns

The Mystery

Swinre Publishers
Zwinderen

Manuscript copyright 2011 - 2020
Author: Edward C. Petrovics
Cover: AVC Support
Publisher: Swinre Zwinderen
First print: June 2018
First print US version: February 2020
ISBN/EAN e-boek US version: 978-90-828698-8-0
ISBN/EAN paperback US version: 978-90-828698-2-8
NUR code: 332

Time ticks
back and forth
slow fast
time like stone
or like bridge
time lives
do it over
time gives
then
time smothers.

The Huns

The Mystery

Sometimes, things cannot be explained. Sometimes it's better to just leave it alone. But when you start looking for the truth, start digging into the past, you have to accept the consequences. During a vacation in the rural province of Drenthe in the Netherlands, a young archeologist makes a mysterious discovery. A mystery that's out of this world. A discovery that will drastically change his life forever.

"The future has already changed,
I just have to still do it."

1　The hunt

Four feet rapidly follow each other like antelopes on the soft moss and the crackling leaves. Dead twigs succumb under the weight of the large, animal skin-covered feet and break the cold silence in the forest. The feet run like their lives depend on it. Now and then, the sounds of rustling leaves and snapping branches are complemented by terrifying screeches of a black crow and the mating call of an owl. The feet keep running imperturbably and make everyone believe they are running from something or initiated a chase. Thick trunks of ancient trees pass by in the background of the inexhaustible feet. The trunks are so large they are impossible to put your hands around. All those giants combined form an endless forest in which time has stood still for centuries, where time and space come together in a fourth dimension, where Albert Einstein's theory of relativity can triumph. A forest in which different events take place in the same place, at different times. Or where the same things happen in the same place, at different times. Nothing is what it seems, everything is causally linked. There is no distinction between the current, past and future. The sun shines through the dark canopy in this Minkowski forest. A fog of mist and moisture is lit up by the clear rays of sunlight. A shadow of a fallow deer shoots through this fog, startled by the approaching feet. An aardvark that's quietly scavenging in the bushes, almost invisibly, lifts his head and beholds the scene in shock. The spectrum of sound of the rustling leaves and the snapping twigs is audibly supplemented by fatigued panting and moaning. The back pair is unable to stop in time and slams into the forerunner, followed by nagging and grumbling.

'Shh,' it immediately follows. It echoes deeply into the woods. The one making the *shh*-sound is a tall, slim young man, covered in animal pelt and wearing an old rumpled hat on his head. He's holding a spear in an attempt to achieve the status of a tough, indestructible hunter. But he's not that indestructible. His long, slim posture gives him a lanky appearance. His kind face however makes up for this. A face masked by black mud smears, similar to military forces, in an attempt to become one with the surroundings. Long blond hair come out from under his hat. A single lock falls across the face. All this running visibly cost a lot of energy, because his forehead is covered in thick drops of sweat. Simultaneously with the *shh*-sound the hunter places his hand on the mouth of the grumbling grouch who bumped into him. Also a hunter, but of a much different stature. A somewhat shorter man with short, thick little legs, a stout figure and a dirty, round, balding head. He's also carrying a spear and wears an outfit of woven flax and animal pelt. He has a wide leather belt around his waist with a funnel beaker canteen. His round face is camouflaged, just like the other, mixed in with some visible cuts and lashes from branches. A plea can be read from his eyes. He's almost unable to breathe. After the hand of the tall young man is removed from his mouth, he remains quiet and subordinate.

The tall, lanky, but friendly hunter goes by the name of Hunze and is one of the warriors of the farming funnel beaker people who resides a bit farther down along the curvature of a creek. He's hunting a wild aardvark with his companion Ems. There's a feast in the village tonight. A spit roasted aardvark is the highlight of the feast, so Hunze and Ems cannot come home empty-handed. In that case they would lose all credibility as the hunters and warriors of the village. Furthermore, no food means no feast, so they must capture an aardvark. Hunze and Ems were given this responsible task by Chief Borg, a smooth-talking decisive warrior, with the persuasiveness of a true leader. He's a leader who however has a flip side. He enjoys good and especially a lot of food and beautiful women, the latter of which are scarce in the village. Most women in the village are farmers, so not at all the fairest. Borg's wife, Ambra, is a cozy, heavy housewife with frizzy hair. Some rotten teeth and molars are put on display whenever she laughs, and she often does. Her laugh can make the ancient trees in the forest shake. Ambra spends her days on taking care of the two children and cooking for her husband Borg. Ems' wife Driek is not much better. The large wart on her nose puts her dead last in the beauty category. She is lazy and doesn't do anything all day. She's only good and insatiable in one area… Nevertheless, Driek and Ems can't seem to have children.

An exception to all these natural disasters is Strum, the daughter of Zara and her husband Lute, the village musician. Strum is an exceptionally beautiful woman in her early twenties, with long, blonde hair, a perfect waist, an attractive face and a dazzling smile. Strangely, the villagers call her by a completely different name. They call her Aa. This name originates from her birth.

'Push Zara! Push!' Lute screams.

'Hgrrgghh… I can't push any harder.' Zara cries.

'I see the head… it's coming, it's coming.'

'Aahhh…' a proud Lute sighs, while hovering his thin face over the baby.

'We will call her Strum.' Lute solemnly vows.

'Aahhh…' Zara sighs.

The adorable aahhh-ing continued during Strum's childhood. An overwhelming 'Aahh' could be heard whenever someone came to visit and saw her lying in her cot. As a little girl she liked to play in front of the hut with dolls made from woven twigs. Every passerby just had to 'Aahhh' at the sight of her. She once ended up covered in manure between the pigs as a rebellious adolescent, and still everyone shouted 'Aahhh…'. When she paraded in the village square for the first time, with her long blonde hair in the golden sunlight, 'Aaahhh…' all over the place. And so it remained.

Aa is responsible for the laundry in the village. She works at the bed of the creek to make sure all clothes of the villagers are clean and smell fresh. She does this with love and devotion. It's almost impossible to imagine that Aa is the daughter of the two Funnel beakers Lute and Zara. Lute is the village musician, a slim, lanky guy with curly hair of medium length. He's completely nuts and conceives the strangest musical instruments. He's touched everything that can make even the slightest sound. His newest creation is an instrument consisting of a number of hollow branches with different lengths, which create different pitches when blowing on the branches in a certain way. He did not yet come up with a real name for this musical instrument, so he calls it the pff by Lute for now. The 'pff' stands for blowing on the branches.

Hunze gestures to the bushes of which some twigs are in motion. He assumes a stealthy position and Ems humbly follows suit. Step by step they very carefully sneak towards the bushes without making a sound. That's at least what Hunze hopes, because Ems is in fact a dirty, stinky little man with sounds coming out of him from above and below every so often, including at this crucial moment, to the annoyance of Hunze. Fortunately this doesn't seem to affect the prey, which is probably unaware of the approaching assailants, sitting in the bushes. The spears of Hunze and Ems assume an attacking position, mere feet away from the bushes. Then Hunze decides to charge.

'Aaaaahhhhh!!!'.

'Aaaaahhhh!!!' right after, Ems' battle cry.

Two spears ominously point to the bushes.

'Aaaaaaahhhh!!!', it sounds from the bushes.

A white pointed cap shoots up, with a long, grey beard underneath. Two frightened eyes in between, looking in the direction of the two piercing spearheads.

'Holy funnel beakers!' it sounds from under the pointed cap. 'Have you gone completely heretic? I can't even do my job in peace.'

The old greybeard with the white pointed cap is Das, the druid of the Funnel beaker people.

'Eh, yeah, sorry,' Hunze stutters. 'I... we thought there was an aardvark in here.'

'Do I look like an aardvark?' the druid exclaims. 'I'm here just looking for some herbs.' In the meantime he grabs his sickle, bag of herbs and his other belongings and walks away from the two confounded hunters while cursing and raging.

In Borg's village, everyone is busy preparing for the feast later that night. The big leader himself is starting a fire to spit roast the aardvark on. Ambra, Borg's wife, is baking bread. The smell of the freshly baked bread reaches far into the forest. Aa is doing laundry by the creek. She will make sure everyone will be eating aardvark in clean garments. Village musician Lute is busy practicing and unsuccessfully attempts to get some sounds out of his self-made instruments. He's pretty successful in disorienting the village animals. A shepherd struggles to get his sheep out of the creek and onto dry land. These are a special breed, ancient sheep that carry a heavy coat during winter, but are now completely shaven. Although, completely... they still have plucks of wool on their heads. The flock now looks more like a hilarious carnival parade. The musical squabbling of Lute complements this bizarre spectacle.
All this bustle is remarkable in this otherwise quiet and peaceful village by the creek, on a timeline dating over five thousand years back. Borg's village is located in the middle of a large forest that borders the high north of the Nether Lands and in the south-west extends to the lower parts, where the fishing people of the twelve seas reside. The higher north is home to the Huns, a bunch of wild giants who are no friends of the Funnel beaker people from Borg. When Huns and the Funnel beakers run into each other in the forest, during searches or while hunting, it could lead to bloody confrontations. Not just because they don't want to yield their hunting grounds, but also because the Funnel beakers consider the Huns to be repulsive monstrosities. They are disproportionally large and strong, have frightening roars and deal deadly blows with their clubs. Conversely, the Huns see the Funnel beakers as a dangerous enemy because of their mysterious forces,

knowledge of herbs, and secretive rituals. Fortunately, both peoples live at least a twelve-day walk apart, therefore making clashes an exception.

Hunze and Ems approach the village. A huge aardvark hangs on Hunze's back with its mouth open and facing down, with a trail of blood running back, deep into the forest. Both hunters eventually managed to overpower an aardvark. Hunze is visibly proud. Ems trails behind and carries both spears. The villagers are thrilled and welcome the hunters. Among them is Aa, who quickly ran from the creek to join the welcoming, but mainly to greet Hunze. She stares at him with dreamy eyes, at his slim, slender body and his enchanting smile. Suddenly a loud noise comes from a hut:

'I'm glad you're here.' Borg is visibly surprised by the arrival of the two hunters. He rushes out of his hut and swiftly puts on his uniform. A rumpled Ambra stoically observes the event from the opening of the hut. God knows what happened in there just moments ago.

'You are invincible! Our hunters, our heroes! Eh… yeah, just put that aardvark over there, dear Hunze…'

Borg then faces Ems, walks around him, checks his back, takes another lap, just to be sure, and looks surprised.

'And where's yours?' he asks Ems, 'Or will it arrive shortly?' He sounds sarcastic and takes a look at the forest. Everyone laughs, except Ems. He shamefully looks at the ground.

'To be honest…' everyone turns their eyes to Hunze, 'Ems caught this aardvark. It was a dangerous chase and a bloody hunt. That's the reason why he's now so exhausted and I had to carry the aardvark to the village on my back.'

Ems looks at Hunze in surprise. He doesn't understand, but wisely keeps his mouth shut. Borg is astonished as well and looks as if he has to think about this for a second. His face shows disbelief, but he leaves it be.

'Come people. Let's continue the preparations for the party. We have a lot of work to do.' In the meantime Borg directs everyone back to the edge of the village where the festivities will take place.

'Where's your father by the way?' he asks Hunze in passing.

The old druid Das walks left and right through the bushes of the forest, a little hunched over, mumbling and talking to himself like an absent-minded professor. He whacks his sickle around in order to clear a path, while looking for herbs he could use during the banquet tonight. But he's also looking for herbs with medicinal effects. He is a druid after all, and therefore responsible for the health of the villagers. He discovered a new type of herb, a type of alliaceous vegetable that quickly and very effectively cures damage to the skin. No one knows of this herb, so he proudly named it after himself: *Allium ursinum.* His little bag is starting to fill up nicely, when he hears some unclear sounds. He's vigilant, but calmly picks some sea lavender. It'll go great with the meat of an aardvark, he believes. The indefinable sounds increase. In addition to birds taking off and changing gusts of wind, he detects a typical unpleasant smell he can't yet describe. How does he know this foul smell, he thinks. In a mere second it gets dead silent. Then, the druid is startled by a horrible roar rumbling through the forest. He takes off right away and makes a run for it. He runs as fast as his old feet allow him to.

The unrecognizable aardvark spins around over the blazing fire. All Funnel beakers gathered around the fire. They sing, dance, drink and eat. It's a true feast. Borg cuts large pieces of meat off the aardvark and passes them around. He takes a little bite himself every now and then. 'Not too much!' he laughs, while simultaneously slapping his big belly. Village musician Lute brought some of his instruments and formed a small orchestra with some of the villagers. They appear to have practiced because it doesn't even sound bad. It has a good rhythm to it. Hunze uses the rhythm to smoothly move his slender, muscular body. He takes Aa's hand and they put on a real show. Little Ems and his wife Driek also jump around like a couple of bouncy balls, to the beat of the drums.

Completely out of breath and with cold sweat on his forehead, the druid keeps on running. 'To the village, to the village', he stammers to himself. The ground thuds with every step he takes. It seems like the ground thuds increasingly harder and faster. The screams and roars come from mere yards behind him. He can't run any longer. The lactic acid overtakes his old legs. Lactic acid he ironically found a remedy for. Some special herbs, a bit of sugar beet and a secret recipe and there you go. The resulting drink prevents the buildup of lactic acid in your legs. One should however drink this three times a day and the druid hadn't drank it in a while. Why would he? Why would he still run at his age? The druid is having a hard time. He falls, crawls, stands back up and falls again. The roof of the forest is getting darker, even darker than it usually is. Something big approaches from the sky. He looks up behind him in fear, but he can't see what it is. There's a ringing and then suddenly, an enormous thud. His hand feels it's a hard material... it feels cold... it seems to be..., but the old druid's thoughts end there. A second later it's red-hot, like his hand is being branded and his eyes see blue.
The night falls, the moon lights up from the dusty mist, the village drums die off.

Current

2   The beginning

Four wheels roll over the black tarmac. A famous hit song sounds from the car radio. Although singing isn't his strong suit, the driver sings along with the chorus. The weather is nice, which is why he opened a window. The wind blows through his blond hair. The journey has taken him passed varying landscapes, villages and quaint towns for quite some time. He enjoys the peace and the space Drenthe still has to offer in spades, away from the bustle and the crowds, the rush of the big cities people are being sucked into. Suddenly, the phone rings.

'This is Danny de Vries.'

'Mister de Vries, this is Esther Schipper from the University of Groningen. I have the complete record for you regarding your research on the recent excavations at the Vork in Haren'.

The conversation continues for a while, but Danny is only half-listening. He's more focused on the driver ~~who's~~ driving next to him. A bizarre appearance behind the wheel who's busy emptying his nose. It makes Danny shiver. Gross, the things people do behind the wheel, he thinks.

'Okay, Esther, thank you. If you can make the record available at the site in Haren, I will pick it up there.'

Danny holds the phone for a little while and thinks. Then he dials anonymously. He hears the dial tone a number of times.

'This is Anne de Vries'.

'Hello madam,' Danny unrecognizably warps his voice, 'this is travel agency De Haan. The five-star bungalow you booked for next week at vacation park De Koperen Ketel, that reservation fell through. The park is overbooked. I'm sorry.' It's quiet for a bit.

'But, but, that can't be. We made the reservation and arranged everything. I'm with the kids and...'

'I understand your reaction, madam,' Danny can barely hold back his laughter, 'but we can offer you an alternative, we still have a mobile home available.'

'A mobile home? So will we actually be mobile or do we have to stay in the same place?'
Anne is turning red and almost starts hyperventilating. The children are in the kitchen watching their mother almost boil over.
Ow, Danny thinks, it sounds like I should stop it right here.
'Eh, hello,' he says with his normal voice, 'this is Da-', but he can't get through to her.
'You know what, mister De Haan, you can shove that mobile home up your ass!' The connection is terminated. Danny is baffled. He didn't mean to upset his wife that much. He calls again, but this time not anonymously.
'Danny!' Anne shouts. 'You'll never believe who just called me. Travel agency De Haan just called me to tell me our bungalow is overbooked... But they still have a mobile home available. A mobile home! You know what I told the guy...?'
Eh no, I don't want to know, Danny thinks.
'A mobile home Danny! Goddamnit, what was that guy thinking?'
Danny wisely decides to keep his mouth shut for a while, followed by a hypocritical 'Seriously?'
'I'll just talk to this De Haan. Leave it to me.' He checks his watch, a nice, sporty model of a famous brand, it has no hands however. 'I just have to go to the site in Haren and I'll come home.'

A sandy building site surrounded by large fences with signs that say 'No Entry', a small tent near the entrance of the area, men and women in white overalls, it looks like a scene from the show *Crime Scene Investigation*. Only the cameras are missing. Some people in white overalls are squatting and digging in the sand with little shovels and dusters. They seem to have found something and are carefully unearthing it. It's still indefinable, but going by the 'oh' and 'ah' sounds, it must be something really special.

'Beep beep' sounds the horn of Danny's rugged 4x4 truck. He's in front of the entrance to the area. The gate opens and Danny parks his car at a reserved parking spot. Before he's properly out of his car, a woman in one of those CSI overalls rushes to him and exclaims with a quite shrieking voice:

'Danny! Danny! We found another femur!'

The enclosed area is a building site for a new industrial and railroad complex. Remains from ancient history were discovered during excavation work, including pots, tools, human bones and coins from the 16th and 17th century. A special team from the University of Groningen, led by the young archeologist Danny de Vries, is charged with the excavations and mapping of the ancient objects. The construction of the complex is postponed by a month because of these archeological finds. So time is scarce. This is Danny's first project after his studies, so he's particularly motivated to ensure the successful excavations.

Danny and the screeching lady in the white overalls walk farther onto the site.

'This is truly awesome,' she screeches. 'My first conservative estimate is that this femur must be over two thousand years old. Ohhhhh, even older than we expected.' she continues. Danny stands still for a bit and gives her a probing look.

'Are you very sure, Hellen? Because nothing in this area points to the existence of a village or stronghold over a thousand years ago.'

Hellen is Danny's assistant. A young, twenty-five-year-old woman with decent looks. Not really the type of woman that uses her hands to dig in the clay, looking for old pots and pans. She has beautiful, blonde hair, put up with bumpits and further stands out because of her dazzling makeup, including fiery-red lip gloss, dark eyeliner and a lot of foundation. All this, behind a high-gloss polished, fashionable pair of glasses with large, square lenses a professional window cleaner would have to work on quite a while. The high-gloss polish is carefully extended to some spectacular nail extensions. She hops after Danny on her red high heels, who already walked over to ~~a place where~~ two man ~~are~~ squatting in a hole.

'Look, there it is.' Hellen points to something that's halfway sticking out of the ground 'Because of a certain mineral deposit on the bone, which I examined, it must be over two thousand years old.'
Danny grabs his magnifying glass and critically studies the bone from all angles. After several seconds he gets up and silently walks to the tent. Hellen follows him.

'Where is the research report Esther would put here for me?' Danny asks, while nervously searching through piles of paper, boxes and in the drawer of a desk.

'Eh, is this what you're looking for?' Hellen takes a big envelope out of her purse. Danny takes it and quickly scans the document. He draws his conclusion.

'Ok, Hellen. You know we are under enormous time pressure, which I hate, but you may investigate this further.' Hellen has the greatest look of enthusiasm on her face.

'Ahhhh, you won't regret it.'
As she says this, she slowly brings her glasses down to the tip of her nose. She provocatively and seductively looks over her glasses at Danny. My God, she's hot, he thinks.

'You have to do something in return though.' Danny says.

'Hmmm, tell me...' Hellen quietly moans. 'What is the boss up to, what do I get to exam-'
Before Hellen can finish her sentence, Danny grabs her and presses his mouth onto hers. He really shows her what he's made of, the primitive man inside him comes out. His hands firmly grab Hellen's breast. After

an intense French kiss, Danny's head moves down, along her neck over her breasts and to her stomach. The white overalls tear open and his face disappears into the divine. Hellen throws her head back and moans. Her hands ferociously run through Danny's blond hair. Outside the tent, the other white overalls continue to work. Even though the tent is violently shaking, they aren't aware of the scenes going on inside. The two in the tent continue unabashed. Danny has Hellen pressed against the desk and has both her legs firmly clamped around him. The mating ritual has started and all evidence suggests the climax is approaching…

'Danny?' Hellen shouts out surprised.
Danny stares straight through her square glasses into her questioning eyes. Once he realizes the here and now, he abandons his thoughts and draws his conclusion.

'Ok Hellen. You know, we are under enormous time pressure, but you may investigate this further.' He repeats. Hellen jumps around Danny's neck and kisses him on his lips.

'Not here!' Danny hisses with fear. He pushes Hellen away and anxiously looks around to make sure nobody saw.

The vacation preparations are in full swing in the De Vries residence. While Anne tries to select some items in the kitchen, their two children, Thomas and Benjamin, run around the house like unguided missiles. Without knowing what's actually going on, the fifth member of the family, miniature schnauzer Bor, chases the kids as if he was a guide dog. First up the stairs, then back down. He can't get enough of it. Anne however can.

'Enough now! To your room and pack your suitcase. One, two, three, dismissed!' She could've easily served in the military as a sergeant-major of the infantry with that persuasive power. The children get the message and march upstairs. Anne takes a seat to blow off some steam.

'Oh crap,' she exclaims all of a sudden, and rushes through the kitchen to the oven like a savage. A black cloud escapes from the oven once it opens. A charred apple pie appears from the cloud of smoke. Anne sighs at the sight of this disaster and wearily leans against the kitchen sink.

'Beep beep.' The horn of the 4x4 sounds for the second time that day. Anne gawks at the kitchen clock.

'Daddy, daddy' followed by barking, it sounds from upstairs. The two run down the stairs to eagerly greet Danny. Before Danny can get a foot in the door, the three already hang from his neck and his pants.

'Ha-ha, hello you silly guys! Ha-ha, who is the funniest, most brilliant, handsome and sweetest dad of all the land?' Silence ensues.

'Mom baked an apple pie.' Benjamin says with an innocent look in his eyes.

'Ha-ha, well, let's go have a taste then!' Danny runs after the children into the kitchen and yells: 'Hey there, chef.' Anne looks disappointed.

'You can leave the chef part.' She slides the charred apple pie across the kitchen table to Danny, who gives it a little sniff.

'Hmm, yum. How are we going to survive the vacation in our mobile home without apple pie?' Danny asks while looking at the children. They scream: 'Nooooo, mommy has to make a new one!' Danny turns his head to Anne, who leans against the kitchen table, gravely distraught.

'Don't worry, I arranged things with the travel agency. We will get the bungalow just like we booked it.' As Danny says this, he embraces Anne. He looks over her shoulder in despair. How in God's name do we go from here, he thinks.

3   The Slate

The first rays of sunlight break through the morning mist in Borg's village. Most villagers are still sleeping off the festivities from the night before. Snoring sounds come from the various huts and little houses. It was a wild party. Some villagers didn't even manage to make it to their house and are sleeping against a tree. Lute, the bard, is one of them. He's lying underneath a tree in an impossible, reverse split. He's still holding a funnel beaker that apparently still contains some ale, because a dog is eagerly slurping from it. The only person who's still showing signs of life is Aa. She's carrying a basket full of laundry to the creek. She quietly sings a cheerful melody her father wrote, and visibly enjoys the beautiful weather and lush surroundings. Upon arrival at the creek she starts doing the laundry, observed with surprise by the various animals living in and around the creek.

'You're up and running early!' it sounds from behind her. She is startled, looks up and sees Hunze. She laughs.

'Ha-ha, you scared me.' She runs her hand through the water at the same time and throws it in Hunze's direction. He tries to dodge the splashing water. The game leads to a merry water fight.

After some time, Aa and Hunze are standing on the bank, tired and soaking wet, and look into each other's eyes for a moment. Aa averts her head in modesty and shyness. Hunze also doesn't really know what to do in this situation.

'Come on, let's go to my father's workshop.' Hunze decides. He takes Aa by the hand and pulls her along.

'But the laundry...' Aa exclaims.

'It's ok, it can be done later. I'll help you.'

Together they walk back to the village where the day has started. Everyone amicably greets one another, and the villagers sweep the place clean. It's quiet at the house of druid Das. Hunze takes Aa around the back, to the workshop. It's a small place, full of all kinds of little pots, dishes and cans. Various herbs and flowers are hanging from the beams to dry. It has a pleasant smell. Aa sniffs up the herbal scents and smiles at Hunze. There's a charred chimney with some semi-burnt logs on the other side of the workshop. Someone made a fire here recently. Hunze looks at some little pots, especially at their content.

'Where is your dad, by the way?' Aa asks.

'No idea. I saw him yesterday in the northern forest. Ems and I were hunting there'. Hunze looks at Aa with a reassuring look on his face.

'It's not uncommon that my dad is gone for a couple of days, looking for herbs, flowers, mushrooms and all that kind of stuff. Don't worry, he'll be back soon. Look, this is a new herb my father found recently.' Hunze takes a little pot and smells it. He then puts it under Aa's nose.

'My dad named it after himself, *Allium ursinum*. He just doesn't exactly know what you can do with it and how it works.' Hunze laughingly states with modesty.

'You know quite a bit about it as well.' Aa says and looks at Hunze with little eyes from under her thin eyebrows. 'You're not just a tough hunter, but you're also an herb specialist.' Hunze looks shyly to the ground and thinks hard about how to continue.

'Come, I have to show you something.'

'What is it?' Aa asks with curiosity.

Hunze walks towards a cabinet, turns a wooden handle and opens a door with much creaking and crackling. He takes out a small wooden box and lifts its lid.

'Look, my dad once found this in the woods when he was looking for herbs. It looks like a piece of slate, it's all smooth and shiny. The stone has a symbol engraved in it.' Hunze's fingers glide over the characters FTC.

'My father discovered the meaning behind the symbols. The F stands for fence, the gate to the afterlife. This one, the T, is a cross, a sign of danger. And the C is the half moon. He hasn't yet figured out the exact connection between them. But there is more. My father told me that when he found this stone and let it slide through his hands, the slate suddenly lit up and a ghost, a man, appeared who yelled something unintelligible.'

Aa listens to the story in awe.

'You know Aa, my father has experienced a lot, like witches, Witte Wieven (elf like beings), the Huns, enemy neighboring peoples, but never something as strange and magical as this.'

'Can I hold it?' Aa asks.

'Yes, of course, be careful. But don't talk about it with anyone. I expressly promised my father I wouldn't tell anyone.'

'It's pretty. So smooth. How did your father do it? With his hands over the slate?' Aa tenderly slides her hand and fingers over the mysterious piece of slate. There's a serene silence in Das' workshop, and a force field between Aa and Hunze is tangible.

'Ah!' Aa suddenly looks shocked.

'What is it?' Hunze yells, equally startled.

'I saw something light up.'

'What? Let me see.'

Hunze carefully inspects the slate from all angles. His face shows he's scared, imagining his dad actually saw it. What if there really is a ghost or wizard hidden inside the slate? The doom this could cause. The entire village could be cursed. And it would all be his fault, because he just had to show the stone to Aa.

'Ha-ha.' Aa is in stitches.

'That's not funny!' Hunze yells, who now realizes he's been fooled.

'Yes it is. You really believed it.' Aa laughs.

Hunze places the slate back in the little box and closes the cabinet. He wants to grab Aa, but she beats him to it and is already back on the other side of the workshop.

'And what is this?' Aa takes a little red pot off the shelf.

'Oh, that is something very special. An energy drink… still in its early stages though,' Hunze laughs. 'It's a brew made of various herbs and

sugars. If you drink this you will get huge amounts of energy and strength. It however has a quite nasty side-effect…'
Aa frowns and longingly looks at Hunze, who takes a second to think, and then whispers something in her ear. Aa starts laughing.

4   Distraction

There's a 4x4 on the side of the highway, with Benjamin behind it in the high grass, pants down to his knees. He doesn't look very happy.

'You shouldn't have let him eat from that apple pie.' Danny yells.

'I scraped off the charred parts!' Anne yells back. This back and forth continues for a while, they can't agree with one another. In the meantime, Benjamin excreted his entire intestinal content in the most liquid form possible. Thomas is still in the car with a clothespin on his nose.

'Nice start of the vacation.' Danny complains.

'Come one, just leave this mess and get back in the car.' Anne tells the pale Benjamin in a more moderate tone. She tries to comfort him a little.

'Everyone and everything back on board?' Danny asks, and without waiting for the answer he floors the gas pedal.
Upon arrival at the vacation park they enter their five-star bungalow and immediately forget about all the drama that occurred an hour ago. The children claim a room, and Danny and Anna are amazed by all the luxury. They park their somewhat overloaded suitcases in the bedroom and let themselves fall onto the large waterbed. Both let out a deep sigh and stare at the ceiling. How to go from here?, Danny thinks.

The phone rings. It startles Danny, who jumps up. He had fallen asleep. Damn, he thinks, and picks up the phone.

'Hey baby...' it sounds from the other end of the line.

'Who is that?' a still sleepy Anny asks.

'Ehh... work. Hellen. I have to discuss something regarding the recent excavation'.

Danny quickly walks down the stairs into the living room.

'You shouldn't call my like this, Hellen. Anne was lying right next to me.' Danny looks around to make sure he's alone.

'Oh… were you doing naughty things I don't know about?' Hellen cynically asks with a sultry tone.

'What is it?' Danny asks. 'I'm on vacation. Why are you calling?'

'I emailed the research results of the excavation in Haren to professor Dijkstra and he contacted me. He's excited and wants to discuss things with you.'

Danny is thinking.

'But ehm… I'm happy to discuss things with you as well… Danny…' Hellen continues, even sultrier than before.

'Yeah, yeah, I'm sure you do Hellen. Make an appointment with professor Dijkstra for next week.'

'Is that the Hellen?' Anne suddenly stands behind Danny. 'From the office?' she says with a seemingly innocent look on her face.

'Eh, yes… I have to discuss some things with her… I mean with the professor about the excavations.' Danny wants to put away his phone, when he receives a text message.

'*Hottie!*' the display reads.

'Done,' Danny says, sounding very excited all of a sudden. He quickly changes the topic.

'I have a good idea for this afternoon. We are going to make a nice road trip to Aa in Drenthe and explore the area. And after that we can have some delicious pancakes.'

'Yeeaah', is the loud and harmonious response of the kids. They entered the living room during their parents' talk.

A while ago

5   The search

Borg's villagers are starting to wonder where the druid is. He's known to leave town for a while, but he hasn't been seen in a week. The bard blows his horn, telling the villagers to assemble. Head villager Borg has an announcement. He stands on a wooden stool, so he can oversee his people.

'Borgers and outsiders. For those who haven't noticed…'
The crowd chuckles. Borg stops his rhetoric and thinks: am I this funny? He however doesn't see that a village dog was sniffing the wooden stool during his speech, lifted his hind leg and took a decently sized pee against the stool. When Borg notices he calls the crowd to order by firmly pounding his stick on the ground.

'This is a serious matter, people. Our druid Das hasn't been seen for six sunsets now. That is extremely disturbing to me.'
The villagers mumble to each other and apparently agree with their great leader.

'We have to search for him, because I'm afraid something happened to him. Who volunteers to go on the search?'

'I will look for him,' the shepherd passing by earlier with his flock of sheep shouts.

'Have you lost your mind?!' his wife yells. 'It's dark and dangerous in the forest. And what about the sheep?'

'I agree.' Borg confirms, 'We need you here, here with the sheep.'

'Eh, I, ahem argh…' Lute clears his throat. 'I would want to look for my companion.' His voice trembles.

'Most definitely not!' Borg sounds decisive. 'We'll end up looking for you as well.'
Everyone laughs, except the bard.
'Come on people, I think we have to look for him with at least two parties.'

'I'm going!' Hunze's voice sounds clear. Aa looks terrified.

'I'm going as well.' another hunter exclaims.

'I'll go with Hunze.' Ems says, and instantly joins Hunze.

'Good. Hunze and Ems go north, and I will take my brave friend here to the east.'

Borg hits the brave friend's meagre shoulder, which almost causes him to collapse.

'We leave tomorrow at sunrise.'

Borg jumps off the rickety wooden stool and walks towards Hunze.

'Are you sure you want to do this?' He asks Hunze while they walk towards Borg's hut.

'Of course! It's my father.'

'Exactly, that's what I mean. You could be too emotional, too involved.'

'Not at all, everything is under control. No worries Borgy.'

Borg arrives at his hut, stops and thinks: Borgy?

Hunze keeps walking to his father's workshop to gather some stuff for the search.

'It could be dangerous.' Aa is suddenly behind him.

'I know.'

'I've heard stories about the Huns… they're savages.'

'Don't worry Aa, I'm prepared for everything. Besides, Ems is coming along with me.'

'That helps?' Aa asks with a worried tone. Hunze laughs.

'I can trust him and he helps a lot.'

'I don't want to lose you' Aa says while looking into Hunze's roguish eyes. 'Good luck tomorrow, and think of me.' She kisses him on the cheek and leaves the workshop, dismayed. Night falls.

The following morning, four feet follow each other across the soft moss and crackling leaves. A familiar scene, but a very different occasion this time. Hunze and Ems are not looking for an aardvark this time, but for Das, Hunze's father. They packed a lot for the tough and long journey, well-equipped with spears, a backpack full of food, herbs and flint stones. A funnel beaker filled with water dangles from their belts. They're looking for traces the druid could have left, foot prints in the sand, broken twigs, beds of herbs of which parts are cut off with a sickle, sounds or perhaps a glimpse of the druid in the distance.

'So what is the deal with those Huns?' Ems asks curiously. 'Have you ever seen them?'

'I've never seen them, but I've heard them. They have quite a loud roar. They're big creatures, people like you and I, but like giants. They're very strong.'

Ems anxiously looks straight ahead, brushes some flies off his nose and asks: 'Where do they li-'

He doesn't finish his sentence because he realizes he's alone.

'Hunze?' he shouts, and looks around, all puzzled.

How is this possible, Ems thinks. We were walking together on this path two footsteps ago...

'Hunze!' he shouts again. 'Where are you?'

He carefully walks a bit further while vigilantly looking around. The sounds of the forest start to make him nervous. He changes the spear he's carrying into a defensive position.

There, he thinks, something is moving behind that big tree.

'Hunze?'

Step by step, with cold sweat under his armpits, he walks towards the tree. Once there, he sees a little hedgehog crawling around behind the tree.

'Shoo!' he yells to the hedgehog and pokes it with his spear. He turns around towards the path, when suddenly a huge roar fills the forest.

'WHHHOOOAAAHHH...'

Ems collapses to the ground in fear. He squeals like a skinny suckling pig, face down in the sand. 'Oh my god, oh my god, there they are, it's all over now! Bye sweet Driek, now I'll never see you again, I love you sweet Driek.'

Hunze jumped out of a tree and roars as he stands over Ems, with both hands high in the air. He laughs.

'Oh, come on. It's me, Hunze!'

Ems quivers on the ground. Hunze takes his hand and pulls him up.

'That's not funny, Hunze.' Ems brushes the sand off his clothes.

'Well, it made me laugh. *Oh I love you sweet Driek,* ha-ha.' Hunze tries to imitate Ems' sobbing tone.

'Well, I do! I love Driek. I can't help it that you have nobody.'

'Hey, you stuffy twit!' Hunze shouts. 'I do have someone, ok? And we happen to be looking for him right now!'

'Yeah, yeah, it's ok.' Ems mumbles while he brushes some more sand out of his ears. They continue across the path in silence.

The silence is however quickly interrupted.

'By the way, speaking of *nobody...*' Ems continues, 'There is someone I believe has a crush on you.'

'Eh? Who?'

'You know her.'

'I do?'

'Yes. Aren't you aware of it? How she's always looking at you.'

'Aa?' Hunze asks.

'Could be.'

'No...' Hunze looks doubtful, 'that's not possible.'

'Why not?' Ems asks in surprise. 'She's a pretty woman, I mean, she's a gorgeous...'

A loud fart echoes through the forest.

'Oops... sorry.' Ems chuckles.

'Yeah...' Hunze looks even more doubtful.

'I know what I'd do if I were you, Hunze.' Ems thinks for a second. 'Why did your father name you Hunze?'

'That's a long story.'

'I have time.' Ems laughs and points around as if he's the only one in the world and nothing is going on.

Hunze hesitates for a moment, but starts his story.

'My father found me in the forest when I was a baby. I was wrapped in jute. Nobody knew where I came from or where I belonged. My father initially considered abandoning me somewhere…' A tear runs over Hunze's cheek, 'But he eventually decided to raise me and give me an upbringing. I am still grateful for that. As you know, I don't have a mother. My father named me Hunze because he suspects I was rejected by the village of the Huns. Again, this is a suspicion, he never explicitly told me this in those words.'
Ems' mouth falls open in shock.

'So you might be one of them??? But you're not a giant. And you're very nice. Why did they abandon you?'
Before Hunze can answer these questions, a dull thump sounds through the forest and the ground starts shaking. The two Funnel beakers stop in their tracks.

'Oh my, oh my, that's them, holy funnel beakers. They're coming to get you Hunze.' Ems yells.

'Don't be silly! Shut up and come on!'
They walk in the direction of the thump. They hear voices in the distance. It sounds like singing. Hunze and Ems crawl through dense bushes towards the singing. As they get closer, the flickering light of a fire emerges. They vaguely see a number of shadows walk back and forth in this light. Ems and Hunze keep a safe distance to get a clear picture of what's going on. Out of fear, Ems lets another one of his loud farts rip into the great wide open

'Be quiet!' Hunze urges, 'They're going to hear us.'
Ems just shrugs his shoulders and gestures it isn't his fault. Another huge dull thump echoes through the forest. It causes the ground underneath Hunze and Ems to violently shake. One of the shadows was carrying something on his back and dropped it on the ground.

'What are they doing over there?' Ems whispers. 'Who are those people?'

'Shh!' Hunze places his hand over Ems' mouth. 'We have to go back to the village.'

They turn around and sneak back through the bushes. Despite their cautiousness, a branch cracks underneath Ems' weight. He stands paralyzed with fear. Holy funnel beakers, he thinks, I hope they didn't hear that. Anchored like a statue, Hunze and Ems let the time pass, fervently hoping nobody noticed them. At that moment, on that spot they only have one major wish: disappear into nothingness, into a completely different dimension. Unfortunately, one of the shadows probably did hear the crack and looks in the direction of the bushes in which the still frozen Hunze and Ems reside. The sparkle of the fire make it seem like the eyes of the shadow are glowing, and they pierce the backs of the couple like blades.

'Do you feel anything?' Hunze whispers.

'It's getting warm underneath my feet.' Ems answers.

'Run!'

They don't hesitate for a second and start running.

6   The confrontation

Five shadows move along deserted wagon tracks through the heather in Drenthe.

'How much longer?'

'Stop whining' Danny says.

'It's so beautiful here' Anne sighs. She presses herself against Danny some more during the walk, to feel safe.

'Just look at this, this view. And smell this…' Anne inhales deeply to take in the fresh outdoor air, '…Delicious. We should've done this a long time ago.'

'Look mom,' Thomas shouts, 'Sheep. Over there!' He points across the heather to a flock of sheep. It's an impressive sight. The woolly animals are obedient, and meekly follow each other. A shepherd walks in front, wearing a long, dark, tanned coat. A black, dented hat rests on his head. He blows his whistle every now and then. The signal tells the shepherd dog, a beautiful Border Collie, to come into action and bring several renegades back to the group.

What Danny and Anne don't realize, is that their own dog got wind of the sheep and the Collie. The shepherd's whistling drew his attention as well. The animal sprints across the heather, towards the flock, loudly barking and growling. Danny will not stand for this.

'Bor, come here!' he yells.

'Bor! Bor!' Thomas and Benjamin add to the yelling and run after Bor in an uncoordinated fashion.

The dog doesn't seem to care about the yelling and runs like a crazed bull for a red rag.

Anne looks at the scene in fear.

'Oh no, Bor is going to drive the herd apart. We're going to have an angry shepherd to deal with.'

Danny's worries turn into laughter.

'Oh, I'd like to see that, Bor chasing sheep. I think it's more likely the sheep will take on Bor.'

Meanwhile, Bor, followed by Thomas and Benjamin, approaches the flock of sheep. The shepherd also noticed the approaching trio and frantically blows his whistle. The Collie reacts instantly and purposefully heads towards the intruders. He cuts Bor off, starts to bark defensively and secures the border between Bor and the flock of sheep. It works. Bor is apparently impressed and takes on a subordinate role by lying flat on his belly.

'Wow, did you see that' Thomas exclaims. 'Good job Bor, good boy!'

'Good? Not good at all!' Danny yells. 'That stupid dog just runs away and doesn't listen when I call him.'
He firmly grabs Bor by his collar and attaches it to the leash.

'Well, he's listening now, right' Anne says, clearly annoyed. 'No reason to be so harsh on him now.'
Meanwhile, the shepherd approaches the family at a swift pace. The closer he gets, the bigger he becomes. He looks grumpy and is clearly not amused by this disruption of public order. With each step, his cane firmly pokes the ground. The wind blows up the back of his tanned coat. His oncoming appearance looks impressive and threatening. The shepherd stops at a mere three feet from the de Vries family. It's a huge guy.

'Ehm, my apologies' Danny stammers, quite overwhelmed. 'He never does this. He usually listens really well.'
The shepherd observes the scene with squinted eyes from under his heavy, dark eyebrows. He grunts something unintelligible and bends over deeply towards little Benjamin. The boy jumps back and can barely hold his pee.

'It unfortunately happens more often, so I'm quite used to it' the shepherd says. 'And this is just a small dog. I've had Bouviers des Flandres and Belgian Shepherds disrupt my flock. That's a bigger deal, you know. In those cases, even my good old Hendrik can't help it.'
The shepherd speaks with a deep, dark voice while he keeps his piercing eyes on Benjamin.

'Good old Hendrik?' Danny asks surprised.
The shepherd laughs and rewards the Collie with a doggy snack.

'I have to move on. Have to get a roof over my sheep's heads before the thunder starts. I would quickly go home as well if I were you, now that it's still dry.'
The shepherd gets ready to leave.

'Oh, before I forget…' he says, slowly turning back towards the family, 'keep your poodle on a leash from now on. This is a nature reserve, you know.'

'Yes, we will…' Danny stammers. 'Thank you.' He politely and hesitantly raises his hand. The shepherd leaves. In a blink of an eye he's all the way at the other side of the heather, where he turns around one last time and looks at the family. As if he wanted to say something, but wasn't able to.

'What a big guy. He looks like a giant.' Anne says.

'Yeah, very remarkable' Danny looks doubtful. 'Something's not right about that shepherd.'

'He actually just gave me goosebumps.' Anne shakenly says.
Danny checks his handless watch.

'Come on boys, it's time.' he firmly says.

'Dad, why did he call Bor a poodle?' Benjamin asks.

The adventure with the sheep made quite the impression on the de Vries family. They continue to talk about it during the remainder of their walk across the heather and through the woods of the nature reserve in Drenthe. Danny looks at the hiking map.

'We can take a little break a bit further on.'

'Oh, what's there?' Anne asks.

'You'll see.' Danny casually responds and quickly stores the map in his backpack.

'Don't be so lame.' Anne gives Danny a little nudge.

'Easy, easy!' Danny starts to walk faster. 'Come on then!' He challenges Anne, who is visibly enjoying it, and hurries after him. They play around for a bit along the trail, until Danny stops walking on the top of a hill. He looks down with an astonished look on his face.

'What is it?' Anne asks, but Danny doesn't respond. She pokes him a bit. Danny still doesn't respond and keeps staring down, so Anne decides to also look down, with Thomas and Benjamin by her side. Time stands still, seconds feel like centuries. On the top of the hill stands a young family, around two centuries AD. Below them, at the foot of the hill, a monstrous structure that has been dormant for more than five thousand years. A resting place for those who roamed the green earth back then. They were hunters and farmers. Unsuspecting Roman soldiers walked by here without a clue about the past and the meaning of the structure. Through the millennia, many explorers and crusaders from all parts of the world passed by. Thieves, murderers, plunderers and 'white wives' from the Middle Ages hid out here, hoping to not get caught. During the Eighty Years' War it was a silent witness of all death and destruction in the area. The first horse-drawn carriages of the Dutch Postal Service, which raced through the country to distribute mail and valuable goods, passed here. Not much longer, Ford Model Ts parked here. Americans and Germans hid here during WWI and WWII to take a stand. For years, and especially in the last years of the current century, tourists from all parts of the world have come here to stare in wonder at the giant structure and fill their digital cameras with selfies. Their children sacrilegiously climbing on top and running over it. To them, it's nothing more than a fun object to climb in the middle of a sandbox.
Danny, Anne, Thomas and Benjamin take another good look. Underneath, at the bottom of the hill, giant stones that spontaneously washed up during the ice age lie orderly stacked.

'A dolmen...' Danny gulps, and continues with a shaking lower lip 'A megalithic crypt.'

Danny, Anne and the children descend and take a lap around the impressive structure.

'History was written here' Danny says with a degree of conviction and pride. And he should know. He's an archeologist, a scientist at heart. He's read a lot about these during his studies and saw many photographs and depictions, but strangely has never seen one himself. Now he's standing face to face with rock solid history. Chills of emotion run across his back.

'What is this, dad?' Thomas asks amazed.

'This, my boy, this is a dolmen. The oldest dolmen you can find here in the Netherlands.' and explains it to him.

'I'm going to sit down for a bit' Anne sighs. 'I'm worn out. Who wants a drink?' She takes some bottles from the backpack that find a ready demand. Danny continues his story.

'A very long time ago our ancestors lived here, in this area. In prehistoric times they roamed around as wild hunters, wearing animal skins, holding clubs and axes. But over five thousand years ago they started to develop into farmers. Agriculture and livestock farming started a true cultural revolution. They built farms made of poles and loam, with thatched roofs.'

'Grandma and grandpa also have a thatched roof on their house.'

'Very good Benjamin. Nostalgic thatched roofs, as we can still see on many farms in Drenthe today. The farmers used fields in the immediate surroundings of the farms. They grew flax, beans and peas, but also forgotten crops, such as einkorn wheat and emmer wheat. They kept oxen, sheep, aardvarks and goats. Even back then they held dogs as pets.'

'Oh, so Bor's grandmother and grandfather also come from here.' Benjamin wisely responds as he brushes the dog's head. Danny laughs.

'Eh, yeah, that's possible. But that's not all. In addition to their agriculture and livestock farming, they managed to develop a unique craft. They became excellent potters.'

Thomas and Benjamin cling to Danny's every word, who is completely immersed in his own story. 'They made many pots, dishes, bottle pouches and beakers that can be distinguished by a very peculiar funnel-shaped neck. And here it comes…' Danny increases the suspense.

'Oh, I can't hold it any longer' Anne yells. 'I have to go take a pee' and walks towards the bushes. This annoys Danny, who watches her leave, but then quickly continues his story, because Thomas and Benjamin are pulling his jacket. 'Go on, go on.'

'All right, so thanks to this special funnel shape in their ceramics, the people who used to live here are now known as… the Funnel beaker people.' Danny spreads his arms in the air to emphasize a eureka moment. 'They traded with fellow people to the east from Sleeswijk and the northern ones from Denmark. They for instance traded their ceramics for large axes. The Funnel beakers also traded with the people from Rijckhold, the current South Limburg. The fire stones, or flints, that were used as spearheads and sickles came from the mines over there.'

'Fire stones?' Thomas asks. 'How can stones catch on fire?'
Benjamin laughs, but doesn't really have the right answer.

'No, not really catch on fire, of course.' Danny continues. 'The name fire stone was used, because these stones are so hard, that sparks fly off when you bang them against each other. This can be used to make a fire. These stones also have very sharp edges, so they're ideal to use as weapons or tools.'
Anne rejoins the company. She clearly shows she's relieved.

'Look mom, I'm going to make a fire.' Benjamin runs towards her with two little stones and starts to bang them against each other. Anne has no clue what's going on and throws a surprised look towards Danny.

'But what does this doll man have to do with those Funnel beaker people, dad?' Thomas asks.

'It's dolmen, Thomas. And that's a very good question. This is still a big mystery. See, it's clear how these stones ended up here. During the third ice age these stones slowly glided over here with the ice from the north. The entire North of the Netherlands, especially the part of

Drenthe, was littered with these types of large and smaller boulders. What we now know, is that the various farmer peoples, such as the Funnel beakers, used these large rocks to build crypts. To give their loved ones a final resting place. But how did those little Funnel beakers – they were only 5 foot 3 inches tall on average – manage to turn those enormous rocks into this structure, in those times, without the help of cranes or bulldozers? That's still a big mystery.'

Danny is so consumed by his own story that he doesn't realize the mouths of Thomas, Benjamin and Anne are wide open in amazement. They are completely captivated at Danny's feet. Some seconds pass before Anne "returns back to earth". She blinks her eyes for a bit and then thinks of something that makes her shiver. She jumps up and takes a couple steps away from the stone she was sitting on.

'So… people are buried here?' she asks, looking bewildered.

Thomas and Benjamin also suddenly realize they have been sitting on a sort of cemetery all this time, and quickly cling onto Anne.

'Yes, but there's nothing left of it' Danny laughs. 'Those rocks and everything underneath are as dead as can be.'

'Danny, how could you tell our children a story about making fire, dead people and burial grounds. Gross!'

'It's just history, Anne, don't be so lame.'

'Come on, boys. It's time for something else.'

Anne directs her children to an old, half-fallen oak tree.

'Who is able to climb this tree?' she rhetorically asks.

Danny is left alone with the dolmen.

'Ugh, women!' he thinks to himself.

But when he turns around and looks at the dolmen, he's so excited to finally see one, feel one and smell one. He walks around, climbs on top and crawls through. The entire history and his stories run through his head again. He takes a seat in the middle of the dolmen, against one of the stones. He closes his eyes, with in the background the sound of laughter of Thomas and Benjamin, who are climbing a tree. Only for a little bit, because after a couple of seconds he opens his eyes again.

'Okay, enough, we're going home.' He gets up a bit awkwardly, causing him to bump his head on the roof of the crypt.

'Darn it, those Funnel beakers were indeed little people.'
Danny rubs his head with his hand. A dizziness overcomes him. Dark, light, blurry.

'Great, I should've eaten more today. Now I'm seeing the light… it shouldn't get any crazier than this.'
While Danny is wobbling on his feet in the middle of the dolmen, he believes he sees a glow from underneath a small rock. He smacks himself in the head in order to wake up.

'See, I'm hallucinating.' he laughs to himself.
While he laughs it off, another faint glow lights up. Danny crawls towards the stone and starts to dig at the bottom, where the glow is coming from. The soil is hard, so he grabs a little stone to loosen the soil. What is this?, he thinks, as he keeps digging. After some serious effort he manages to expose a little piece. He backs off in order to get a good look at it. A little spot of the rock he just exposed shows a strange glow. It has a peculiar icy blue color, giving you the idea that it must feel very cold. But what if it feels hot? Danny can't resist the temptation, a horrible dilemma, but he has to know. What is it? What does it feel like? He slowly but determined crawls closer to the stone. Closer to the glow. He extends his arm to touch the glowing part of the stone. Wait, he thinks, all of a sudden. He takes out his phone and quickly snaps a picture. 'Always good to have' he says with confidence. He again extends his arm. His hand, his fingers touch the stone. The glow draws into his fingertips. He feels dizzy again, but a different kind of dizzy this time. Light, stars, turmoil in his eyes. He sees a vague shadow in a flash, a frail, young man wearing a hat. The young man also has his hand placed on the stone. A shock runs through his body. This whole ordeal only lasts a mere second. Danny gets startled and lets go off the stone. Everything goes dark.

'...Danny? Danny?'

Danny opens his eyes and sees Anne standing in front of him. He's in the middle of the dolmen, squatting against a rock.

'What's going on, sweetie?' Anne asks with a worried tone. 'We've been looking for you for over half an hour. We kept calling for you. And you end up taking a nap here.'
A nap, Danny thinks. He tries to remember what happened and looks at the stone. No glow, nothing. I must've dreamt it, he thinks.

'The picture!' he shouts out and grabs his phone.

'What picture? What are you talking about?' Anne asks.

'No, never mind.' She won't believe me anyway, he thinks. She'll think I'm hallucinating. Who's going to believe I saw a blue glow in a rock? If I tell her I stood hand in hand with a shadow wearing a hat, she'll think I'm completely crazy. No, I first have to find out what happened.

'Danny, you're acting so weird.' Anne sounds even more worried.

'It's all good. I just fell asleep.'

'And you have blood on your head, Danny! What happened?'

'I indeed hit my head. Nothing serious.'
In the meantime, the sky has darkened and they can hear thunder in the distance.

'Hmm, how is that possible? I checked the forecast this morning, and they predicted clear skies all day.' Anne barely finished her sentence, when big droplets start falling down.

'Come on, let's run to the car.' Danny yells.
An hour later, the car drives onto the parking area of a pancake restaurant in Aalden, a typical village with old, nostalgic farms with thatched roofs, peacefully located under old oak trees, the crowns of which are intertwined. The thunderstorm has passed and the sun shines through the foliage. The de Vries family gets out of the car and walks towards the entrance.

'Well, that's great, we're soaking wet.' Anne complains.

Danny says nothing.

'The kids are going to be ill tomorrow.' she complains again.

'Why didn't you bring any umbrellas?' she continues.

'I...' Danny wanted to say something, but changes his mind.

'Yeah, you! With your great ideas.'

'How was I supposed to know there was going to be a thunderstorm?'

'Well, you always know everything, mister archeologist.'

'Archeology has nothing to do with the weather, Anne.'

'Yes, I know that,' she hesitantly responds, as if she knew.

'But that's not the point. You should always bring umbrellas when you go outside.'

'Oh?' Danny says and thinks to himself: just let her talk, it'll blow over.

'Who wants a pancake with syrup?' He asks out loud.

'Meeee!'

They walk through the door into a hall with a desk made of old oak wood, with an old-fashioned bell on top. Thomas gives it a good whack. It instantly disturbs the peace. A few moments later – as if they were already eyeing the approaching guests – a lady appears, wearing a traditional costume

'Can I help you?' she asks politely.

'Yes, we're looking for a room for four people.' Danny says.

The lady looks at Danny in surprise.

'This is not a hotel' she says.

'Oh, then just a table for four, please.'

'Right this way.'

'You do have pancakes, right?' he asks, just to be sure.

The lady guides the family towards a small door.

'Watch out for..'

'Ouch, crap, hit my head again.'

'Once bitten, twice...' Anne can't complete the saying.

'Yea, yea, just rub it in.'

'I wanted to warn you' the lady says. 'Also look out for…'

'Ouch, ahh, my ankle.' Danny moans.

'…the step' the lady resumes.

After this crippled entrance, the family eventually manages to get to their table. The table is covered with a gingham check cloth, a little candle, and utensils wrapped in a napkin with a gingham check pattern. A corny combination, but it all matches well. The restaurant is located at the back of the farm, the part where the farmer used to run his business. The roof rests on large oak uprights, which still show beautiful, old trusses. The sides, where the cows used to stand, have a lowered part, which made it easy to shovel their shit.

'I bet you they don't have a Michelin star here.' Anne says.

'Stop it!' Danny says. 'You're complaining again.'

'Would you like to order something?' a friendly young man asks. He is also dressed in traditional clothes, with a dark grey plus-fours and old-fashioned Dutch wooden clogs. He's also wearing a black collared shirt and a nicely tied handkerchief around his neck with the familiar gingham check motif. He's wearing a cap and is holding a digital order pad, wirelessly connected with the kitchen.

'What happened to the notepad?' Anne asked.

Danny is visibly annoyed about her behavior, but wisely keeps his mouth shut and places the order.

'We'll have twice the 33 and twice the 41.'

The young man types in the numbers and lights the little candle. Danny rubs his head some more. That second head butt didn't do him any good. The room is spinning.

'I knew that people used to be a bit shorter than they are now.' he says, 'but how tall can that door be? I'm guessing about 5 feet… the farmer that used to live here must've been a midget.'

'Let me see this.' Anne runs her hand through Danny's hair and moves some blond locks aside to assess the damage. 'I think it's not that bad.'

'Well, I don't think so.' Danny groans.

'You're being a baby. There's nothing there.'

'But I feel what I feel.'

'Yeah, I wish you'd feel something.' Anne hypocritically looks up.

'What is this about?'

'About feeling. Feeling something for each other.' she clarifies.

'You're starting this again?'

Anne doesn't really know if she should respond to this. She mumbles something like 'Yeah, I should start this.'

'Aahh! Women! I'm going to the bathroom. I'm not feeling well. My head is spinning.'

Danny gets up and throws one more intrusive look towards Anne.

'Women's voices!' he clarifies, while he makes a *blah blah* gesture with his hand. He then walks away, past the kitchen where the smell of sweet pancakes meets his nose, following the signs that say *toilets*. The sweet air now almost makes him gag. Usually he's able to eat up to five pancakes in a row. He feels lightheaded and notices he's wobbling. Two blurry doors appear in the distance, dressed with a little man and a little woman... Which one should I take, he thinks. He randomly opens one of the doors and walks inside. The toilets sharply contrast the rest of the interior. The floors, tiles and ceiling are bright white. Large light fixtures hang from the ceiling that fill the room with a ton of light. The walls hold stainless steel urinals and sinks. Which ones are the sinks and which ones are the urinals? You can't even see the difference anymore, damnit, Danny thinks. The bright light forces him to squint. He walks to a mirror to check out his injury. 'I'm perfectly capable of assessing whether something is wrong with me or not.' Danny mumbles. As he stands there, he hears a toilet flush behind him. A door opens and someone gets out of the stall. The man walks to the sink with determined steps and does his thing. Danny doesn't pay too much attention to it. He stares at the mirror and checks out his head, where he can see a little wound. Some blood seeped out of it, but that already coagulated. He takes out his handkerchief, wets it and tries to clean the wound a bit.

'You should've just gone home.' the man says.

'Eh?' Danny looks in the direction of the voice, in surprise. Because of the bright light and his squinted eyes he's unable to properly see who or what is talking to him.

'You can still go home and forget what happened.'

'Who are you and what do you want?' Danny stammers.

'Don't worry, I won't hurt you. I'm merely giving advice.'

'I don't need advice.' Danny assures him. 'Everyone always wants to lecture me and give me advice. I've had enough!'
He rinses his bloody handkerchief under the faucet and frantically wrings it out.

'And if I may give you a piece of ad...' but he doesn't finish his statement. The man is gone. Danny looks around, opens some stall doors. But the man is really gone, up in smoke. He didn't even hear him leave. Danny looks at himself again through the cracks of his eyelids and tries to get his confused state under control.

'That voice...' He turns on the water and throws some cold water in his face with both hands. 'I've heard that voice before somewhere.' While he walks back to the table in confusion, Danny regularly looks around to see if he can spot the guy from the voice. He couldn't have disappeared from the face of the earth, right? he thinks. Anne starts again when Danny arrives back at the table.

'What took you so long?'

'I had to freshen up a bit.' Danny says.

'That takes you half an hour?'

'Half an hour? It felt like five minutes to me.'

'We ended up eating the pancakes.'

'I can see that.' he mumbles, looking at the empty plates.
Danny wonders: what should I tell them... that I saw a man in the bathroom... who advised me to forget everything... what the fuck did he mean with 'everything' anyway? Anne will never believe me, especially after what happened earlier this afternoon. She'll think I'm seeing ghosts.

'Come on, let's go home.' Danny decisively exclaims.

'Home?' Anne asks surprised.

'I mean to the bungalow park. I'm tired.'

'Ahh, the man is tired. I guess that's what we'll have to do then, right?'

'Anne! Just leave me be for a bit' Danny responds annoyed, as he puts on his coat.

'Are you paying?' He quickly follows up.

'I have to pay?' Anne asks.

'Yes, you three ended up eating everything.'

Anne sighs, but pays the bill. The staggered family gets in their car.

'Tomorrow we're going home.' Danny decisively says.

They leave the pancake site with a large cloud of dust behind them.

7   The blue

A string of air bubbles continuously float up to the water surface. This seems to end for a moment, when it becomes quiet. But then it continues. The air bubbles get bigger, and suddenly the coughing face of Ems emerges from the water. Driek is standing behind him with a large brush. A number of villagers along the waterfront are amused by the ordeal.

'Well,' Driek says 'let's wash this little aardvark.'

'Do we have to do it this way?' Ems coughs.

'Come on man, half the forest can smell you. I'm not going to lie next to you in the box-bed.'

'You don't smell like roses either.'

Driek doesn't appreciate that remark and hits Ems in the head, which generates a great applause from the waterside. Hunze and Borg are among the villagers on that waterside.

'Come,' Borg says to Hunze, 'Let's go for a little walk and tell me again what you saw exactly.' The two trudge from the river bed in the direction of the forest.

'It was quite dark, so it wasn't perfectly clear' Hunze says. 'But those shadows were building something. That is what caused those huge tremors.'

'Do you have any idea what they were building?' a concerned Borg asks.

'No, not at all.'

'Who were they? Huns?'

'Possibly, but it was too dark.'

'Hmm' Borg ponders. 'Who else could it be?'

'Maybe the fellow people from Sleeswijk?'

'Would they have captured your father?'

Hunze shrugs.

'They won't do anything like that, right?... I really don't know.'

A sad look in Hunze's eyes reveals that he's quite upset about his father's disappearance.

'We have to go back to that place to see what's going on there.' Borg suggests. 'The whole village will go! We will form one big army!' he now exclaims combatively.

'I'll go back.' Hunze cautiously says. 'Alone.'

'Alone??? What is this nonsense? Do you have a death wish?'

'Alone I'm inconspicuous and agile. This way I can first investigate it.'

Borg thinks.

'You make a good point.' he eventually says.

'Also,' Hunze continues, 'I would like to know what happened to my father. I have to know.' He sounds determined.

'We'll do it this way!' Borg decisively says. 'Tomorrow, before the first rays hit the foliage, you depart. But be back before sunset! This stays between us and you report directly to me.'

Borg wraps his arm around Hunze's narrow shoulders.

'Come, let's have some tasty einkorn bread at my sweet Ambra.'

Before the rooster can celebrate the morning with his crows, Hunze silently sneaks out the village. He knows exactly where to go because of the position of some stars and the moon. For now, he doesn't let anything distract him and purposefully walks through the forest. He just has to find out what's going on in the woods. And whether his father is there.

The weather is clear, with a slight morning mist here and there. The first rays of light from the sun pierce the mist and quickly heat up Hunze's slim face. The warmth and the peace in the forest are in starkly contrast with the tension and fear that are ruling Hunze. He stays alert. This peace can end at any given moment. Someone can cross his path at any given moment. Friend or foe. *Always stay vigilant* is one of the wise lessons his father taught him. It can't be much farther, he thinks. This is where I gave Ems the biggest scare of his life. He chuckles. He can still see poor Ems on his knees and shout: 'Oh, I'm never going to see my sweet Driek again'. Hunze walks a bit further off the path and deeper into the woods with a wide grin on his face. The grin quickly turns into tension and unrest on Hunze's face. This is where the thumping started. This is where they heard the voices and the singing for the first time. Hunze's heart is pounding. Weird, because there's nothing going on now. It is quiet, nobody around, total silence, and total emptiness. Hunze crawls through some bushes and pushes some branches and twigs aside. The blinding sunlight forces him to squint his eyes to still be able to see his surroundings. Hunze takes another step forward, which gets him nowhere. He falls forward, accompanied by much crackling and moaning, his stomach hits the ground and his face falls in the sand. His hat flies off his head. His foot got stuck behind something. When Hunze returns to his senses, he tries to get up with much cursing and ranting. He slowly turns around and sees the cause of his fall. 'A stone?' he rants to himself. 'Just my luck. A damn stone.' He brushes the sand off his shoulders and wants to retrieve his hat that flew off. But as he walks towards his hat, he looks forward and is left speechless. He gasps. A few foot lengths from him lie giant boulders, orderly stacked on top of each other. Not simply in a big pile, but neatly arranged in a row and on top of each other. Hunze had seen these types of giant rocks in the forest before. Legend has it that the ice gods took the stones thousands of years ago from the mountains to use them as a table, to put their chalices filled with divine drinks on. The gods often sat around the stone table completely drunk, just roaring at each other. All that yelling and splashing caused the thunder, followed by snow and hail. There's one of these giant rocks in his village, but this many of them is really bizarre.

'Holy funnel beakers,' Hunze stammers. 'What is this?' With caution, but also with some curiosity, Hunze walks towards the rocks. He takes a lap around them, looks in between and walks around them again. He then thinks to himself 'How the heck did all these huge stones get on top of each other?' While he continues to think about this, he's overcome by a haunting feeling. He takes a little step back and sits on a smaller rock. Could it have been those legendary ice gods after all, he wonders. But there was no snow, no ice, it's not winter now… and those shadows… those weren't ice gods. Without finding an answer, Hunze continues to sit on the rock, defeated, quietly staring at the structure for a while. As he's sitting there, darkness slowly falls. He suddenly realizes he made an agreement with Borg to get back to the village before dark. He gets up, grabs his stuff and gets ready to return home. But then something he has never seen before happens. He looks towards the stones, from where a faint glow lights up his face. As if the stack of boulders hadn't caused enough amazement, another phenomenon takes place that astonishes Hunze. His mouth slowly opens in awe. Points of light glisten in Hunze's eyes. A spectacle in which dozens, no, hundreds, of little lights appear from behind the stones and dance up and down like frolicking bees. What is this? I've never seen anything like this, Hunze thinks to himself.

Once he realizes there's no immediate threat, he carefully walks towards the stones and the parade of lights. As he gets closer, their numbers seem to increase. The lights now also start to float around him, which makes him a bit dizzy. Suddenly, Hunze notices one of those lights is sitting on his hand. He intently observes it. It's a type of fly, he thinks, but one that lights up.

'Hey, little fly. Where do you come from?' he asks quietly, to avoid scaring them off.

A feeling of euphoria takes hold of him, a 'wow' feeling. Hunze climbs on top of the stones to get even closer to the wondrous natural phenomenon. He quietly starts to laugh. He is filled with a sense of joy and freedom. He starts to laugh louder and louder. The flies dance around him like ballerinas while pleasantly buzzing. Hunze feels light as a feather, as if he's being carried by the little flies. But suddenly they're gone. As suddenly as they appeared out of nowhere, they disappear into nowhere again. Hunze looks in between the rocks to see if he can catch a glimpse. He walks around the dolmen and crawls through to find out where they went. Ah, there they are. He discovers a faint light on the other side of the dolmen. The light coming from the stone is different however, a light blue light, opposed to the white light of the little flies. Hunze continues to crawl, but the light dims before he can get to the stone. He is unable to find out where the little flies are hiding and decides to return to the village. It's late and dark, but the moonlight will guide him home safely.

The rooster has never crowed as loudly as this morning. It's as if he feels he's going to be slaughtered that day and that today is thus his final performance. He already crows as loudly as he can as soon as the first rays of sun find their way through the trees to Borg's village. Slowly but surely the sleepy village awakes and the villagers poke their heads out their huts. High-stepping Chief Borg walks to the well like a true headman, and fills a bucket. He takes a sip from the bucket and pours the rest over his weary head. He roars loudly, the water is freezing cold, and shakes his head back and forth, like a buffalo that just stepped out of a puddle.

'Good morning Borg.' a villager says, who also throws his bucket into the well, pulls it out with a rope and carries out the same ritual as his predecessor.

'A good morning to you too.' Borg says.

'Good morning Borg.' It's Lute, who greets the head of the village with a sing-song tone. He's also carrying a bucket and throws it into the well. Borg and the other villager look at each other in surprise and then look at Lute.

'What?' Lute hesitantly asks.

Borg and the villager stick their heads over the edge of the deep well, look down and start laughing. Then, Lute realizes. He threw his bucket into the well, but forgot to tie a rope to it.

'Good luck!' Borg roars to Lute, and walks back to his hut. On his way back, Aa calls out to him.

'Borg, have you seen Hunze? He didn't come home yesterday.'

'Damn, you're right. He didn't call in. Have you checked his hut yet?'

'Yes, nothing. His bed wasn't slept in. Now what?'
Borg thinks.

'Hunze is smart, I can't imagine something happening to him. Let's just wait for him today, dear. If he hasn't shown before the end of the afternoon, we'll go looking for him.'
Borg feels uneasy. First the druid and now the son of the druid, of all people. This does not augur well, he thinks.

'But ehh... How come you're so interested in Hunze all of a sudden?' Borg asks Aa.
She shyly looks to the ground.

'Aa?' Borg asks again.

'Isn't it important that Hunze is safely back at home? And to find out whether he found the druid?' Aa responds with carefully chosen words.

'There's more to it, girl. You can't fool Chief Borg.'

'There's nothing, really.'

'You're in love with Hunze?'

'No, I'm not. That villager is beneath me.'
While Aa says these words, she resolutely turns around to avoid further discussion.

'By all druids!' Borg exclaims. 'Lute's daughter may choose to love whomever she wants. Share it with me! Shall I discuss it with your father?'
But Aa is already out of sight.

Several hours later, Aa's two small feet drag along the creek. She looks sad and worried. She wipes off a tear that runs over her cheek with her sleeve. She doesn't know what to do and walks through the forest without purpose. She decides to return to the village via the dark path. She stays clear of Borg's hut. She doesn't want to see him for a while. Without noticing, she walks straight towards the druid's hut.

Thoughtless, she arrives at the entrance. She hesitates. Should I go in?, she thinks. She however believes she has no business in there, and turns around. At that moment, a rumble sounds from the hut. Aa gets scared and freezes. A couple of seconds later she thinks she just imagined it, and gets ready to leave. But then she hears the rumbling again. She's now certain somebody is in the hut.

'Who is there?' she asks.

No answer. She carefully walks to the door and grabs the old handle to open the door. It's dark inside and it smells like burnt oak, coming from the wood stove.

'Is someone here?' she asks again and walks farther into the hut. It's familiar territory to her, because she's been here before. She regularly visited the druid's hut to taste new concoctions. Whenever he discovered new herbs, he proudly spoke about their various uses. Suddenly, someone grabs Aa from behind and firmly presses a hand against her mouth to shut her up. She tries to call for help, but all she can get out is a 'hmm hmmm mhh'. She struggles and tries to get away like a wild aardvark that just walked into a trap. Eventually she sees an opportunity to turn around and looks her assailant straight in the eyes.

'Hunze?'

'Aa?'

He lets her go in terror.

'What are you doing here?' she asks.

'I could ask you the same thing.'

'I heard noises and…' that's all Aa is able to get out. She grabs Hunze and presses him against her.

'I'm so happy to see you. We were worried. You didn't come home yesterday.'

'I did, but it was very late. I didn't wake anyone and slept here.'

'Why here?'

'I miss my father. I haven't found him yet.'

Aa looks into Hunze's eyes. She feels his sadness transfer to her and throws her arms around him in an attempt to comfort him.

'But I do have something else I'd like to show you.'

'Oh, what's that?' Aa asks surprised.

'I can't explain it. It's something you have to see!' Hunze says in delight.

'Come to the well when the moon rises, and I'll take you.'

'Tonight? In the dark?' Aa asks, sounding worried.

'Because you can only see it in the dark. Trust me.'

'I do.' she says.

She carefully kisses him on the cheek as she giggles and trots out of the hut.

'You still have to report to Borg, though.' she tells him.

Hunze is left confused. A kiss, he wonders. He wipes his cheek with his hand.

The moonlight pierces through the branches. The sounds of crickets fill the forest.

'Psst.'

'Yes, I'm here.'

Two dark figures are standing near the well in the middle of the village.

'Is that you, Hunze?'

'Yes, come on, before we wake up the whole village.'

'Quite exciting.' Aa giggles.

'This way.' Hunze takes Aa by her hand and walks into the forest along the dark path.

'What is it you want to show me?' Aa asks.

'It's a surprise. You'll see.' Hunze whispers, followed by a quiet 'I hope'.

'I like surprises.' Aa laughs.

After having walked for a while, Aa starts to worry.

'You weren't able to find a trace of your father?'

'Nothing,' but he immediately corrects himself. 'That's not completely true. I did find some traces of him using his sickle.'

'Oh, but…'

'They were fresh cuts, that's why.' Hunze clarifies.

'What if something happened to your father and he's not coming back?'

Hunze sighs. He takes a break at the old oak tree to navigate their position.

'This way.'

Hunze and Aa carefully make their way through the bushes along a small path. They have to dodge branches and twigs to prevent them from smacking them in the face.

'We're here.'

Aa tries to get a good view of the surrounding in the faint moonlight, but doesn't see much more than trees and bushes. Hunze walks away from her, a bit farther into the open field, and climbs on top of the dolmen.

'This is it!' he exclaims like a small child. Hunze stands on top of the boulders with his hands spread wide, like a god atop a mountain.

Now Aa sees it as well. Her mouth falls open in surprise. She's also familiar with the enormous erratic rocks from the ice age that are found in the forest every so often, but she's never seen a giant structure of these rocks before. She approaches the dolmen taking small steps.

'How… what… who…?' she quietly stammers.

'Don't ask me, I have no answers either. Come on! Come up here.' Hunze extends his hand and carefully pulls her up, onto the rocks. Aa starts to giggle quietly, coming from a fear of the unknown instead of a feeling of excitement.

'This is not all.' Hunze assures her.

'Well, I think this is impressive enough. Can I get down now?'

'Wait!' Hunze thinks. He wonders how it happened the last time. What did he do to cause these fireflies to appear? He nervously walks back and forth on the rocks, stomps his feet here and there. Nothing.

'Why are you pacing? You're scaring me.'

'There's something else you should see, Aa.'

'Hunze…' she shyly laughs. 'I'm only seventeen.'

'No, it's light. Flying light.' Hunze clarifies, as he stomps his feet once more.

Aa looks at him in surprise.

'I know the druid was an eccentric man, but I didn't think his son would also lose his marbles… Hunze, I want to go back home.'
She jumps off the rocks, lands with both feet firmly on the ground and takes a few steps into the woods. Then, Hunze suddenly shouts.

'Aa, look!'
Aa looks back and sees something she's never seen before. A wondrous spectacle, dozens of lights that frolic upwards from between the stones. It's a magical ballet performance that makes the Bolshoi Theatre pale in comparison. More and more fireflies appear from the caverns of the dolmen. The fearful and uncomfortable feelings Aa had a few moments ago, made room for amazement and euphoria.

'Come' Hunze says, as he reaches out his hand to Aa.
Aa climbs onto the dolmen again. The lights dance around her, making her feel light as a feather. It's like a fairy tale. She is the princess and Hunze is the prince. She firmly holds on to Hunze's hand as they dance on the stone, through the frontline of fireflies. Hunze laughs, it worked. The thing they came for in the dead of night worked. Aa's jump onto the ground woke up the fireflies. Aa sees Hunze's great big laugh, his twinkling eyes under his hat, she feels his warm hands and melts. She's been having intense feelings for Hunze for a while now, but wasn't able to express them. Now, the moment is there. The entire setting, the feeling, everything feels just right. While dancing on the dolmen, guided by the lights, she brings her body increasingly closer to Hunze's. She continues to intensely look into his eyes and sees the sparkling reflection of the fireflies. Now, she thinks. She gently closes her eyes, purses her lips and carefully places them on Hunze's. Time stands still for a couple of seconds.

Hunze reacts surprised and clumsily. He pushes Aa away, which causes him to falter and almost fall. He barely manages to remain standing and looks at Aa, perplexed. The euphoria and liberating feeling have completely disappeared. The fireflies apparently sense this moment. They silently return to their home, underground near the dolmen. Hunze starts to stammer.

'You kissed me?'

'Seems like it. That's what they call a kiss.' Aa says.
Hunze is completely befuddled and touches his mouth with his fingers to see if everything is still okay.

'But why?'

'Why? Why?' Aa repeats.

'Yes, why did you do that?'

'Don't you realize anything? That I might like you, find you attractive and sweet... Hunze, I love you. I want you to become my husband... the father of my children.'
Father? Children? Hunze thinks.

'Wow! This is going a bit too fast for me.' he interrupts. 'I can relate to the like and love part. But your husband... children...'
Hunze is horrified and doesn't know how to act. To Aa, this is a completely unexpected and disappointing reaction.

'Don't you love me?' she asks.
Hunze hesitates to respond. His face clearly shows deep contemplation.

'It is... it is difficult. Marrying, children... I'm not really thinking about those things. You know?'

'Let's just skip that, then. But you love me? You would want to be with me?' Aa asks, nearly pleading.
Hunze sees a tear run down her cheek. It hurts him to make her sad. He thinks she's pretty and a kind, cool girl, but there's something keeping him from getting closer to her. He doesn't really know what it is. What he does know, is that he's a man, a hunter who likes

adventure and excitement, that he might become the next chief of the village and that he has a secret desire for…, for what exactly? He doesn't really have the answer yet. He looks into Aa's disappointed eyes.

'We have to go back to the village.'
The journey home is long and silent.

Another good old-fashioned ritual at the well. Villagers come and go to rinse of the morning dust. Lute also drags his feel towards the well. He looks over the edge and sees that his bucket is still in there, deep, deep down.
Crestfallen, he helplessly looks around. The villagers try not to laugh.

'I've heard this is a bottomless well?' Borg yells, who entered the village square and addresses Lute.

'Well, well, well,' he continues, looking very serious. 'We have to get to the bottom of this problem'. Borg throws his big arm around Lute's narrow shoulder as they walk away from the well. Borg sneakily turns around towards the remaining villagers, and yells with a smile on his face: 'Come on my dear Lute, just don't kick the bucket.' The villagers can no longer keep a straight face and roll on the ground laughing.

Hunze walks a bit farther down the village. He's thinking about whether or not he should walk towards Borg and tell him about the pile of rocks. He decides to wait for a better moment and walks straight to the druid's hut to possibly find any clues that give more information about his father's disappearance. He runs into Aa, who's carrying a bucket. She's going to get water from the well. She says nothing as she passes Hunze and continues walking, looking directly to the ground. Hunze feels guilty, but knows there's currently no solution. Once arrived in the druid's hut, he doesn't really know where to start or what to look for.

He's rummaging around the funnel beakers, pots and caldrons, feeling helpless. The sickle, he suddenly thinks. Hunze isn't sure anymore, did dad take his sickle? He eagerly looks for it in the corner housing some tools. No sickle to be found. So that could mean he did take it with him. He will at least have something with which he can defend himself. That calms Hunze down. He decides to return to the pile of rocks one last time, this time alone, and then report to Borg. The pile fascinates him. He has a feeling, a suspicion, something more can be found there. Maybe there's a trace that leads to his father.

It's peacefully quiet in the village around sunset. A goat walks around, looking for a place to sleep, and some chickens eat some final grains before they go home to roost. A little fire is burning next to the well, with two villagers beside it, warming themselves. Hunze passes them and greets them as if nothing is going on. Once he passes some tree trunks, he looks behind to make sure the two aren't looking at him. He then quickly walks to the other side, along the winding path, into the forest. He has brought his spear. Not to hunt an aardvark this time, but to protect himself. He doesn't know against whom or what. Against the Huns? Hunze wonders whether those giants are actually the greatest threat at the moment. There's something else going on in the forest, he's sure of it.

Once he gets to the big oak, he abandons the familiar winding path and makes his way through the bushes. He tries to not make too much noise in order to hear the sounds around him. *It's always better to be a step ahead of your enemy and the great unknown*, as his father taught him. Dad... where are you?, Hunze sadly wonders. The Northern forest is immensely large. It extends to the Frisians in the west and to the dangerous Northern Sea in the north. Hunze can remember this. He's been there once during an exploration, with Ems and two other hunters from the village. Ha-ha Ems, that short fatty with his short legs could only keep up with the greatest difficulty. The exploration lasted at least three seasons. They reached the Northern

Sea exactly during the storm season. The waves were high as huts and pounded the forest. The trees were devoured as if they were kindling. We had to be careful to not get swept away by the water. That's why we went back into the forest, towards the east. After two sunsets we arrived at the mouth of a river on the Northern Sea, with very calm water. We camped out there for a while on a little beach. It was beautiful there, swimming in the cold water. And there were fish… so many fish. My stomach still hurts from eating all the fish, ha-ha. Only Ems was afraid to go into the water, that poor thing. He always kept watch, because well, you never know. In order to give him some of the experience of the sea we named the little beach after him. We carved the letters of his name into a large rock, in funnel beaker style: *Ems.* After some sunsets we departed and followed the banks of the river, further east, so we could map the forest in eastern direction, where the East Frisians lived. We have no problems with these people. They're peaceful and we trade things with each other; food, pelts. Materials. Hunze laughs, I still remember that when my father visited the East Frisians, he always brought fragrant and medicinal herbs with him and returned with a peculiar material. *Bronze* he called it. As a little boy, I had no idea what you could do with it, but dad threw it on a fire and eventually made it into a sickle. Wonderful, that father of mine is very arty. I once cut my finger on that sickle. Aa patched me up with a rag to stop the bleeding… Aa… Anyway, so we headed east. That's where we first encountered the Huns, the giants. I remember it well. We walked over a hill and saw the settlement on the other side. We didn't know who they were at first, but then I saw a couple of those giants walking… By Borg, such monsters. Some of them carried huge clubs. The ground shook whenever they took a step. Ems, the coward, wanted to turn around right away, but we remained on the hill a bit longer to explore the surroundings. It was a settlement with huts made of logs, at least three times the size of the huts of us Funnel beakers. Some Huns used a large hill as a hut. The top of the hill was open, with plumes of smoke coming from the hole.

Weird fellows, those Huns. Who starts a fire in their own hut? In a certain spot in the middle of the settlement, some Huns were sitting on big rocks in a circle. I don't remember it exactly, but they were singing. Not like how we sing after some brews, and also not like how the Bard sings. It was more like buzzing, humming, grunting, I don't know. It didn't sound very pleasant, not to my ears at least. We jokingly called their whining *Hun sing and so.* That's how we remembered this settlement as *Hunsingo.* Ha-ha, we eventually got the hell out of there. We didn't feel like getting clubbed in the head.

All these memories make Hunze laugh. It keeps him going during the journey. He suddenly stops walking. Besides the call of an owl, the howling of a wolf and the crowing of a black crow he believes he hears something else. A squawk or fizzle, far away from him. A sound he doesn't know, which puts him even more on guard. He holds his breath for a few seconds, but is unable to detect anything else suspicious. He's only several steps away from the dolmen. He takes another couple of steps through the bushes and it appears. It looks exactly the same as last time, like a silent witness. Hunze is increasingly fascinated and slowly walks towards the magical pile of stones. He gently runs his fingers over the rock formation. He still has no clue as to how those giants managed to stack these rocks like this, and why. He studies their position relative to each other, but can't make anything of it. His heart is pounding in his throat. He feels the blood coursing through his veins. After walking around and through it a number of times, he climbs on top of the largest rock. He has a good view of it in the clear moonlight. The structure is oblong and extensive. It looks peaceful and deserted. That enormous immovable mass radiates peace. When Hunze stands still for a couple of breaths, a tiny light flies by very subtly. He doesn't even realize it at first. Until a second and a third light pass by. He suddenly sees the presence of the fireflies, which quickly multiply.

'Hey there, little pals.' he whispers.

The fireflies appear from all nooks and crannies and again entertain Hunze with a magnificent ballet performance. He realizes he didn't stamp or jump this time. They just spontaneously appeared. He extends his arm and gently runs his hand and fingers through the swirling lights. They seem to glow stronger than last times.

'What do you want to tell me?'
A firefly lands on one of his fingertips. Hunze tries to get a closer look of the little creature, but it's so tiny that nothing can be distinguished.

'Just tell me, show me what you want me to see.'
The spectacle is so impressive that Hunze forgets about the world around him. The peace is suddenly brutally disrupted by a huge banging. The fireflies sense doom and disappear between the rocks. Another bang makes the ground shake.

'By Borg, what is this now?' His euphoria turns into fear, the way a beautiful, sunny day can turn into an ominous thunderstorm. Hunze flees into the bushes and keeps quiet. Two dark figures approach the dolmen. From the size of it, they seem to be Huns. He raises his ears in order to hear the conversation. He managed to learn a bit of their language during one of his father's many wise lessons, as well as the explorations.

'It has to work this time.' one says.

'I'll try my best, Lofar.' the other responds.

'Make sure you get that ceeflex generator up and running, we have to get out of here.'

'But, in which circles should I mingle?'

'Try it with the notables and politician, they always do well. But keep quiet and stay in contact with Milan.'

'Ok, Lofar.'
Generator, notables… Hunze has no idea what they're talking about. In the meantime, the two arrived at the dolmen and look around as if they're looking for something. They also look in Hunze's direction. He holds his breath.

'Come, it's time.'

'Definitely. We'll see each other later.'

'Oh, one more thing…' The man called Lofar grabs the other guy by the arm and dominantly bends over, '…watch out for that old troublemaker. If you run into him, you'll know what to do. Call me.'

'No worries, Lofar. You can trust me, you know that.'

Having said that, the subordinate one disappears between the rocks. Hunze watches the events unfold in complete silence. He shouldn't gasp or snap any branches, because he will be in big trouble. He doesn't stand a chance against those giants; he'll definitely lose. His father taught him to not even displace the wind, and to keep so quiet that time seems to stand still. The man who calls himself Lofar looks at the bedrock. What's he waiting for, Hunze thinks. The other giant is still hiding between the rocks. Hunze cramps up, because he has to stand in the same position for too long, when suddenly a blinding blue hellfire-like light appears, accompanied by soft sizzling and crackling. The bright light burns Hunze's eyes. He squeezes his eyelids, keeps his hand in front of his face and tries to catch a glimpse between his fingers. The blue light disappears after some breaths, but he still needs some time to get used to the twilight of the evening. He eventually sees that the other Hun is still standing by the rocks. The Hun looks in between the rocks and yells something, and leaves after he gets no response.

Hunze sits down with his back against a tree. The whole thing has to sink in. Right now he's unable to make anything out of this. What were those two Huns talking about? What was that blue fire? Where did that one Hun go? Questions he is unable to answer. When he comes to his senses a bit, he realizes that he has two options. Either he goes back to the village, or he checks out the rocks. His insatiable curiosity and yearning for answers make him choose the second option, although he realizes this could become a very dangerous mission. After having carefully observed the environment, he gets up, takes his spear in defense into his right hand and gradually makes his way towards the stones.

'Hello?' Hunze yells. His own voice scares him, because it echoes against the rocks and sounds louder in the silence than he expected.

'Do you need help?' he quite naively continues.
Since there's no response, Hunze decides to get in between the rocks. The Hun should be here somewhere, he thinks. He didn't see him leave. It's quite dark between the rocks, but he's still able to see a little bit because of the moonlight… He glances to the left, to the right and then again to the left. When Hunze is certain there's nobody here, he sighs to release the tension. Hunze doesn't understand it at all. That giant couldn't have just fallen through the ground…

'That's it!' he utters in a eureka moment.
He scours the ground and kicks some sand aside in some places. There's a trapdoor or a secret passage in the ground here somewhere. There must be. Hunze is convinced he's right and starts his investigation. A couple minutes later Hunze is sitting with his back against a rock. Defeated and distraught, sweat and dust sticking to his forehead. He stares into space and thinks it all must have been a dream. But… what if it was all a dream, what's that firefly doing there then? Hunze sees the light come from under the soil near a stone, swirling up and down in a haze. A besotted firefly, he thinks. When the little animal approaches, it disappears just as quickly as it appeared. Hunze starts to dig with his bare hands, dig into the hard soil until his nails break. His little hat falls off his head and drops of sweat splash off his face. His face starts to glow, not red but blue. Bright blue.

The news spreads like wildfire through the village. Most villagers have gathered near the well. Borg, Ems, Aa, Driek, Lute, they're all there. They eagerly gesture and all speak at once. The bustle and panic also seems to rub off on the animals. The sheep and goats bleat, the roosters fight each other and a dog runs around the scene, barking. It's chaos and disorder.

'SILEEEENCE!' Borg raises his voice and climbs on top of a log. It has no effect.

'SIII…' he now seems to have the attention and adjusts his volume, 'lence'. He clears his throat.

'He was eaten by the wolves!' a villager starts.

'The Huns got him.' another rambles.

'No, that's impossible. He's just looking for his father.' Aa assures everyone. 'Hunze is smart, he won't let himself get caught.'

'But the Huns, no one stands a chance against them!' Driek shouts. Borg uses his hand to tell everyone to be calm.

'There's only one way to find out where Hunze is. We will have to look for him.'

'I agree!' Lute exclaims, a bit too cheerfully. He tries to keep the mood up, but it doesn't really take. The villagers start to mumble amongst themselves. Their best hunter is now gone.

'Who should look for him then?' Ems asks.

Borg thinks. He realizes it will be a dangerous search, but comes up with a solution, like a true village chief.

'We will search, each time with a group of three villagers. Each with their own strengths; a hunter, a scout and a woman'.

'Broads coming along on the search???' one of the men shouts.

'Yes, she can look after the food and care. But she remains in the background! But you'll find this will benefit you' Borg assures them. 'And not unimportantly, we only search between sunrise and sunset. We set up camp in the dark.'

After some internal scheming, the villagers accept his proposal. They determine who will go with whom, and leave the center of the village, towards their huts.

The following morning, the first group heads out. They return after several days. The villagers are waiting for them, hoping they have Hunze with them, but the search was unsuccessful. The following group departs, but they also return defeated after some days. The third group starts their search. They don't have different news upon their return. The villagers return to their huts, completely defeated. Aa is inconsolable, her tears run into the little river, where she usually does the laundry so cheerfully. She swam, played and had fun with Hunze in that same river. She had a major crush on Hunze, but was never able to clearly tell him. Now it seems Hunze is lost in time and will never return. That sweet… sweet Hunze, I will never see him again, Aa sobs. She walks along the river bed. She sees his smile and those twinkling eyes under that ever-present little hat in the reflection of the water. She can no longer stand it, the unbearable pain of the loss of her loved one in the prime of her life. She no longer feels a warm future, just the cold water on her feet. An inconsolable Aa merges with the river's clear water. The running water meanders through the forest to an infinite destination.

Suddenly, a firm hand grabs Aa's arm, who's floating through the water, and pulls the seemingly lifeless body from the creek onto the land. The soaked clothes continue to seep for a while. The body slowly regains consciousness. Aa carefully opens her eyes. She looks into the sunlight and everything is blurry. A very peaceful smile appears. I'm in heaven, she thinks. It's so beautiful here. Now I'll see Hunze again. When she sees the figure above her, she's certain.

'Hunze? Is that you?'

'Yes, sweet Aa. Why did you want to drown yourself?'

'Because I want to be with you.'

'Well, that's strange,' Hunze laughs, 'because then you should *not* drown yourself. Good thing I saved you.'

It takes a while before Aa comes to her senses.

'Saved?' she asks. 'I'm not in heaven with you?'

Hunze laughs.

'You're in heaven with me… in Borg.'

Aa jumps up.

'Hunze?' She looks around in horror. 'Where were you? Everyone's been looking for you. We thought you were gone, dead.'

'That's what I thought as well. But I've seen something, you won't believe it. I saw the hidden city of Hunsingo, the city of the Huns. It was impressive but scary at the same time. With strange animals that loudly follow each other without legs, large birds the Huns walk into, huts stacked on top of each other, sometimes as many as thirty on top of each other, and…'

Aa looks bewildered at Hunze and has no idea what he's talking about. She thinks for a second and then wisely responds: 'I can believe you saw Hunsingo. But ehm… all that other stuff… I would keep quiet about that for a bit if I were you. Come on, let's go home. Don't ever go to those rocks again!'

8   The dream

Danny is back at the dolmen for further research. The events that transpired during his vacation really got to him. The strange blue glow on one of the rocks, the vague images he saw in his thoughts, his temporary loss of consciousness, the strange shepherd, the man in the toilet. All these things run through his head. A vacation that will not soon be forgotten, he thinks, while checking his handless watch. Just like the last time, he walks around the dolmen a couple of times, but today it's extremely hot outside. The sun is almost right above the dolmen. A crow aimlessly circles around above the dolmen and breaks a moment of silence with its cawing. The blistering heat however doesn't stop him from climbing on top of the dolmen, walk over it and then crawl inside in between the rocks to get a closer look of the abnormal stone the blue glow came from.

'If I may give you some advice.' it suddenly sounds from somewhere outside the dolmen. It scares the living daylight out of Danny, he crawls out of the dolmen.

'Forget what you saw.' it sounds again, now from the other side of the dolmen. Danny just manages to see a shadow disappear behind the stones.

'Who's there?' Danny shouts. It's as if his voice fades into the distance. He sees the shadow move between the rocks and runs after him. The shadow is too fast. His heart is pounding. He wants to know who's there, so he runs around to the other side, hoping to cut the shadow off. He is shocked to see his own dog there upon arrival.

'Bor? What are you doing here?' Danny walks towards him and wants to grab his collar, but Bor runs off, between the rocks.

'You should keep a leash on that poodle,' the stranger sneers, this time again from the other side of the dolmen.

Danny is starting to become slightly paranoid and wants to chase after Bor through the rocks. But then he walks into a huge wall of blue light that completely blinds him. He hears Bor barking in the distance, the barks fade into quiet howling. Danny, who is now panicking, tries to find his way. He then sees that face again in the blue light, the face of that young man wearing a hat. He's trying to say something, but it's inaudible. It seems like he wants to warn him. But the only thing Danny hears is extremely loud ringing that seems to be coming from the sky. He looks up and sees a large, dark colossus descend towards him. He feels an enormous thump.

'Ahhh!' Danny jumps straight up.

'Whuh huh ohw...' His heart is beating at 150 beats per minute and his breathing resembles a steam engine. He bewilderedly looks around, with fear in his eyes. He's sitting upright in his bed, in his own bedroom, back from vacation in his own house in Loppersum. His pajama is drenched in sweat. Anne is still sleeping next to him, undisturbed. It takes a while before Danny comes to his senses and realizes where he is. He looks at Anne again to make sure she's indeed sleeping.

'Unbelievable' he whispers to himself.

Danny checks his handless alarm clock on the nightstand. He roughly runs his hands through his hair to wake up more quickly and wipes the sweat off his forehead with the sleeve of his pajama. He gets out of bed, puts on his slippers and looks outside through the curtains. It is still pitch dark, it's only 3 in the morning. He walks to the bathroom. He turns on the light and looks in the mirror.

'Blood?'

A little line of blood seeps over his forehead. The wound on his head opened up. Time heals all wounds, he thinks. Well, not for me. He wipes off the blood with a cloth and dabs the wound in order to clean and dry it.

'I'm getting good at this.'

He looks at himself again and lets everything get through to him.

'What the fuck?' he yells out loud, but he gets no answer. He takes two paracetamol from the medicine cabinet and takes them with a bit of water. He then walks back to the bedroom. On his way there, he opens the door of his children's bedroom a tiny bit and sees the boys are fast asleep. Suddenly, anxiety overwhelms him.

'Bor?!'

Danny runs down the stairs in a panic, opens the door to the utility room and flips the light switch. The dog basket is empty.

'What the f…' He takes another good look around the utility room.

'Bor?'

Nothing.

'Anne!' Danny shouts, as he runs up the stairs.

'Anne! Where is Bor?!'

Anne, who woke up from all the ruckus and shouting, is standing at the top of the stairs.

'What's going on, Danny?' she asks, half asleep.

'Bor's not here!'

'Bor's not here?' she repeats, taken aback. 'What do you need Bor for in the middle of the night?'

'What do you think? To take him out, go for a walk with him!' Danny sarcastically shouts.

Anne stares at Danny with disbelieving eyes.

'Go for a walk?' she asks, as she looks back at the heavy rain coming down onto the bedroom window.

'Where is Bor?!' Danny shouts again. He stampedes to the children's room and turns on the light.

'Thomas, Benjamin!'

The boys jump up. The duvet flies off the bed. On the bed in between the two children, Bor is lying down, happily wagging his tail.

9   Controversial research

It's quite 'cozy' at the breakfast table of the de Vries family. Not really. No one has said a word all morning. Anne takes some rolls and a glass from the jug of juice, which she puts down in front of Danny with so much force that the juice splashes out the jug. Drips of orange juice hang from Danny's nose. He closes his eyes for a second and visibly clenches his teeth to prevent himself from saying something. He grabs a napkin and wipes his face clean. He promptly looks towards Thomas and Benjamin on the other side of the kitchen table. Danny gives them a threatening look to let them know they shouldn't even think about saying anything. Message received. The children don't move their lips and clam up. Awkwardly they continue to chew on a piece of bread they can't seem to swallow. They're afraid to ask for the jug of orange juice, although they yearningly look at it. Anne throws the last burnt rolls on the table as she uneasily leans against the countertop. The children look at her.

'What?' she nonchalantly asks.
The children look at the burnt roll.

'They've spent a bit too much time in the oven' she says. 'So what?' Danny looks at the handless kitchen clock.

'I'm going to the university.' he decisively says. He gets up and roughly shoves the chair under the kitchen table.

'Eh?' Anne mumbles. 'But we're still on vacation.'

'There's something I need to find out. It keeps running through my head. I have to find out. You go do something fun with the boys today.'

'Do something fun?' Anne asks. 'Do something fun??' she asks again, now visibly annoyed. 'Mister is going to work during his vacation and we just have to do *something fun*?!'

Thomas and Benjamin follow their parents' verbal hostilities by turning their heads from left to right, from one to the other. Danny takes his phone and puts some stuff in his bag.

'You're such an unbelievable ass.' Anne shouts.

'I'll call you when I'm on my way back.' Danny snippily responds as he walks away.

Anne is left stunned in the kitchen. But not for long. She takes the bowl of rolls and chases after Danny, who in the meantime got into his car and put it in reverse.

'Here!' She throws the bowl of rolls to the car. 'You forgot to take your lunch, honey!'

Annoyed by this violent act, Danny drives off with a bit too much throttle. A curtain of smoke shoots from under the tires and a red-faced Anne is left alone in the street.

'And don't think we'll be here waiting for you, dick!' she yells at him, knowing Danny won't hear it anyway. When Danny goes around the corner, Anne is still furiously stomping the ground. She turns around to go back inside and sees the children watching her from the kitchen window.

'What? What?!' she threateningly yells at the two, who duck in fear.

It's busy on the highway to Groningen. The warm summer sun heats up the tarmac. Waves of heat rise up from the tarmac between the cars. The road surface looks like one giant black mirror. In the distance you can see things that aren't there, a mirage. Traffic is *'slow to stationary'* as the traffic reporter on the radio phrases it. Danny joins the traffic jam. He uses the delay to call the university.

'University of Groningen, good morning' a friendly woman's voice says.

'Good morning, it's Danny de Vries. Could you connect me to professor Dijkstra?' He sips from a cup of coffee he just got from a gas station. He winces in disgust and spills some coffee on his suit. The coffee from the machine tastes awful. What a shame, he thinks. As he wipes the spilled coffee off his suit, the voice says: 'I will connect you to professor Dijkstra, one moment please.'

Yeah, yeah, Danny thinks as he checks his handless watch. I know those 'moments'. All those minutes of waiting add up to a big chunk of your life. Time is valuable, lady. If we could just turn back time it would not be a problem and we could just do it all over again, perhaps even better. What if it were possible... we'd have all the time in the world. The thought makes Danny laugh.

'This is Dijkstra', Danny hears from the other end of the line. It's a deep, unerring voice, an authority you instantly respect. Professor Dijkstra works at the University of Groningen. He was Danny's supervisor when he graduated in archaeology. Danny stayed in contact with the professor after his study, and they work together on the current project.

'Professor' Danny responds. 'There's something I'd like to discuss with you. It's a bit difficult over the phone. Oh, and there's something else I'd like to show you to possibly examine.'

'Is it urgent?' the professor asks. 'I'm quite busy these upcoming weeks.'

'Eh, quite' Danny says. 'Is this afternoon possible?'

'Just come right away then.' the professor answers.

'Great, thanks. I'll see you soon.'

Danny tries to throw his phone onto the passenger's chair just in time, because a cop on a motorcycle popped up out of nowhere on the other lane. The officer looks at Danny from under his helmet, and it looks like he caught Danny using his phone while driving. Danny gives the officer a sheepish look. He gestures Danny to the side of the road.

'Good morning, officer.'

'License and registration, please.'

Danny hands over the requested documents.

'Do you have any idea as to why I'm stopping you?'

'I seriously have no clue.' Danny says without shame.

The man in blue looks inside the car and nods in the direction of the passenger's seat where the HTC lies.

'That's two hundred and ten euros, sir.'

'Eh, not really, this one was on sale for hundred and fifty.'

The officer keeps writing unflappable.

'Here's your ticket. You'll receive the payment order at home. Call hands-free in the future. Or even better, don't call at all. Have a nice trip.'

Danny grudgingly takes the ticket and crumples the paper outside the view of the officer. After the officer drives off on his motorcycle, he furiously throws the ball of paper out the window.

'Shit, shit, fucking shit!'

After a long and expensive car ride, Danny arrives at the University of Groningen. He parks his car and walks to the entrance. He reports to the porter's lodge.

'Good afternoon, I'm here to see professor Dijkstra.'

The lady on the other side comfortably checks all the paperwork on the desk in front of her.

'What's your name?'

'De Vries'

Again, the lady takes her sweet time.

'Do you have an appointment?' she asks, looking over her reading glasses.

'He is expecting me. I just spoke to him on the phone.'

Danny gets slightly annoyed.

The lady thinks and slowly picks up a red phone from her desk. She wants to dial a number, but realizes she doesn't know professor Dijkstra's extension. She puts the phone down again and looks up the number at a glacial pace. She browses through a book.

'Kleinstra, you said?'

'No, Dijkstra! With a D, like Dirk.'

'Dirk Kleinstra' the lady responds with a raspy voice.

For a moment, Danny seems to be capable of grabbing the lady by her red scarf and pull her over the desk, reading glasses and all.

'Miss, I... Dijkstra... professor Dijkstra'. Danny starts to hyperventilate.

'Take it easy mister Dijkstra. And you're here for?'

'Danny?!' a surprised woman's voice exclaims. He turns around and sees his lifesaver.

'Hellen!' Danny excitedly yells. 'I'm so happy to see you, now, here, at this very moment. You shouldn't have come a second later, because in that case they could've put an ad out for a new receptionist.'
He embraces Hellen, a bit too firmly, and cuddles her. Hellen is somewhat surprised by Danny's extraordinary behavior, but doesn't resist.

'Could you get me in? I have an appointment with professor Dijkstra, but I didn't bring my pass.'

'What do I get in return?' Hellen asks without any shame.

'Hmm, yeah ehh... not now Hellen. Maybe later.'

'I'll take you up on that. In the broom closet!' She clips a visitor's pass onto his lapel.

'Broom closet...?' Danny mumbles.
After the security checked their passes, they step into the elevator. Luckily I'm not alone, Danny thinks, as he stares into Hellen's eager eyes.

'Dijkstra's on third. I'm going to my office on the fourth floor. I'll see you later.' Hellen gives him a big wink. Her eyeliner almost flies off.
Upon arrival at the professor's office, Danny checks his pocket to make sure he still has the scraping of the stone. He then knocks on the door, which is actually already ajar. A nice custom at the university, all doors are open and everyone can just walk in. But out of politeness and respects he still knocks.

'Come in' a testy voice responds.

Danny enters the room. It's actually a large workspace. A large desk with a work lamp and a computer sit on one side of the room. Behind those, a bookcase with dusty books that, from the looks of it, haven't been touched in recent years. On the other side, a large worktable holding test tubes, a bubbling Erlenmeyer flask, a burner, a fume hood and another computer. It strongly reminds Danny of his high school's chemistry classroom. Benno Heethuis was the name of his chemistry teacher.

'Professor? Danny de Vries, we just spoke on the phone.'

'Oh yeah? Oh yes, sorry man. Come on in.'

They shake hands.

'Cup of tea?' the professor asks.

'Eh, no thank you.'

'You wanted to ask me something, correct?' As the professor asks this, he pours two cups of tea.

'Tea broadens the mind.' He gives Danny a cup. 'But if you wanted to ask me something, you could've also just called me, right?' The professor raises his voice. 'That would save you a lot of time.'

'Eh, yeah, no. I wanted to ask and show you something!'

'Video calling!'

Danny gives the professor a confused look.

'You could've showed me during a conference call.' the professor explains. Danny thinks of whether or not he should respond, but concludes that this jibber-jabber about video calling adds nothing to the issue at hand.

'Look, this is what I wanted to show you.' He takes a little bag out of his jacket and puts the scraping on a petri dish. The professor puts on his glasses and looks at the substance. He shakes the dish back and forth and mumbles *'ahem'* and *'mhm'*. He thinks, types something on the keyboard and then gazes at the screen. After a couple of seconds he walks back and forth along the worktable. He then picks up the dish again, smells it, dips his finger in the gravel and tastes the substance with the tip of his tongue. The professor's eyes suddenly start to circle. The whites of the eyes of the old man are magnified by his glasses. He starts to speak gibberish and brings his hands to his head. His glasses fall off his face. He wobbles on his old legs and eventually falls to the floor, where he mutters some *'argh'* noises. Danny is scared senseless.

'Professor?!' he yells, as he leans over him.

'Professor?! Can you hear me?' He listens to make sure he's still breathing. He is, albeit very slowly. Danny grabs his phone to call 911.

'I could go for a cup of tea' the professor suddenly says. 'I got you good, man!' he roars, while he clumsily gets up and puts on his glasses. Danny is completely befuddled and doesn't really know whether he should laugh along or punch the professor in the face. He sneakily clenches his fist to launch it right between his eyes, but he manages to restrain himself.

'What do you think it is?' he ends up asking.

'Eh, well, sand, dust, smells like nothing, tastes like nothing. Where did you get it?' the professor asks.

'In Drenthe. Scraped it off a dolmen rock.'
The professor gives Danny an interested look with bulging eyes behind his glasses.

'A dolmen? Really??' he asks surprised and curious.
But then his tone changes.

'And you bother me with this?! Waste my precious time? Time I could've used on other useful cases.'
Danny starts to tell the entire story. The professor becomes more interested as the story unfolds. He Googles things every now and then on his computer. Danny finishes his story after about ten minutes and sees the professor staring at him.

'Danny, I've always thought you were a brilliant student. You were eager, curious, inventive and very accurate in your research and reports. Great! You've graduated cum laude for a reason.'
Danny feels excited. Nothing stands in the way of further research into the dolmen stone. Together with the professor he will make history,

travel the world, give lectures, write a book and have signing sessions. This discovery will change his life. He can see it all happening.

'But this, this is total crap!' The professor brutally interrupts Danny's evolving thoughts.

'Mush! Nonsense! Did you have a bad night? Have a wet dream? This would be the last thing I'd expect from you. Well, I have to hand it to you; you do have a great imagination. If you had come to me with this as a freshman, I would've had a laugh… but from you…'

'But I have proof, check my phone, this picture…'
Danny shows the photograph of the dolmen, but it shows no blue glow. Danny is flabbergasted.

'But couldn't you at least examine the gravel?' he asks in a frantic attempt to persuade the professor. 'Some extraction research isn't too much to ask, is it?'
The professor dramatically shakes his head.

'I'm so disappointed.' He puts the petri dish next to the microscope, walks to the coat rack and puts on his plaid jacket.

'I'm going for a walk. I need some fresh air. You can find your way out, right?' He turns around and exits the room.
Danny is left defeated. He kicks over a chair in anger and furiously walks around the room. He stops in front of the window and looks outside. It's busy on campus. Students riding their bikes back and forth, without a care in the world, unaware of what just happened here in this room. Not knowing what happened here thousands of centuries ago, at this location. There wasn't a campus here back then. Back then, the Neanderthals, bears and wolves called the shots. Imagine a bear walking across campus right now… Danny sniggers. Those innocent little students wouldn't know what to do. They would run and cycle away at top speed while crying for their mothers. It's pathetic. Danny comes up with a plan. He grabs his phone and calls a number from his contact list.

'This is Hellen.'

'I have to talk to you right now.' Danny snippily responds.

'Hmmm, so do I...' just leaving out the word 'baby'. 'You know where to find me...'

Upon arrival on the fourth floor, Danny exits the elevator and decisively walks to Hellen's office. His own office of all places, which he doesn't see three hundred and sixty days of the year. The few days he does visit his office, he spends finalizing projects and to have some boring meetings with the university's management. He now has other business to take care of. He'll show her who's in control. Danny slams open de door and walks in at a steady pace. Hellen is sitting on his desk. She's wearing a fiery red short skirt and has one leg pulled up, strongly tempting one to see underneath that little skirt. She senses Danny's rage, which visibly turns her on. Her tongue glides over her red lip gloss, making her lips shimmer even more as she purses them.
    'Hellen, you must...'
    'Yes, I must!' Hellen responds as if she's climaxing right there on the spot. Before Danny can say anything, she grabs him by his button-down, pulls him towards her wild body and presses her juicy lips onto his mouth. Danny lost once again. Room 4.69 of the campus is now the theater of Lady Lust.

Danny stands in front of the window and tries to look outside, but the window is all fogged up. He wipes a part of it clean. It's warm inside...hot and sweaty. He opens the window a bit and checks the handless office clock hanging on the wall. His anger turned into surrender. He thinks about what occurred shortly before. Is this what I want?, he thinks. Danny turns around and sees how Hellen closes the last buttons of her blouse. She shakes her head to straighten out her tousled hair. My god, this chick is so hot, he thinks.
    'This is not what I came for.'
    'But you did come.' Hellen assures him.
    'Is that the only thing you can think of?'

Hellen laughs and puts on her black Gucci sunglasses. At least she looks like a feisty secretary again, Danny thinks. He tries to keep the follow-up all professional.

'Hellen, I helped you with your research on the site in Groningen. Now you have to return the favor.' Hellen frowns and listens.

'I'm on to something. I don't yet exactly know the details, but it's something revolutionary... out of this world. But before I continue, you have to absolutely promise me you will keep this a secret for now. Don't talk to anyone about it.' Hellen sees that Danny is being serious. She looks at him over her glasses.

'My lips are sealed.' She slides her index finger over her lips, makes a locking gesture, and throws the invisible key over her shoulder.

'I discovered a special stone at a dolmen in Drenthe. It stands out because it doesn't look quite like the rest. I just visited professor Dijkstra to ask him to examine a sample. But he won't go for it.'

'So what do you want from me?' Hellen interrupts.

'I want you to get the professor to carry out an extraction research on the gravel I gave him.'

'And how am I supposed to get him to do that?'

'Whatever it takes.'

'Whatever it takes?'

'Whatever it takes, yes.'

Danny takes a step back, spreads his arms towards Hellen and runs his eyes over her body like a scanner.

'Ooohh no! No no!' Hellen takes a lap around the room.
She can't believe that Danny is asking this of her.

'Listen, Hellen, the professor is quite in to green leaves.'

'I'm not a green leaf!' Hellen shouts.

'But you could use your charm to get him to do it. Please, Hellen, he's the only one who has access to the extraction laboratory. You have to help me!' Danny sounds desperate.

'I'll have to think about it.' Hellen says hesitantly.

'You're the best.'
'I haven't said yes yet.' she emphasizes.
'I know you won't let me down.'

10 Thunder

Smashes, clashes, swooshes and blammos; computer game sound effects blast from the speakers at de De Vries residence. It's the beginning of the evening. Thomas and Benjamin jump up and down on the couch while playing their new computer agility game Speedlimit. They have to complete a course as quickly as they can, while defying all kinds of obstacles. Danny is sitting next to them and gives his sons pointers, just like a dad should. Anne is making coffee in the kitchen.

'Look out! A scaffold! Go around!' Danny loudly shouts.

'A bridge! Quick, it's still open! There, a police boat! Try to avoid it!' It looks like Danny is even more immersed in the game than the boys are. In front of you! A buoy!' he yells.

'Whatever...' Benjamin whispers, hoping his father doesn't hear. He's grown bored with this game.

'Don't let the boys play on the computer for too long,' Anne worryingly says while handing Danny a mug of coffee.

'Ah, just let them be. They're not on the computer that often,' Danny yells in their defense.

'They actually have to go to bed soon anyway,' Anne concludes.

'Ahh, dad?' Thomas whines with a sad look on his face.

'Just let them play. It's their vacation.'
Anne shakes her head and walks towards the kitchen.

'Boys, I have a surprise for you.' Danny sounds excited.

'What is it? What it is?' Thomas and Benjamin yell. They know exactly how to manipulate their father in order to stay up another hour.

'I have a new game. I actually wanted to save it for later, but fuck it.'

'DANNY!' it sounds from the kitchen. 'Watch your language.'

'Sorry,' he says, ashamed. The boys giggle, they are having a great time. Danny walks to the cabinet and takes a DVD-box out of the drawer.

'It's a super cool, exciting game...' He holds up the DVD-box with both hands, as if he's lifting a trophy.

'It is...'

'GODZILLA' the boys scream, just before Danny can reveal his carefully kept secret.

'Right. Godzilla. I was about to say that.' Danny puts the DVD in the computers and starts the game.

'Cool.'

'Super cool,' Danny adds. 'It's actually a pretty violent game, especially right before bedtime, but oh well. It's important in this game to keep Godzilla under control.'

'Yeah, we got this, dad,' Benjamin responds with such conviction Danny almost believes it.

'Of course.'

Danny shows them how it's done.

'So that's how you do it. Now it's your turn.'

After the monster hurtled across the screen for a number of minutes, causing a lot of damage, Danny hands the controller to Benjamin.

'So is this monster also from the dolmen era?' Thomas asks.

'Eh, yeah, something like that. It's actually from a bit longer ago... but only a couple billion years,' Danny says with a smile. 'Godzilla is actually a Brontosaurus, but a very mean one.'

As he says this, he grabs Benjamin while doing a Godzilla impression and gives him a good shake. The boys laugh.

'It's your turn now, Thomas.'

Thomas takes the controller from Benjamin and swings the monster across the screen.

'So bad ass,' he exclaims, sounding like an accomplished Godzilla hunter.

During a certain scene, Godzilla stands on his hind legs, with his fore legs high in the air. The beast threateningly stands in front of the New York police office. Thomas is in control and lets the enormous fore legs of the beast land on the building with a simple movement of the controller. Godzilla flattens the building with overwhelming force. The speakers boom, sparks fly from the 80-inch flat screen television, the couch Danny and the boys sit on shakes, pieces of plaster float down from the ceiling, the glassware in the cupboard rings, and Bor starts to howl.

'Crisis.' Thomas throws the controller down with force, as if he was just electrocuted by thirty thousand volts, and stares at the smoking flat screen like a zombie.

'WOW…' Benjamin exclaims, perplexed. 'How do you do that?' Danny is looking at Thomas, scared and speechless. A couple of seconds later the shakes and tremors start again. This time even more intensely. Outside, a car alarm goes off. Danny jumps up and Anne comes running into the living room.

'I have a leak in the kitchen!' she screams.
Danny runs with her into the kitchen and sees water spraying all over the place from a ruptured pipe

'Shut off the water main,' he yells.

'ME?' Anne screams.

'Is there someone else here?' Danny asks, very annoyed, while looking around. 'Never mind, I'll do it,' he adds and hurries to the basement to close the stopcock.

'Did the water stop?' He yells from the basement.

'Yes.' Anne sounds shocked and realizes the severity of the situation. She looks like a drowned dishrag.
When Danny returns from the basement he gently and cautiously walks around, as if he expects another tremor at any moment. He looks around and observes the damage, cracks in the walls, plaster from the ceiling, broken glassware in the cupboard, a cracked living room window, not to mention the water damage in the kitchen.

'What happened?' Anne asks concerned.

'An earthquake…? No that's impossible. Could this have to do with the drilling by GasCo?'

'That intense?'

'You're right, this is really intense.' Danny runs his hands through his hair and rubs his face. He's visibly gutted.

'Let me see if there's something on the local news.'

Danny surfs through the channels and stops at the regional network. *'…extends in the area between Siddeburen and Stadskanaal and has a significantly greater force than before. At this moment our team is trying to get in contact with a spokesman of GasCo. Once we manage to do so, we will get back to you right away. Furthermore, our journalist Eric Roeleveld is on his way to Loppersum. Our newsroom received a striking number of earthquake reports from this municipality.'* The dolled-up lady behind the news desk keeps rambling on.

'That's here,' Anne says.

'Yes,' Danny diffidently responds.

'This is not normal, right Danny?'

'No, you're right. Let's just clean up a bit for now. Tomorrow I'll see if I can get answers from somewhere, from GasCo or someone else.'

The next morning Danny is having a cup of coffee in a café in the city. He still has a heavy head and has to recover from the previous night. He looks around, to the morning traffic which completely congests the city. Inside, a voluptuous waitress is walking around with coffee and rolls. A student of about nineteen year's old, working for one of those hip student temp agencies. Exploiters of students, who pay them a measly 9 dollars an hour and submit an invoice for 26 dollars an hour. Danny checks her out, especially when she has to bend over to place the tray on the table. Her high heels make her look taller than she actually is. Danny lets his mind run free.

'More coffee, sir?'

Shit, she's at my table all of a sudden, he thinks.

'Yes, please pour me another cup. Thank you.'

He's getting warm, so he loosens his tie a bit.

'Everything ok, sir?' While the waitress asks this question, his phone vibrates in his pocket. He clumsily tries to retrieve it from his pants. The girl shyly looks at it. Danny gestures that everything is fine and waves her off.

'This is Danny de Vries.'

'Amice.'

Amice? No one has ever said that to me, Danny thinks.

'This is de Vries!' he clarifies once more.

'Yes amice, we're going to make history, all over the world! It's amazing. Can you come to the lab right now?'

Danny recognizes professor Dijkstra's voice.

'I can do that. I'll be right there. In about thirty to forty-five minutes.'

He quickly puts his phone away and grabs his wallet to pay the waitress. He then makes his way out the door and decides to take the bus to the university's campus. As he walks to the bus stop, he gets the distinct feeling that someone is following him. When he looks behind him, he sees a crowd of city folks that all seem to look at him. A woman carrying a grocery bag, a construction worker wearing a yellow helmet, a man with a long, black jacket, a student on a moped. They all have their prying eyes focused on him. He turns back around in fear and keeps walking. Illusions, delusions... why would anybody follow me, he thinks. I'm a nobody.

When he gets to the university complex he reports to security. There she is again, that woman with the little red scarf. Weird that they haven't kicked that hard of hearing Holly yet. This time however he wisely says nothing. He looks at her and gives her a mean grimace. That's because he actually brought his pass with him this time and waves it in front of her face. The lady doesn't even recognize him. Oh no, not Alzheimer's as well. Sad. He continues his path to the laboratory.

'Professor, good morning.'

'Ah, you're here. Good. I want to show you something. Look!' The professor slides a microscope slightly towards Danny. As Danny looks through the microscope he manually sets the focus and tries to discover what he actually should be seeing.

'What is this?' Danny asks surprised.

'This is phenomenal. Something that isn't even included in our periodic table.' The professor reveals.

'All I see is a swarm of bacteria fighting each other.'

'That's correct, amice. Isn't it wonderful? This will change evolution and will baffle people.' But then the professor corrects himself. 'Eh, what do you mean? Bacteria? Let me see.'
He looks through the microscope.

'Ah no, sorry, this is the wrong microscope. This is the one you should see. Here, check this one.' Danny looks through the other microscope.

'This is the gravel I gave you?' Danny asks.

'That's right, amice.' The professor sounds elated. 'I had the scrapings extracted in the centrifuge. Besides common silicon they found traces of four unknown structures. Four unknown metals to be precise. See, here's the computer printout. And did you see the structure of these metals?' Danny again looks through the microscope.

'This is very special,' he assures him, 'I've never seen anything like this before. What is it?'

'Exactly! What is it? This is out of this world, extraterrestrial. Do you remember that meteorite impact a while back in Chelyabinsk, in the Urals in Russia? All kinds of amazing discoveries were made there, but this… this supersedes all! Look, watch this! These metal particles have an unparalleled magnetic field. And see what happens when I keep a regular earthly piece of metal close… do you see?'

Danny sees a bright blue glow he clearly recognizes as the glow in the dolmen. The professor continues.

'It needs further examination, but it's certain that these metals have a special characteristic, qualitatively better than all our precious metals combined.' He turns to Danny. 'That dolmen of yours… that's almost certainly a meteorite, or…' The professor is clearly very excited and can barely breathe. He takes a seat in order to calm down.

'Or what?' Danny asks.

'Parts of a space ship! Space, Star Wars, ET phone home…'
Danny notices the professor is losing it a little bit and tries to oversee things reasonably.

'Ok, professor. Whatever this ends up being, we have to keep this an absolute secret for now, until we are certain of what it is and we can scientifically back it up.'

'Good idea. Eh no, sorry,' the professor stammers.

'What is it?' Danny asks.

'When I realized this had to be something extraterrestrial, I asked my American friend and colleague at Harvard to have a look at my research results and give me a second opinion.'

'In other words, the news is already out?'

'Well, no…' the professor ponders. 'He assured me his discretion. He won't publish it…'

'Then we'll just have to trust him,' Danny sighs.

'But Danny, you have to tell me, where is this dolmen of yours and what is with that blue glow?'

'I don't know any more than what I originally told you. It's not clear to me either. I plan on going there again, to have a closer look of the stone.'

'I'm coming with you!'

'That doesn't seem necessary, professor. After all, the fewer people who know where it is, the better, at this point.'

'Try to take some pictures.'

'I will do that. Thank you, professor, I will keep you updated.'
Danny gives him a firm handshake and leaves the university.

'Boys, boys!' Danny yells.
Benjamin and Thomas are having a massive pillow fight on their parents' bed, with Benjamin being the clear losing party.
'Calm down for a bit. Sit!' Danny gestures to the two.
'But dad, I was winning,' Thomas complains.
'Listen. Your mother's birthday is coming up… do we have a present yet???' Danny emphasizes the *we*.
'But don't you always take care of the presents?' Benjamin asks.
'Exactly! So what's going to change this year? You're now old enough to arrange something as well. Or at least help me. Does mommy perhaps give you any clues about what she would want to get for her birthday?'
The two boys look at each other and shrug their little shoulders.
'Right. Mommy basically already has everything. But there must be something we can get her that makes her happy.'
'A new oven, to make actually delicious rolls,' Thomas yells. Danny gives him a questionable look.
'No, the oven it's fine. It's her own b…' Danny doesn't finish his sentence.
'A car!' Benjamin exclaims in a eureka moment.
'You don't give people cars for their birthday,' Danny assures him. 'It has to be something small, something personal.'
Thomas suddenly politely raises his finger. Danny looks surprised and gestures that it's not necessary to do so at home.
'Mommy once said that she would love to be home alone for a day. Have some time to herself.'
'A day home alone??? Why would she want that?'
Danny doesn't give himself the time to wonder. He even starts to gloat.

'Great! That's actually a VERY good idea. If mommy wants that, then that's the best present we could give her, right? You two make a pretty birthday card!'

It's early in the morning when the alarm goes off in the De Vries house. It's not an annoying buzzer that makes you jump out of bed, it's also no annoying tune from a morning radio show, but it's a cheerful children's choir singing *happy birthday*. Anne sleepily presses the snooze button and checks the time with squinted eyes.
  'Hm… I wonder what time it is. Danny?'
  'Thomas?' Anne remains dazed. 'Benjamin?'
Slowly but surely, Anne starts to realize she hears something she usually never hears. Silence.
Anne turns around and sees an empty bed on the other side.
  'Danny???'
There's a birthday card on her nightstand. One of those absurd cards with a picture of a huge dog with a head that's much too big for its little body, holding a rose in its mouth. The crooked handwriting reads *To the sweetest.*

Dear Mommy,

Happy birthday.
You get from us the present you wanted to have for a long time.
A veri nise day, all for your self. Alll alone.
Do what you want to do.
See you tonigt, kiss.

Thomas and Benjamin and also daddy

  'Yes!' Anne jumps out of bed, all of a sudden she's wide awake.
  'How did Danny know that?' she wonders out loud.
She's so euphoric, she doesn't really know what to do first.

'I'll stay in bed and read a book.'
She jumps under the covers. Two seconds later she jumps back out.
'No, first I'm going to make myself a nice breakfast.'
'Or should I take my sweet old time in the bathroom, without Thomas or Benjamin pounding on the door?'
It gets Anne all restless and excited.
'But I don't have to… shit!'
'I know! I'll tidy the cupboard with my collection of tin teapots.
Anne walks to the cupboard and yanks the little door, to no avail.
'Damn, it's locked.' She walks to the kitchen. 'The key should be in this drawer somewhere.' But the drawer is stuck. Anne walks to the shed, to Danny's toolbox to grab a screwdriver. She opens the closet and all tools fall out. It's a big mess, with tools lying all over the place.
'Just what I need.'
She starts to sort the tools and hang them from the little hooks. Over an hour later she's finally back in the kitchen, holding a screwdriver. She wants to jimmy open the drawer to find the key to the cabinet with the tin teapots, so she can finally tidy it. After some prying the drawer starts to move and comes loose. The drawer is completely stuffed.
'Hm… that's going to take a while…'
Another hour later all junk is removed from the packed kitchen drawer and everything is neatly organized. Anne also found the key to the cabinet.
'I could go for a popsicle right now,' she sighs.
She opens the freezer door and stares at a deep container with frozen ice accretion on the sides. The popsicles are completely snowed in.
'Ow, that doesn't look good.' She starts to hack away the ice accretion. After a couple of powerful taps, her beaded bracelet comes loose and disappears underneath the fridge. When Anne gets on all fours to check under the fridge, she can't see anything, because it's too dark. She hopelessly starts to look for a flashlight.

'In Thomas' room,' she thinks. She checks the entire room. In addition to the flashlight, she also finds a huge pile of dirty laundry.

'Ah, might as well do some laundry, why not?'
After the washing machine is set to do its lengthy job, she grabs the flashlight to check underneath the fridge. She presses the on/off button. No light. She smacks the thing. Still nothing. No batteries.

'There are batteries in Danny's nightstand!' she sighs. She stumbles upstairs and opens the little drawer.

'Oh, no!' Anne moans painfully. There's something in the drawer she didn't expect and also didn't want to know about. She closes the bedroom door behind her, with a grim look on her face and stumbles back downstairs.

Anne takes a seat on the couch. She's exhausted. What should I do now, she thinks as she deeply sighs.

'The dentist gave me some magazines from the waiting room. I still have to read those!'
She takes the magazines, an almost 2-foot high pile, puts them on her lap and checks her watch.

'Oh my, it's 7:30.'
She quickly rushes through the magazine on top without reading it. Before she reaches the last page, she throws the entire collection on the ground.

'Arggghh!' she yells, imitating a riled-up monkey that just came from under an exploded drying hood.

'Hello! We're home!' cheerful voices sound from the kitchen.
Danny and the boys bounce into the living room.

'Ello ello,' Anne says with a fake smile and a limp-handed wave. 'And where are you coming from?'

'We went to the Enchanted Forest in Zuidlaren!' Benjamin reveals.

'Enchanted forest??? Oh, that's fun. I want to go there with you once.' Anne gives Danny a piercing look. 'To the Enchanted Forest, just like that?'

'Eh, yeah… we were just driving… and suddenly we were close to the Enchanted Forest,' Danny hesitates.

'Oh, that's fun,' she says without meaning it.

'Look mommy!' Thomas shows her a picture.

'Ohh, that's so cute. The entire family on the rollercoaster. Mommy would like that as well, a picture with mommy and her entire family. Mommy would like that a lot indeed. Mommy, Thomas, Benjamin, all of us in a picture together. Mommy and the children.' She throws another mean look in Danny's direction, who still doesn't realize what state Anne is in.

'And how was your day? Your birthday!' Danny coolly asks.

'Amazing! I've had a lovely day all to myself!' Anne tries to say it with dry eyes. 'I wanted to get going with my own trinkets, but I ended up defrosting the freezer, fixing the kitchen drawer, tidying your tools, looking all over the house for batteries for the flashlight and running three big loads of laundry for the boys…other than that it was a great birthday… all alone.

Danny stares at Anne with amazement. 'What did you need the flashlight for?'

The knife frantically tries to make its way through the fibers of a bloody steak towards the white chine of the plate, with inevitable consequences. The pressure of the knife forces the red life juice to come out of all sides of the piece of meat, which once was a great Drenthe Highlander, with a beautiful coat and elegant horns. Once grazing the juicy heathers of Drenthe, now the virginal earthenware. Danny asked Anne out to dinner to settle their recent outpourings. He picked a small, picturesque establishment that allows them to grow closer without being disturbed.

'It's because of the children,' Danny unravels with a sigh. He puts down his knife and fork.

'The children?' Anne responds in surprise.

'Yes, it's just too much for me. They're all over the place, you know. I can't take it anymore. Everything is getting too busy, at work, everything.'

'But then it's not because of the children! Yes, they're getting bigger, sometimes a bit rowdy yes, but what do you expect…?' Anne takes a little breather after this rhetorical question. 'You can't blame your kids for the fact you get too caught up in your work. And then we're not even talking about me. How do you think I feel? You're gone a lot lately, you don't talk to me anymore, you, you… we haven't had sex in weeks… Danny, what's going on with you?' she asks, all upset.

'It's not you either, Anne…' That's all Danny can say. He picks up his glass of wine and effortlessly chugs it.

'But I want to make it up… with the kids! Tomorrow is the last vacation day, I will take them, so you can have a day of peace and quiet,' he assures Anne.

'I still love you a lot Danny. Don't disappoint me and the children.' They decide to end their dinner and head home. Once home, the lights are quickly turned off.

The next morning the De Vries house is buzzing. Thomas and Benjamin are frolicking through the kitchen like two wild bulls, while Anne cleans the breakfast table. Danny just took a refreshing shower and is coming down the stairs.

'Who wants to do something fun today?' he yells. His question did not fall on deaf ears.

'Yeeeeeeessss!!!' the children loudly roar.

'All right! Put on your shoes and coats, let's go!'

'Here, take some stuff for the road.' Anne puts some bottles and cakes in a backpack and hands it to Danny.

'Take good care of them. Where are you going, anyway?' she asks. Danny looks at her with a big grin on his face and raises a condescending finger.

'I'm going to give them a day they'll never forget. It'll be fun!'

With open mouths and large, amazed eyes, Thomas and Benjamin stare at *Wheatfield with Crows*, a masterpiece by Vincent van Gogh, painted in mid-1890 in Auvers, France. The work stands out because of its darkness and subconsciousness. Some extreme art critics classify the work as his farewell letter and see it as one of his most controversial paintings.

'The black crows in the stormy sky are a great mystery. All art critics on earth wonder whether the crows fly towards the painter or away from him,' Danny explains, wildly gesturing. 'Only the master knows!' he mysteriously adds.

Thomas and Benjamin get chills at the sight of this morbid painting.

'I told you it would be fun! Vincent van Gogh is a great master. Misunderstood in his own time, but his works are now priceless and are shown all over the world, including here at the Vincent van Gogh Museum. Come, let's move on.'

'Do they have a ball pit here?' Benjamin asks.

'Look, this is one of the paintings that made Van Gogh famous. This will get you a bit more cheerful.'

The trio stand in front of *Vase with Fifteen Sunflowers*. The flowers desolately hang their little heads and are beginning to become immortally brown. It's the faded version. Danny looks at it for a moment as he ponders.

'There are more paintings of sunflowers, in bloom and much healthier. I think it's that way.'

He walks towards another room as he makes this statement. The children trudge after him.

'I enjoy going on a trip with you. This is much more interesting than Wildlands or Six Flags. I really admire Van Gogh.'

Thomas and Benjamin, both with long faces, raise their lip and make a *blah blah* impression of their father.

'Look, this is Van Gogh himself.'

Danny looks at a self-portrait of the painter.

'Van Gogh is always very recognizably depicted wearing a straw hat. He was so vain that he made thirty-five self-portraits. He painted this in 1887 when he resided in Paris, in the apartment of his brother Theo.'

The children look at a bland, dismal, old man with a straw hat and a pipe, with no smoke coming out. They look at the sign next to the painting; *Self-portrait with straw hat. Arles 1888*. They sigh, getting a little tired of their father's endless babbling.

'Daddy, can we have a bottle of coke?' Thomas asks.

'Shhh, don't talk so loudly, son, you're in a museum here. You have to respect the silence that allows people to daydream, surrounded by all this beauty. We will go outside later and you can have your coke there, in the sun in the Vondelpark.'

Having said that, Danny walks along the collection of drawings. His attention is drawn by *Church in Zweeloo*. He stares at it, motionless. It's a characteristic little structure from the 13th century. Characteristic because of its gothic pointed arches and the small tower with that striking cavalier. He recognizes that little church. After their walk on the heather and the incident at the dolmen they drove by this church on their way to the pancake restaurant. He wanted to take a picture back then, but it was raining cats and dogs. He's intrigued by the clean pen strokes Van Gogh put on paper here, and gets fully immersed in the scene. It feels as if he's in Zweeloo in 1883 right now. But his attention is suddenly drawn to something else. There, next to the church, stands a shepherd with a flock of sheep. Danny takes another good look at it. His heart stops and his breath is taken away. The shepherd, he thinks, as he looks at the figure, now only inches removed from the painting. The few seconds he stands motionless in front of the drawing seem to last hours. The shepherd!

'The shepherd!!' he now loudly yells through the gallery. The other visitors are left shocked and annoyed.

For a while it looks as if Danny is aimlessly wandering around the gallery of the Van Gogh museum like a fool. But he quickly comes to his senses. He recognizes that shepherd, no matter how small he is in the drawing. It's the shepherd they encountered during their walk on the heather. It's the exact same shepherd that woke Danny up from a nightmare. It's the shepherd of Zweeloo. The shepherd… Van Gogh… the shepherd… Van Gogh… He keeps repeating it in his head, searching for some kind of connection. Danny thinks of what he should do now. He has to further investigate this, because he's certain there's a connection between the shepherd and Van Gogh, he just doesn't know what it is just yet. He decides he has to investigate and that he should look for the letters and memoirs written by Van Gogh. There must be some kind of information about the shepherd in there. He swiftly walks out the museum and – in his madness – leaves Thomas and Benjamin behind.

11   The letters

Danny is driving to the university's library not thirty minutes later.
He's on the phone.

'Yes sweetie, sorry, sorry. I don't know what happened to me. Some
sort of black out I guess, I don't know.'
Anne can be heard from the other end.

'How could you do that, you dick!'

'I'm sure Thomas and Benjamin were properly taken care of over
there. There was a friendly security guard walking around there.
They're probably being spoiled with coke and candy.'

'And who came up with that... *do something fun* with the kids?'

'Well, yeah... it was really interesting though,' Danny assures her.

'To a fucking museum. Who does that?!'

'Anne, be reasonable. Do you want to pick u-'

'Oh, stop it, you asshole! I don't want to see you any time soon.
And you won't get to see the boys again either!'

'Sweetie, they're just in the museum, everything is fi-'
Anne ends the call.

The adrenaline starts to rush through Danny's blood. His intuition tells
him he's on to something big, but he himself doesn't have a clue what
it is yet. Van Gogh... The shepherd... He gets the feeling that he's
experienced certain things before. In his thoughts he sees Van Gogh
shaking the shepherd's hand and sees how they start talking. The flock
of sheep is herded and kept together by a dog. It's exactly the same
dog the shepherd on the heather had with him. Van Gogh and the
shepherd are very busy talking and make wild gestures... what would
they be talking about? Danny speeds up some more in the last miles
to the university.
Upon arrival at the university, he quickly walks in and passes the lady
with the red scarf. He runs up the stairs to the second floor, where he

opens the door to the library with his passkey. The space is deserted. He quickly gets a cup of coffee from the machine. His brain reaches a boiling point, and so does the coffee machine. He has a strong urge to filter an answer from his beany brain. Ten seconds later, Danny sits behind a desk that supports his cup of coffee, a reading lamp, keyboard, mouse and a monitor. He turns on the computer and types in *'Letter Van Gogh Zweeloo'* and frantically starts to scroll.

The evening progresses, after visiting many useless websites about Van Gogh, his life and numerous pictures of paintings, Danny finishes his fifth cup of coffee. In the meantime, a cleaner has arrived at the library, ready to use his cart full of chemicals, brushes, rags and a broom to clean up the place. The cleaner hunts for coffee rings, dust and cobwebs, things that shouldn't actually be part of a utilized library. For the moment, Danny is not disturbed by the cleaner and continues his hunt on a different website. He suddenly seems to have found something. A letter from Van Gogh to Max Liebermann, his friend and art colleague. And its's about dolmens. Danny looks at the historical document and starts reading. He is so into the letter that he has no clue the cleaner is also remarkably interested in what Danny is doing. Danny is lost in Van Gogh's letter.

'Dear Max, we left Het Hooghe Veensche yesterday. My journey continues across the new Hooghe Vaart towards the German borders and the Nieuw-Amsterdam Field. My mistress Gertrude by my side (ps. This is between us, my friend, nobody knows about Gertrude and I).'

Danny frowns. Van Gogh had a sweetheart on the side? Hm, a well-kept secret. That rascal. He continues reading.

'I hope to draw some nice pictures during my journey, but I'm especially looking for a puzzling mystery that is hiding between the magical rocks in the Veensche landscape...'

...The wooden tow boat slowly makes its way over the babbling water of the Hoogenveenschevaart, pulled by a horse that walks over the cart track along the bank. Quiet music sounds from the boat, from a small barrel organ with Italian design by Ludovico Gavioli. The music dies off over the barren landscape.

'I want to dock later,' a man shouts from the tow boat to the driver, who pulls the horse by hand. The driver mumbles something like 'moi' and continues to trudge with his raggedy shoes, next to the horse's heavy hooves. A lot of dust flares up. The man on the boat stoically observes the ordeal. He has reddish hair and a reddish beard. He's wearing a crumpled straw hat to protect his pale skin against the sun.

'Vince! We should also find some food and a place to sleep before it gets dark,' a woman yells from the other side of the boat. She's wearing a white skirt, blouse and a white hat with a sunflower on it. She dances across the boat with little catty steps, like a drunken butterfly.

'Ai sweetie. According to the map we're close to the Amsterdam Field. We will dock there.' Vincent puts down his pen.

'You think they have nice stores and jewelry there?'

'Don't expect too much of it, darling,' Vincent laughs. 'They're not as advanced here in the peat area. Enjoy, enjoy the beauty that nature has to offer.' The driver on the shore chuckles.

'Yeah, yeah. You and nature, flowers, painting, ahh, blah blah...' As Gertrude babbles, the group approaches a swing bridge near the Zwinse Drift. An old, hunched bridge operator slowly walks up and discusses with the driver.

'It's a guilder, sir!' the driver shouts to Vincent.

'A whole guilder??? ... to turn the bridge???'

'I'd do it for that, Vince,' Gertrude exclaims.

'Not a chance,' Vincent throws a guilder to the driver.

'I'd like a receipt,' he says.

'Moi.'

The bridge squeaks and cracks as the bridge operator turns the crank.

'It doesn't open very often, sir,' the old man apologizes.

He's breaking a sweat.

'No worries, good man. We have time, all the time in the world.'

'Well Vince, I'm really hungry though,' Gertrude yaps. 'Hmm, a nice, juicy pork skewer…' she tackily adds.

'Easy Gertrude. Behave! Otherwise I'll just put you on the bank with all your suitcases.'

It doesn't impress her. She miserably starts to sulk on the bow. The driver chuckles. The boat slowly slides between the pillars of the Drift bridge. The music glides along with it.

A lot of noise breaks Danny's glide. The cleaner's cart fell down from an elevated part of the library. All spray bottles, brushes and buckets are spread out across the floor. That's one way to clean the floor, Danny thinks. The cleaner is however nowhere to be seen. Weird, Danny thinks, as he takes another good look. He then believes he sees someone to the side, behind a bookshelf. Danny gets up and walks in that direction.

'Hello?'

His call is answered with some rumbling.

'Are you there? Do you need help?'

Danny walks around the bookshelf. No one. This is crazy, he thinks. Why would that cleaner just leave his fallen cart behind? Then the lights go out and the library is pitch dark.

'For f…' Danny rants. 'Hello?!'

The emergency lighting switches on after mere seconds. At that exact moment, Danny sees a shadow duck behind a bookshelf, followed by some rumbling and tumbling. This is all getting a bit too much for Danny. He can feel something isn't right. He reluctantly walks towards the bookshelf the shadow ducked behind. As he makes his way over, he takes a heavy book from a shelf, with the idea to give someone a big whack if necessary. He firmly holds the thick book on shoulder height.

What the hell am I doing?, he thinks, three more steps away from the shelf, almost wetting himself. Now then. Danny jumps forward with the book in the air.

'Who are you?' he yells out in fear.

There's no one.

'What the fuck,' he sighs.

The lights come back on. The power outage seems fixed.

Danny puts the book aside and notices the title; *Age of Anger, Pankaj Mishra.* Danny chuckles, I know that book. A lot of pointless anger in this world. He looks around and walks around the room on his tippy toes. He sees that the fallen cart is gone. No cart, no mess, no water marks. No cleaner either. Nothing at all, as if time and events didn't happen for a bit.

'The cleaner wiped himself out,' he sniffs out loud.

He leaves the whole cleaner situation be and decides to consult some more books and references about Van Gogh from the library. It's always easier to read from a book than off a screen, he thinks. Once he gets back to his desk he stretches out and leans back in his chair. He grabs his mug and takes a sip of his coffee, rubs his eyes and runs his hand through his hair.

'Pff... that Van Gogh is on to something. He must have known something about the dolmens beforehand.' Danny keeps looking, this time in the books, between the letters and notes. *Blah blah blah* and *blah blah blah.* Nothing, hmm, maybe this; *To Gertrude... you are my... I enjoy you...* grrr, Danny sneers, just a lovebird talking, nothing. Then a letter with the name Johan Picardt catches his eye.

'Picardt... Picardt... I've read that name before somewhere.'

He takes the keyboard and googles *Picardt.* A long list of results pops up. Danny hastily browses the fields and clicks some links. *Johan Picardt, preacher in the castle town of Coevorden... writer of korte-*

beschryvinge-van-eenige-vergetene-verborgene-antiquiteten…
mapped the dolmens of Drenthe…

'That's it!' Danny exclaims.

'How much longer?' Gertrude complains. 'It's soo boooooring here.'

'Not too much longer, my love. I can already see the first houses of the Drentsche Veld.' The tow boat slowly glides across the seamless canal and heads for a turn on portside. The kicking of the horse's hooves on the dusty trail and the whistling of the blackbirds are the few sounds that can be heard. However, as the portside turn approaches, a completely new sound slowly adds to the orchestra.

'Do you hear that, Gertie?' Vincent asks.

'Yes, pretty, isn't it, the birds' songs,' Gertrude responds.

'No, I don't mean the birds. Listen carefully!'

'I only hear birds,' Gertrude says, as she takes an ignorant look around.

'You don't hear the singing?' Vincent asks, this time annoyed.

'Yes, of the birds…'

Vincent sighs and shakes his head in defeat. Between the sounds of the gliding water, the blackbirds and the hooves of the horse, singing emerges from behind the portside turn. The singing gets louder and sounds like a choir, a male choir. Vincent stands on a shaky box to see something along the turn, over the collar of reed. He indeed sees another tow boat approaching them, carrying a fifteen-man shanty choir. The men are wearing traditional fishing costumes and are clearly feeling it. They are singing their hearts out, standing tall with their heads held high, as if they were singing in a sold-out theater. It's a colorful and bizarre scene. The conductor stands on the bow of the punt to indicate the pace, which – contrary to the pace of the boat – is nice and quick.

'Moi moi moi
over Hondsrug through Hunze

bare feet through the soggy peat
a bare rock, a cold stone
full of pride, further none
past in a current
yields by a blue light
the path meanders the banks of Aa
gone gone, never there
a memory in the forest
a blue light breathes coldly
alone, in a continuous well
moi moi moi.'

Vincent and Gertrude listen with rapt attention to the impressive singing of the shanty men on their tow boat that smoothly sails by on portside.

'What a pretty song' Gertrude shrieks. 'What's it about, Vince?'
Well, Vincent thinks, as he takes off his straw hat to show his respect and makes a deep, humble bow towards the male choir.

'Beautiful! I'd like to have this merry bunch in front of my easel.'

'Ok, so let's go after them, Vince?'

'No. We have to go forward. I have a mission.'

The driver tightens the reins right before the first bridge of the Amsterdam Field. The horse slows down and brings the tow boat to a standstill.

'We're here. We're docking.' Vincent throws a rope to the drive, who uses it to pull the boat to the side. It's a high dock. The boat is almost five feet below the bank.

'So, how do I get to land, Vince?'

'Oh, stop complaining. The driver will help you.'
The driver looks startled. Me, he thinks. But his fear quickly gives way to a mean grimace. He has a plan.

'Isn't there a ladder I can use? Or a ramp?' Gertrude nags.

'I told you to not think too much of this place. It's simple and meager here,' Vincent sighs. He is about to jump onto the bank and climb up, but realizes the luggage has to go up first.

'You go first.'
Gertrude takes the rope the driver hands her. The boat rocks and shakes when she stands on the edge to jump onto the bank.

'Vince, this is going wrohoo…' Right when Gertrude is on the side of the boat, the driver gives the rope a quick pull, with only his index finger.

'…hooohooo, Viiiince!!!'
Gertrude falls flat onto the slanted bank like a carpet beater, with her face right in the high grass. The driver chuckles.
Vincent sighs. How could I have been so stupid to bring her along, he thinks.

'Dear man,' he yells at the driver 'Could you catch the luggage?' He throws up the steamer trunks, one at a time. Gertrude's trunk is quite heavy, too heavy for Vincent.

'Damn, Ger! What in God's name did you pack?'
She mumbles something. Her mouth is still filled with grass.

'Driver, also take that there!' as he points to Gertrude.

What a bimbo, Danny thinks. He carefully reads Van Gogh's notes. He feels a bit uneasy. He still hasn't found what he's looking for. What's the deal with this Picardt? He takes a sip of coffee and continues reading.

On the dock, Vincent takes out a note with some scribbles on it.

'According to Picardt, there should be accommodation owned by Hendrik Scholte here.'
The trio walks across the bridge to the Amsterdam Field with all their suitcases. Vincent asks a passerby about the accommodation. The old woman points to a majestic, yet somewhat simple mansion on the other side. Upon arrival at the mansion, the driver yanks the bell pull,

followed by a bunch of noise. It looks like the complete bell was pulled from the wall.

'What is going on here???' a bald man in his fifties shouts. 'Who is causing all this ruckus???'

Gertrude sneakily points to the driver.

'Dear sir. Are you Hendrik Scholte?'

'Yes, and who are you?'

'I am Van Gogh, spelled G O G H. Doctor Picardt, the preacher from the castle town of Coevorden recommended this place to me.'

'That quack?!' the proprietor rants.

'Excuse me?'

'He still owes me several guilders.'

'Ah… that is not my business. But let's settle this. Picardt is my friend. We're looking for a place to rest tonight.'

'Yes, and maybe something to eat…?' Gertrude quietly squeaks.

'Moi, come on in then.'

Van Gogh is on the edge of the bed in the room of the accommodation and is searching in the handwritten notes in his messy writing folder. At some point he seems to have found what he was looking for, and rushes outside to a local livery stable.

'Dear woman!' An old woman is sweeping the straw in the stable together, visibly fatigued. The unexpected entrance by Van Gogh startles her.

'Fear not, dear woman. Could you tell me if there's a possibility to ride one of your horses to my destination?'

The woman suspiciously looks at Van Gogh and thinks about it.

'It'll cost you five guilders.'

'Deal.' Van Gogh throws a worrisome look into his pouch, but manages to pull out a coin.

'Simon!' she yells at the person at the bottom of a wooden staircase.

'Simon!!! Where are you, dumbass?!' A young man rushes up the stairs, accompanied by a lot of stumbling.

'You've got work to do. Saddle two horses.'

The young man has a friendly, yet insecure look in his eyes. He's about twenty years old and has a pretty face with a full head of blond hair. He's wearing worn-out work pants and a coarse woolen sweater. He grabs two horses by their harness and saddles them, as the old woman watches.

'Where are you heading?' she asks Van Gogh.

'To Zweeloo. To Picardt's congregation.'

The woman freezes. She looks at the boy and tells him to put the horses back.

'Sorry. I just realized we don't have any horses available.'

Van Gogh doesn't understand.

'But w-'.

'I told you we have no horses available,' the woman yells. 'These are lame.' She demonstratively kicks against the legs of the horse next to her.

'You should try somewhere else,' she raves.

'Do you have any suggestions?' Van Gogh asks, overwhelmed.

'No!!' She disappears behind a wooden stable door that falls shut with a huge thump. Van Gogh walks out, defeated. He looks around and approaches several passersby to ask them if they know another livery stable, to no avail.

Van Gogh hopelessly lights a small cigar.

'Sir,' it suddenly sounds.

Van Gogh looks around, but has no idea where this *sir* came from.

'Sir!' it sounds again. Now Van Gogh sees the source of the *sir* cry.

'This way!' It's the blond boy, waving him to the side of the stable. Van Gogh hesitates. What is this boy up to?, he thinks, and looks around to make sure he's really waving at him and not at someone else. Van Gogh walks over to the boy.

'You're calling me?'

The boy skittishly looks around to make sure no one sees them together.

'I could take you to Zweeloo.' Van Gogh looks surprised.

'Would you look at that? What's in it for you?'

'Nothing...' the boy responds in surprise. 'maw is nuts.'

'Maw?'

'That broad,' the boy clarifies. 'She's insane.'

'Ah.' Van Gogh doesn't really know what to respond to this.

'Ciggie?' the boy asks.

'Ciggie?'

'Yes.' The boy makes a smoking gesture.

'Well, ok then.' Van Gogh takes a little box from his inside pocket and hands the boy a small cigar. He ignites a match and lights the smoke in the corner of the boy's mouth. The young man inhales and starts coughing.

'Well, well, inhale slowly.'

'It's my first one.'

'Your first ciggie?' Van Gogh bursts into laughter.

The boy is ashamed and is ready to walk away.

'Hey there, young man. You're the one who called me, you tell me you can guide me to Zweeloo... tell me, what's your plan?'

'Are you willing to pay those five guilders?'

Van Gogh frowns.

'Is that what this is about?'

'Yes. Maw is crazy and I could really use those five guilders.'

Van Gogh thinks. In hindsight, five guilders was a bit over the top.

'And what do you know about Picardt?'

The boy nonchalantly shrugs.

'That's none of my business. I'll take you to the edge of town, but I'm not going any farther!' he assures Van Gogh.

'But how do we get there?'

'Wait.' The boy walks around the corner. He comes back two minutes later, with two horses.

Van Gogh and the boy mount the horses and urge them to giddup. At that moment the old woman comes outside, ranting and raving.

'Siiimooooon!!!' she screeches, as she approaches, threatening with a broom in her hand.
Van Gogh and the boy don't hesitate for a second and gallop out of there, across the drawbridge and across the heather towards Zweeloo.

Eight hooves move across the heather at a calm pace. It's a bit misty, which complicates their navigation. Simon however, is able to keep a steady course for Zweeloo. There's not even a breath of wind. The combination of mist without wind creates a serene, peaceful landscape.

'What will happen with that woman when you get back?' Van Gogh asks.

'Ah,' the boy sighs. 'I'm not afraid of that old hag. She might look ugly and dangerous and can wake up the whole street with her yelling, but a little mouse would already make her jump on the table.'

'Jump?' Van Gogh wonders out loud.

'That woman can't do anything anymore. She needs me for all the work in the farmhouse. The only thing she's still capable to do is sweeping the floor.'

'Capable of doing,' Van Gogh corrects him.
The boy looks at him in surprise.

'Her husband passed away last year, you know. That's why she's a bit delirious.'

'Are they your parents, or family?'

'No, I'm glad they're not. Orphan.' The boy sighs. 'My own parents passed away when I was five. I didn't know them very well. My aunt tried to take me in for a while, but she was hitting the bottle pretty hard.'

'Bottle?' Van Gogh asks.
The boy makes a drinking gesture.

'The congregation ended up housing me with Fray and Yap after a year.'

Van Gogh now completely lost the plot and frowns. Simon laughs. His bright white teeth shine.

'Yes, that's what I call them. Jannie, that old broad, is completely frayed. And Ger, her husband who's now underground, always yelled: *Just throw it in my yap.* So that's why.' Simon looks at Van Gogh, but he still doesn't seem to get it.

After riding for a while, some questions pop up in Van Gogh's head.

'How do you know pastor Picardt?'

'From the stories,' Simon answers.

'Tell me.'

'He was a humanitarian in the congregation of Coevorden. He helped people, the poor and needy, you know. They said he was a good person. He made sure I could live with Fray and Yap.'

'Have you ever met him?' Van Gogh asks.

'No, I haven't. Also never been to the church. But I've heard the church in Coevorden was always packed.'

'But ehm, was? You keep talking about him in the past tense.'

Simon gives Van Gogh a questioning look.

'Well, yeah, that's true... because the pastor started to change overnight. He became grimmer and started ranting about witte wieven, lazy farmers and layabouts from the chancel during the church services. He called the church a scam. He stopped his philanthropy and has not been seen much among the general populace since. Sometimes he's gone for months.'

'That sounds promising,' Van Gogh mumbles. 'How did that happen?'

The boy shrugs his shoulders.

'Since then it's said he's been living a modest life at the parish in Coevorden. Apparently he's only involved with the stones anymore.'

'The stones?' Van Gogh tightens the reins, causing his horse to stop. The horse steams and moist vapors escape from its nostrils with brute force.

'Do you mean the dolmens?' he asks to confirm.

The boy nods.

'I've heard he can often be found at those stones, and that he draws them on a map. He walks circles around them and takes notes and such.'

'Come, we have to move on,' Van Gogh hastily responds. He urges his horse to move. The two continue their journey across the heather.

Simon stops at the edge of the town of Zweeloo.

'That's as far as I'm going. I don't want them to see me here.'

'As we agreed. Stay here with the horses. I'll be right back.'

Van Gogh gets off his horse and continues his trip into town on foot, searching for the church where he will meet Picardt. It's eerily quiet in the town. No one in the streets. Some oil lamps in farms are lit, but no other signs of life can be detected in the farms themselves. What could that boy be so afraid of, Van Gogh wonders.

The church is difficult to find. A church tower usually towers above the farms and the trees. The pointy tower of the faith can generally be seen from miles away. The higher the better; the greater the faith. The height of the tower is also important for the sound of the clock. The higher the tower, the farther the sound of the bells travels. Convenient for the farmers working on the land. Then they'll know what time it is, that it's time to head back to their wife, who will be cooking by the fire as usual. But the tower is now undetectable, or invisible because of the mist.

Still nobody on the streets I could ask, Van Gogh thinks. He walks out of a little street towards a faintly lit streetlight. Behind it, atop a mound, the church of Zweeloo emerges.

'Ah, there you are,' Van Gogh thinks out loud. 'No wonder I wasn't able to find you right away.'

The church of Zweeloo is a small structure with a very small tower, a cavalier. The Roman and Gothic architectural styles give the church a sturdy appearance. The window frames are in the shape of pointed arches and hold small windows. Magical, Van Gogh thinks. I should make a nice picture of this in the future. He slowly walks up the mound, up towards the dark back of the church. Once he gets there the clock in the cavalier breaking the silence, scares the living daylight out of him. The clock strikes as if it was half past the hour. That's strange, Van Gogh thinks, the hands show it's at the hour. The sound from the fifteenth century Mary clock has a high tone color and will therefore not extend as far. He passes a number of tombstones on the mound. A macabre feeling takes hold of him as he looks at the headstones. He stops at one of them. In the faint light of the streetlight he is just able to read '*Alexander Lodewijk Lexturgeon*'.

'Hee, old scoundrel,' Van Gogh jollily exclaims. Lexturgeon is one of the three podagrists from the fortified city of Coevorden.

'Without those compositors, they still wouldn't know what a book is, here in Drenthe,' Van Gogh laughs. He continues reading. *'Preacher ref. church Zweeloo. Venlo 1815 – Zweeloo 1878'.*

'You darn bastard!' Van Gogh raises his voice to the tombstone. 'Couldn't you have waited for me those few more years?'
The tombstone remains silent.

'He was a nice guy. But that's what they all are when they're dead.' Van Gogh chuckles.
Suddenly, he hears some rumbling sounds originating from the church, as if something is falling over. Van Gogh is curious, but careful. He sneaks along the back of the church, looking for the entrance. Once more, a noise stems from the church. This time it seems like a candlestick falls to the floor. Van Gogh stands at the entrance and hesitates while holding the door handle. Should he go inside or should he knock first? Or should he shout: Who's there? He continues to hold on to the handle of the door, with clammy hands. Ahh, nonsense, Van Gogh thinks. I'm the one who's there, he giggles. He presses down on the heavy handle and pushes the solid wooden door inwards. The twelfth century wood and hinges creak and sigh as if they had never been moved since that time. He slowly walks into the church over the cold stone floor, investigating the area, and walks past the gothic bowl

of holy water. True to his faith, he dips his fingers into the holy water, makes a cross and stands still for a moment, as if he expects a warm welcome from a massive orchestra or something. Nothing happens. It is cold, calm and quiet. A gentle mist of moonlight enters through the pointed arch windows. This gives Van Gogh the opportunity to take a look around. There's a seventeenth century wrought-iron poor box at the start of the walkway. He picks it up and shakes it. Might be something in there, he thinks, with a smile on his face. He continues over the walkway towards the pulpit with nice woodcarving, the numbers *1709* are engraved in it. The altar also houses a thirteenth century baptismal font, made from Bentheimer sandstone. Beautiful piece, Van Gogh thinks. His fingertips carefully glide over the smooth rock. He then sees a candlestick lying on the floor next to the altar. He looks around to make sure nobody is around, and bends over to pick up the gilded candlestick. It's tarnished and dusty. He uses his sleeve to give the candlestick a good rub to give it back its shine. He suddenly sees a shadow in the reflection of the candlestick. He turns around in horror. But there's no one there.

'Reverend Picardt?' Van Gogh yells. 'Are you there?'
It stays quiet. Van Gogh walks through the second walkway back towards the pulpit where the shadow seemed to have appeared.

'Picardt? It's me, Vincent.'
Suddenly, clanging sounds come from near the entrance. He walks in that direction and finds the poor box lying on the floor… it's still rolling back and forth a bit… someone must be here, Van Gogh thinks.

'You shouldn't have come here,' a deep male voice resonates through the church. It scares Van Gogh.

'You can still return home and forget what happened.'

'Picardt?' Van Gogh stammers.

'No worries, I won't do you any harm. I merely give advice.'
Well, that's reassuring, Van Gogh sarcastically thinks.

'This is not funny, Picardt. You invited me here. With respect.'

'Go and forget.' It's a frightening reverberation.

Van Gogh has had enough. He pulls open the entrance gate and takes a last look back into the church. The gate then locks behind him with a dull thump. He quickly walks back to the edge of the village, where Simon and the horses would wait for him. Upon arrival, there's not a trace of the boy.

'Great. Simon?' Van Gogh yells.
The wind starts to pick up. A branch cracks and breaks off an old oak tree. Leaves dance in the wind. Standing here all alone gives Van Gogh a bad feeling.

'Simon!' he shouts again. A worst-case scenario unfolds. Now he has to walk all the way back to the Amsterdam Field... He checks his pocket watch, but it stopped, so he makes a time estimate. It'll be really dark later. He can't go alone across the hea-...

'Sir!'
The boy holding the two horses appears from the bushes.
Van Gogh sighs in relief.
They climb the horses and follow the cart track across the heather, back to Nieuw-Amsterdam.

Danny sits at the edge of his chair while reading Van Gogh's memoirs. But the letter stops here... It's incomplete. So how does it end, Danny thinks. Did Van Gogh end up talking to Picardt and what did he find out about the dolmens? He eagerly searches the archive to see if he can uncover more parts of the letter or other notes. Nothing connects.

'Damnit.' He slams his fist on the table. Coffee remnants splash out of the coffee mug in all directions.

'Just when I'm on to something,' he says while grinding his teeth.
He decides to call it a day, but that's easier said than done. The entire story keeps running through his head. He can't let it go and it's eating away at him. He shuts down the computer and leaves the library. What he doesn't know is that – right after he leaves – someone in the library turns the computer back on and goes through Danny's search history.

Danny is too tired to drive his car. He takes a cab at the university to take him into the city. There, he aimlessly strolls the streets all night and heads into a bar every so often to drink away his thoughts. In one of the bars he meets an attractive, young woman, with whom he starts a conversation. He quickly realizes she's a prostitute. Without any shame, Danny lets himself be seduced and they take a cab to a hotel nearby. It would be kind of an issue to take her to his own house. Anne…, he thinks, as his sperm cells break loose.

A fried egg sizzles on the hotplate. The chef of the hotel, wearing a huge chef hat, is cheerfully preparing a *Special Egg* at the breakfast buffet. Special Egg??? Danny thinks. Just a regular fried egg… must be that little bit of parsley on the edge of the plate that makes it so special. But it tastes fine. While Danny puts butter on a brown roll and hastily sips from his coffee, he takes out his phone and calls Hellen.

'Good morning, it's me.'

'Hey sweet cheeks. Where *are* you? I've been trying to call you.' Danny automatically checks his handless watch.

'Could you cancel all plans for today?' he asks.

'Cancel everything? Naughty plans?'

'Just do it,' Danny says, slightly annoyed by all the *sweet cheeks* and *naughties* from Hellen. 'I'm going into the field for research.'

'Oee, exciting…'

'Quite. I'll report back in when I'm available again.'

'What is it ab-'

Danny ends the call, sips away his last bit of coffee and quickly finishes the last bit of Special Egg on his brown roll.

'Ehm, miss?!' Danny somewhat clumsily waves at a waitress. Despite her tray being packed with dirty plates, cups and glasses, she walks over to Danny.

'Do you have something for my roll? I'm in quite a hurry and I don't want to leave this delicious roll to its fate.'

The lady awkwardly saunters around with her heavy tray. She is thinking of whether she should park it on the table or walk it straight to the kitchen. She gives Danny a bit of a shy and embarrassed look.

'A bag?' Danny clarifies, as he acts out how he's putting his brown roll in a virtual bag.

Thirty minutes later, Danny sits in his own car and drives towards the heathers of Drenthe to pay the dolmen another visit. *The* dolmen he stumbled upon a few days ago with his family. Stumbled upon, because they were just going for a walk. *The* dolmen where a strange event occurred. Where he hit his head and believes he was unconscious for a couple of seconds. That's his belief, because according to Anne he disappeared for almost half an hour. *The* dolmen where a mysterious stone with a strange blue glow caused him to have delusions. *The* dolmen, the scrapings of which showed it wasn't even an earthly material, according to the periodic table of elements. *The* dolmen that has been puzzling Danny up to this point. Fragments of fantasies that keep running through his head and won't stop. He hopes to find more answers with this second visit. He nervously and restlessly peers across the country road, on which he seems to be the only driver. Seems, because once he looks into his rearview mirror, he sees a dark SUV rapidly approaching. He doesn't pay any attention to it at first, but Danny starts to get nervous when the car keeps following him. He slows down a bit to give the SUV the opportunity to pass him. But that doesn't happen. He eventually hits the gas and leaves the SUV behind. Not for long, because the black SUV also accelerates and this time almost meets Danny's trailer hitch.

'What do you want?!' Danny yells out loud into his rearview mirror, as if the driver of the SUV were able to hear it. He can sense something is not right and decides to speed up even more in order to outrun his pursuer. Without noticing it, the speedometer has reached far into the dusty part of the dial; the part the needle never visits. It's effective, because the SUV starts lagging behind. Danny sniggers.

He maintains this high speed just to be sure, flies over a bridge and races past a parking lot, where a motorcycle cop is enjoying a sandwich, well-hidden amongst the green shrubs and afforestation. The officer almost chokes on his sandwich. He doesn't hesitate for a second and furiously starts his engine. Danny remains focused on the road and can only think of his sole purpose: to get to the dolmen as quickly as possible. He no longer cares how he does it. While he checks his navigation system to see if he's reached his exit yet, he hears a police siren behind him. It doesn't seem to bother him for a bit, but he realizes he's in trouble when he sees the blue lights in his rearview mirror.

The officer slowly and very carefully gets off his motorcycle. He clicks the crass colossus onto its kickstand, pulls up his leather pants, struggles to remove his helmet, takes a notepad and pencil from his inside pocket, looks up towards Danny and puts a huge grin on his face. His day couldn't get any better.

'Look who it is, mister phone call'. It's the same cop Danny ran into a couple days earlier.

'Weren't we going a bit too fast? He he he,' the copper chuckles.

'Not me. You perhaps?'

This comment doesn't sit well with the officer. He rips the yellow note from his pad and hands it to Danny.

'I hope I won't see you again,' the officer adds.

With the needle stuck on 50 miles per hour, Danny reaches his exit to the heathland where the dolmen is located. The black SUV is nowhere to be seen. Those folks obviously dropped out as soon as the blue lights came on, at least that is what Danny thinks. The cowards. But it's better this way. At least he won't have to worry about them anymore.

With appropriate speed, Danny drives onto a dusty driveway of a parking lot at the edge of the heather. It's the end of the day, so the place is dead. He sees a couple of buffalos grazing in the distance. Those won't bother him much, because they're in a fenced area. A buzzard circles high in the sky and makes a sudden freefall and flies back up just as quickly, in a loop. A true circus act. Something is dangling from its beak. Nature is beautiful and everything has a function, provided you have an eye for it. Danny is able to somewhat enjoy his walk towards the dolmen, but he still has his guard up. He sometimes skittishly looks behind him to make sure no one is following him. Danny recognizes the hiking trail towards a hill that emerges in front of him. It's right behind that hill, he knows. I wonder if it's still there, he thinks. Nothing will surprise him anymore, he can't help but laugh at the idea. He walked here with his family only a few days ago. A weird thought really, realizing that a hopeless distance between him and his family is developing. That thought hurts him. He regrets the things unfolded the way they did, creating tension in Danny and Anne's relationship. He has to make sure things will get better. He however doesn't have much time to think about that now. He made his way through the soft sand of the hill and arrived at the top. Just like last time, the huge structure of stacked prehistoric rocks is on the other side of the hill. He takes a lap around it to see if nothing has changed. Nothing special here. He didn't expect it to be any different. It's been dormant here for five thousand years, so it would be weird if something changed in this short period of time. He makes his way inside through the narrow entrance and turns on a small flashlight. He lets the faint glow run over the rocks. Danny investigates with a critical eye, and looks for things you'd normally pay no attention to; for carvings, color differences, little cracks, and so on. Anything could be a clue. It smells stuffy and it's eerily quiet inside the dolmen. Outside sounds barely make it in, and anything that does make it through, instantly subsides. It even feels colder. Danny's breath is turned into a chilly mist. He carefully aims the light in the direction of the different stone. He squints his eyes to place additional focus on the stone and keeps his eyes on it for a few seconds, as he stands motionless. Nothing's happening. He slowly walks towards the stone, one step at a time. What is it with this stone? he wonders. Why so careful? It's just a meteorite, quite normal. But that blue glow the last time… that wasn't normal. He squats down in front of the stone and wipes the gravel off it with a brush. He then somewhat hesitantly lets his fingers glide over it. He hopes something will happen now, like in Aladdin and the Magic Lamp, even though he doesn't believe in fairy tales at all. He even hated it when Benjamin asked him to read him stories about Little Red Riding Hood or Snow White. Having to do the voices of the evil wolf and the grandmother… beyond painful. In that respect it's great to have computers and tablets now. Just give your kids one of those and you won't hear from them for hours.

Danny awakes from dreamland with a big sigh and starts to dig around the stone with his hand, without having any idea of what he could find. The soil around the stone is very loose, so he quickly has some more leeway. He eagerly starts digging with both hands, like a dog that caught a trail. But Danny has no idea if he caught a trail. It could all be a waste of energy. He digs deeper and deeper, obsessed by the idea that there has to be *something*. He's sweating profusely and the muscles in his hands and arms start to acidify. All of a sudden he freezes and stays completely still. Droplets of sweat run from Danny's forehead onto his fatigued face. The droplets slowly transform like droplets of dew in the morning light, this time however not because of a red glow of the sun, but because of a sparkling, soft blue light. This enchantment doesn't last very long. He hears a twig snap behind him and in a flash sees a dark figure approach him.

Danny has a hard time opening his eyes. Everything is still blurry. He still feels a dull pain in his head and his ears are ringing. He's on a bed and forcedly gets up to sit on the edge of the bed. He runs his hand through his hair and feels a big bruise on the side of his head. He looks around in a daze and notices he's on his own bed. In his own room, in his own house. Did I dream all this, he wonders. He looks out through the bedroom window. His car is parked in front of the house, as if nothing happened.

'Anne?' he yells.

'Anne?!' a bit louder this time.

It remains quiet. Danny walks down the stairs. Checks the kitchen, the living room and the backyard. No sign of Anne, nor the children. The dull pain in his head flares up. Danny takes a bottle of whisky from the cabinet, pours himself a glass and drinks it in one big gulp. He considers filling the glass again, but ends up bringing the bottle to his lips.

The doorbell rings. Anne, he thinks. But that's weird, because why would she ring the doorbell of her own house?

'Good morning. Are you mister De Vries?'

'Ehm yes. And who are you?'

A well-kept, somewhat heavy man stands at the door, in his fifties, with greying hair, dressed in a dark rain coat. Next to him, a slender, silent, young man, in his twenties, wearing jeans and a strikingly fashionable jacket. He has blond, reddish, wavy hair. There's something unpleasant about the look in his eyes. When you look into his eyes, you feel the urge to quickly look the other way. The two are definitely not the father and son type. The heavy man takes his wallet and shows something that looks like an identity card.

'We're from the police.'

Houtman, criminal investigation the ID says, next to a black and white picture of the grey man, who now stands in front of Danny.

'Anne? Did something happen to Anne?'

'Who is Anne?'

'My wife. I am... I was...' Danny wildly gestures, and wants to explain that he was at home all of a sudden, in an empty house, but then thinks about how in God's name he should explain that to the police.

'May we come in?'

Before Danny can say yes or no, the two are inside. The silent young man instantly starts walking around and observing things around the house.

'Are you here because of the speeding offences?' Danny carefully asks. The old detective gives him a surprising look.

'I didn't really introduce myself,' he starts. 'I'm Dick, I can't help that,' he apologizes as he shakes Danny's hand. 'Dick Houtman. And this is my colleague, Sjoerd van Oranje,' he continues, as he points to the young man.

The older, heavy detective examines the room as he walks through it. He is clearly the authority of the two, although it doesn't show through his appearance and clothing style. His khaki colored pants are quite baggy and look a bit like a feed-sack. The whole thing is luckily held up by white suspenders, which might just as well be retro hip nowadays. The dark blue raincoat is super old-fashioned, but then again, so is the man himself. An age in which the shrinkage and arching sets in. Colleagues at the station jokingly call him *the sack*.

'You work at the University of Groningen?' the older detective asks.

'That's right. I'm an archeologist.'

'What do archeologists do?' The young man breaks his silence. 'Something with old pots and pans, right?' he cynically adds, while holding an old vase.

Detective Houtman averts his eyes from Danny into the direction of his young colleague and visibly shows his discontent regarding this rhetorical question.

'This is a Roman jug I dug up in Romania during my student days. It's a valuable memento to me,' Danny clarifies, as he carefully takes the jug from the hands of the detective and puts it back on the cabinet.

'Do you know professor Dijkstra?' The sack now gets to the point.

'Yes, he's my mentor.'

'When did you last see him?'

Danny thinks for a second.

'Two days ago.'

'Why did you meet him?' The young brat asks in a cross-examination, as he approaches Danny's comfort zone.

'Sjoerd!' The authority calls the young buck to order. It works, because the young detective crawls back into his shell.

'But what is this?' Danny asks, worried. 'Why are you here?'

'Mister De Vries, please take a seat.' The old man kindly gestures to tell Danny to take a seat in the armchair.

'Professor Dijkstra was found dead in his laboratory yesterday afternoon.'

Silence ensues.

Danny blinks a couple of times to find out whether all of this is even real. First that stuff at the dolmen, and then he's back in his own bed, with a bruise on his head, Anne who is nowhere to be found, and now the police in his house, telling him the professor is dead.

Detective Sjoerd attentively observes Danny and looks somewhat disappointed. He apparently expected a different reaction. Something like *huh, how, who, what?* The first reaction by a suspect is always crucial. That's what he was taught during his training. The young detective slightly bends over towards Danny and really tries to get a reaction out of him with his piercing eyes. He eventually gives up and spreads his arms in a gesture of hopeless surrender. He gives his old master a questioning look.

'It doesn't seem to affect you very much?' detective Houtman points out. After a short moment of processing, Danny responds.

'Well, it does. But it overwhelms me.'

'I very much understand. Take it easy.'

'You know, professor Dijkstra is… was my mentor.' Danny slowly starts to come back to his senses. 'What actually happened? What caused him to die?'

'Not what, but *how* he passed away,' the detective corrects him. 'Where were you yesterday afternoon?'

'Ehm, I was doing research… somewhere on a location.' Danny suddenly realizes that he shouldn't say anything about the dolmen or the stone. That would only complicate things even more.

'Somewhere on location?' the detective asks in surprise.

Danny nods quietly.

'According to our information, you are the last person who visited the professor in the laboratory. That shows from the register and the camera footage,' the old detective clarifies.

'But… what happened to the professor? Why is the police involved in this?' Danny asks.

'Mister de Vries, the professor was killed.'

'What? How? You mean murdered?' Danny stammers.
Detective Sjoerd jumps up and finally gets what he was waiting for; the incredible reaction of a primary suspect. The vulture ruthlessly attacks its weakened prey.

'Where were you yesterday afternoon?' the young detective snorts. His piercing eyes closely approach Danny's. 'What was the reason for your visit to the professor? What did you talk to him about?'
The old master gives his student the green light for a bit of this dominant interrogation.

'Ehm, I was in the field, like I just told you.' Danny stammers.

'Do you have witnesses?' the old detective asks.

'Ehm, yes… I mean no. I was alone.'

'What did you talk to the professor about?'

'That is sort of a business secret. We have that at universities as well,' Danny clarifies. 'Am I a suspect?'
Detective Houtman thinks and looks at his young colleague.

'Not for the time being. But you have to remain available. Here's my card. Houtman is my name. Dick, which I can't help… but I think I already told you that…' he hesitantly and apologetically adds.
The two then leave the house.

Distant past

A number of villagers gather on the village square. Chief Borg climbs atop a tree trunk.

'Villagers!' Borg clears his throat and looks around.

'It is with great pleasure to announce that our brave and fierce friend Hunze has returned.'

Surprised mumbling and buzzing arises among the villagers.

'Has he gone insane?' one of them exclaims.

'He's nuts. We have to choose a new chief,' another yells.

'Where is Hunze, by the way?' Borg asks.

The villagers look around and casually shrug their shoulders.

'Hunze! HUNZE!!!'

Hunze and Aa appear from their hut and rush to the village square. The villagers act surprised and are happy to see Hunze again.

'Sorry. I was just… just…' Hunze stammers.

Borg looks at Hunze, at Aa, back at Hunze and back again at Aa.

'Just? What?' Borg asks. Again, he takes a look at Hunze and again at Aa, and believes he has the answer to his own question.

'Ahh, I don't even want to know,' he continues as he shakes his head and shrugs his shoulders and restarts his speech.

'Dear villagers. After a rough journey, Hunze has returned, he has discovered the hidden city of Hunsingo.'

All villagers start talking to each other in disbelief. Borg tries to talk over them.

'We are in the midst of troubled times. We're in a crisis, the trade with the nomads from the eastern regions is not going too well, the yield from our fields is disappointing and there's not much game to hunt, so we don't have enough food…'

The listeners present mumble in agreement.

'…We are fighting with different tribes and are dealing with other ominous issues, such as the heathen witte wieven who cast their demonic forces over our village and our fields from their damned burial mounds, those horrendous man-devouring Huns with their gigantic clubs, and the warlike Sueven with their devastating dragon fires.'

Borg takes a deep breath after this frenzied speech from the throne. The villagers are still mumbling, but cling to his every word.

'Dear villagers, it is time to arm ourselves. We cannot let ourselves and our beautiful village get wiped off the map by these diabolical barbarians. We have to protect our women and children and secure our future!'

The crowd erupts in cheers and jeers, spears and clubs are raised into the air and the bard blows his flute. In the meantime, Borg naturally takes his time and lets the victory wash over him.

'That is why I, as the leader of this village, have decided to strengthen our forces. We will furthermore brotherly unite with our friendly neighboring villages in Eksloo and the Bourtangen Moors, with the conquering of Hunsingo as the ultimate objective. Our group of hunters and warriors need new recruits. That is why I nominate two younglings to join the warriors, Havelt and Jor!'

The young duo is promptly pushed forward by Borg's two strong arms, in order to proudly stand in the limelight.

Havelt is a confident, young man who recently went through puberty. He looks self-assured, but he's still young and inexperienced. His most important character traits are his eagerness and intelligence. Without realizing it now, Havelt will grow to become a powerful leader who will erect his own tribe and settlement in the western part of the northlands. Jor on the other hand, is not as full of character, but he's as strong as a bear. A brute force, about the same age as Havelt.

'Havelt and Jor still need to be thoroughly trained of course,' Borg continues. 'I would therefore like to nominate someone to take on this important task. Someone who has earned his stripes and knows how to act in combat situations. Someone who can transfer his knowledge and skills to these two young recruits.'

While Borg speaks these words, Ems can just feel that this is about him. He meant a lot to the village, went out hunting often, worked in the fields, helped to dig the well in the village square, in short, this is a done deal. The chubby short guy takes a little step forward and shows all the signs indicating he is ready for this responsible task.

'Hunze! I would like to entrust these two recruits to you!'
The villagers cheer in agreement. Hunze looks around in surprise, to make sure Borg is actually talking about him.

'Me?'

'Yes! Unless there's another Hunze here in the village. If so, could the real Hunze please stand up!' Borg laughs.
Ems, who initially is very disappointed, pats his friend on the shoulder. Deep down, he knows Hunze is a much better choice to complete the mission. With his big arms Borg directs the slender Hunze to the wooden podium and lets him climb it.

'I am honored and I won't disappoint you! But I want to include someone to help me with this difficult assignment, a confidant who blindly follows me, with advice and assistance, during good and bad times... Ems!'
For a moment, the entire square is quiet, with everyone looking at each other in surprise. The villagers then erupt into euphoria, followed by a militant feast that doesn't end until the middle of the night.

At the crack of dawn, Hunze and Ems are already very busy to transform a part of a field and the forest into a training camp. They drag logs to the area and make puppets out of reed and straw that serve as enemies and will be the target of their deadly spears. Aa comes over with a basket.

'You guys are doing well,' she compliments while laughing.

'For the village and villagers!' Ems yells from a distance.
Aa walks over to Hunze.

'I brought some food and drinks. I think you could use some on this day.'

'That is sweet of you,' Hunze says, as he takes off his little hat to wipe dry his sweaty forehead. His blond hair moves like a wheat field in the wind. Aa shyly laughs, but Hunze doesn't seem to notice. He is set on his difficult, responsible task of the day and has set his spears to it. His usual cheerful appearance, completed by his little twinkling eyes, have now made room for a serious, worried look.

'Check it out!' Aa enthusiastically opens the basket and shows all the items she's brought. 'I have waldkorn bread I baked myself, sheep's cheese, lard, and a delicious, fresh pearled barley brew.'
Meanwhile, both recruits Havelt and Jor enter the improvised training area.

'Mmm, pearled barley brew!' Havelt licks his lips.

'It's better if you don't stay here,' Hunze tells Aa. 'It could get dangerous. Men's stuff.'
Aa puts the supplies back into the basket with disappointment, leaves the basket with Hunze and heads for the village. She would really like to have stayed there, to help, to treat possible injuries, to provide the men with food and drinks, but especially to be with Hunze.

'Men!' Hunze fiercely yells. 'This is the first day of the many to come. It is my job to show you the ways of the battle. With power and wisdom!'
Hunze's pep rally continues for a while, to finally result into combat training. Ems and Hunze set up a track that serves as an obstacle course. Havelt and Jor have to crawl through thorny bushes, climb in trees and wade through the creek's strong current. They are taught how to sharpen spears, how to aim and throw these spears. The self-made straw men take a rough battering. The recruits learn techniques on man-to-man combat. Ems is also getting the hang of it and manages to keep the two recruits at a distance quite well. In fact, Havelt and Jor actually want to stay as far away from stinky Ems as they can. Every time Ems shows how to hold a spear high in order to attack, horrible farts shoot from his fat ass. You don't want to be anywhere near that.

Tired, but satisfied, Hunze sits on a little hill and sees how the two young bucks develop. Havelt stands out in particular. He's only a bit younger than he is, and he's smart, decisive, handy and strong, and… he's no sight for sore eyes. He uses his slender, muscular body to lift heavy logs with suppleness, and throw the pointy spears a great distance. Havelt has quite a tough appearance. Despite of that ruggedness, he's always friendly and helpful. With intrigue, Hunze observes the boy from a distance, which gives him a satisfied, pleasant and indefinable feeling.

When sunset nears, the satisfied warriors return to the village. Hunze draws his conclusions and prepares for a strategic defense plan he will discuss with the warriors of the neighboring villages. Night falls.

Loud hooting from a horn extends over Borg's entire village. The lute blows with all his might. After some time, all villagers have gathered on the village square, around the well. Borg takes his position on the large wooden block.
　'Villagers! I have an important announcement to make!'
The villagers mumble and wonder what that tubby will be jabbering about this time.
　'This morning, at the crack of dawn, our forces Hunze, Ems, Havelt and Jor left. They are heavily armed with spears and will follow the path through the forest to the east.'
Again, the alarmed crowd mumbles.
　'Why didn't I know anything about this?' Driek, Ems' wife asks.
The other villagers respond in agreement.
　'It's a top-secret mission,' Borg continues. 'They will pay a visit to our allied neighboring villages in Sleeswijk, Eksloo and the Bourtangen Moors and will join their warriors and hunters. The plan I came up with… and Hunze also contributed a bit,' Borg corrects himself, 'that plan comprises of the United Villages against all evils that cross our paths.'

Borg takes some time to breathe and think.

'Dear people, let us request the gods that our warriors will have a successful mission and will safely return to our village.'

Eight feet follow each other at a high pace across the soft moss and the crackling leaves. Dead twigs crumble under the weight of the large feet covered in animal skins, and break the icy silence in the forest, an endless forest in which time seems to have stood still for centuries.

'This is going well.' Hunze shouts. 'We're well on our way towards Eksloo.'

'Shall we set up camp soon?' Ems ask, as he smacks his round head to chase off a big, fat fly.

'Ok, good idea. Then you and Jor can go find some food. I will teach Havelt to make a fire.'

'Do you want meat, fish or vegetarian?' Ems laughs, as he leaves with Jor.

Hunze instructs Havelt to gather firewood in the area.

'Don't go too far. We have to keep an eye on each other and protect each other,' Hunze says.

When Havelt returns with a bundle of branches, Hunze tells him to squat in an open area and shows him two stones he firmly holds in his hands.

'Look, these are firestones, or flints. These rocks are so hard, that sparks fly off when you bash them into each other. If you do this quickly and often enough, these sparks will hit little, dry twigs or dry grass, which will catch fire after some time.'

Hunze is so passionate about this that Havelt hangs on every word.

'Here, you give it a try.' Hunze hands the stones to the young hunter. Nothing happens initially, but Hunze urges him to keep going. After Havelt's forehead is covered in sweat, a tiny plume of smoke appears from the grass.

'Keep going!' Hunze shouts. 'Now blow on it a bit.'

With a smile on his face, Havelt eventually creates a little fire from the dry grass, and adds some small twigs. Hunze looks at his apprentice with pride.

'You learned all of this from your father?' Havelt asks.

'My father was…' Hunze changes his mind, '…is a wise man. Knowledge and skills are passed on from one generation to the next.'

'What's it like to have a druid as a father?'

'It's very interesting at times, because you learn everything firsthand. But sometimes it's not great. He was often gone, looking for herbs. He also regularly left for a long time to attend the meetings of the Order of Druids, where the latest teachings and forms of healing were shared with each other.'

Hunze takes a jug from the knapsack.

'Here, have some barley brew.' He pours some brew into two funnel beakers and hands one to Havelt. At that moment their fingers and hands touch unexpectedly. They get startled and look at each other in silence. Hunze slowly and very carefully moves in Havelt's direction. Their eyes are locked the entire time, creating an intense force field. Flaming light from the fire illuminates their faces. The life's elixir in Hunze's veins runs at an unprecedented speed, while his heart pumps with the rhythm and force of a wolf, one of the few animals the Funnel beakers fear. The cunning, the inexhaustible strength, the perseverance and determination with which the animal sneaks up on, attacks and devours its prey. The hunters from the North are inspired by and learn from the impressive animal. Hunze also respects the animal's cunning ways. The tension between Hunze and Havelt further increases. The hungry wolf approaches the unsuspecting doe.

'We're eating deer!' it suddenly sounds.

Ems and Jor show up to the camp from out of nowhere. The force field between Hunze and Havelt dramatically collapses. Ems looks at the two in surprise, not really understanding what has just taken place. Ems and Jor actually drag a lifeless dear with them, tied to sticks between them. A trail of seeping blood runs back into the forest, to the place the two speared the animal, Havelt jumps up and reacts surprised.

'Holy funnel beakers, did you two catch that?'

'Ehm… no, she walked towards us and tied her own legs to our sticks. *Eat me! Eat me!* she screamed.'

It's quiet for a moment. Ems throws a questioning look at Havelt and then to Jor. A roar of laughter erupts and fills the forest.

The four brotherly enjoy their well-deserved dinner and quickly go to sleep in order to be well-rested. Rest, which is needed to gather the strength they will definitely need the following day. Hunze cautiously keeps one ear and one eye open. Miserable howling and a huge thunder can be heard in the far distance. The ground shakes. Witte wieven and Huns, he thinks. Still far away, for now.

Today

14 The intriguing man

Danny saunters around the house, totally confused. He grabs a bottle of hard liquor and fills a glass to the rim, picks up the newspaper, but is unable to concentrate. He looks outside through the window, while he keeps checking the handless clock. He turns on the TV but turns it right back off. He turns on his answering machine and listens to the messages.

'Hey *Danny, it's Freek. When are we going to another soccer match? I'll hear from you.*'

A beep sounds to indicate the next message.

'*Hellen here.*' Her voice sounds steamy but crackly at the same time, coming from the machine. '*I cancelled your appointment with the rector magnificus as you requested, but he was not amused... and he expects you to call him ASAP. And ehm... call me ASAP as well, sweetie.*'

Danny mimics a cackling chicken to imitate her and finishes the last bit of liquor in his glass.

Beep. '*Good day, it's Van Dijk from the local newspaper Dagblad van het Noorden, I wanted to ask you for an interv-*' Danny demonstratively presses the button to hear the next message.

Beep. '*Danny, it's Anne*'. Danny instantly goes from sleep mode to power-on. '*I'll be at aunt Lena with the kids for a few days... I think it's better for you and I to not see each other for a couple of days. You don't have to call me. I will call you when I'm coming back.*'

Anne gone, Danny thinks. To aunt Lena? That woman is always nagging and complaining. Every family always has a fun aunt, the one who spoils you and coddles you, allows you to do things you're not allowed to do at home, but every family also has a terrible one. And they end up going to Lena, the terrible one. Thomas and

Benjamin will be delighted, Danny sighs. He is however relieved, because now he knows where Anne and the kids are. Now he can completely focus on the case.

Two TV vans and a satellite van with a giant dish on top stand in front of the town hall of Loppersum. The tensions inside the conference room are running high. Camera people and photographers stand at the ready, and the people of Loppersum mumble and gesture to each other about the created situation. Danny walks around and sips from his cup of coffee. A terrible cup of joe, but he doesn't show it. He now understands why civil servants can be so sour, having to drink this coffee every day. He subtlety puts down his bitter pill somewhere and declines a second cup a friendly waiter wearing pants that are too tight offers him. The boy is walking on eggshells.

'Ladies and gentlemen, I request you take a seat.' The town clerk gestures as if he were a chief stable master. 'The mayor and the board of GasCo will first hold a press conference. You can ask your questions after that.'

A number of security officers take their position, as a precaution for what could possibly happen. Before the delegation has set a single step into the council hall, photographers nervously fill their memory cards with pictures, afraid to miss anything, they don't want to miss anything in case a competitor does manage to capture an important moment. Danny observes the whole ordeal. What a charade, he thinks. But he's here anyway, because it is of significant importance to him. The mayor, the CEO of GasCo and another big shot hide behind the conference table and a wall of microphones. They tensely look towards the crowd present. The mayor clears his throat.

'Ladies and gentlemen. Welcome, it's good to see a lot of you showed up. Although the reason therefore isn't a nice one.'

'You can fucking say that again,' an old man yells from the room. All photographers and cameras instantly turn 180 degrees to capture the unknown listener who has the courage to speak out. The security officers start to get nervous. The old man is probably a farmer from the area. He's quite heavy and tall. He's wearing a flat, black cap and has a wrinkled face with quite a sizable unkempt stubble. He's wearing a loden jacket. He's probably one of the tremor victims. Overwhelmed by all the cameras pointing at him, the man slowly sits back down in his chair and remains silent. Danny closely checks out the old farmer. I know him from somewhere, he thinks.

'I kindly ask you to remain calm. You will have a chance to ask all your questions after the press conference.' The mayor continues his speech.

'We understand that the recent tremors could have been quite shocking...' The mayor is startled by his own statement. '...ehm, quite scary, and that these have had unpleasant consequences for some of you. We will of course try everything in our power to compensate any damage to your houses, but we're still researching to what extent cause and effect are related. As long as this is not established, the question of liability will remain unclear.'

Hubbub fills the room. The crowd is now busy talking to each other and clearly show their disagreement with the speaker. Danny looks around to identify the types of people in the room. Very diverse, young and old, pretty and ugly, housewives, farmers, and even a guy from Suriname with a big afro. You don't see that often in this neck of the woods. The man laughs loudly. What could be so funny right now?, Danny thinks. Another man catches his attention, still quite young, around thirty, neat hair, casually dressed; he looks intelligent. The man enthusiastically studies the meeting and takes notes. Probably a journalist, Danny thinks.

'I would like to give the floor to the CEO of GasCo, mister Koster.'

'Thank you, mayor. Ladies and gentlemen, at GasCo we are very aware of the risks that come with drilling for shale gas. But we also know that we carry out these drillings with highly advanced techniques, and according to refined procedures. We track every second of how and where we drill and assess the situation of the soil.

That's why we are able to state with convincing certainty that the recent tremors are not the direct consequence of the drillings for shale gas.'

The crowd erupts in loud jeering and booing.

'You're trying to wipe your own slate clean,' a woman yells.

'Yeah, you don't take any responsibility for the damage to our houses,' another roars.

'We most certainly take our responsibility,' CEO Koster tries to defend himself. Without success. With his hand covering the microphone he consults his neighbor, the big shot. The mayor jumps in.

'Ladies and gentlemen, we understand your concern and I can assure you that we will absolutely take our responsibility. If the damage to your houses is demonstrably caused by the drillings, an independent commission will – in consultation with GasCo – come up with a solution for you. Are there any more questions?'

'Don't you think it's striking that the tremors only occur in the area where the drillings for shale gas are?' a reporter of RTV News asks.

'At this time, no relation between the two has been shown. We also drill in other areas, without any tremors,' Koster responds.

Blah blah blah, such a politically correct answer, Danny thinks.

'Why doesn't GasCo approve archeological research in the areas they drill in?' It's the man with the notepad who asks this question. Danny is instantly intrigued by the question of the honorable man. Why this question? Danny is aware of the refusal to allow research in the area, but what interest does the man have to ask this question on this stage? What does this man have that makes me so intrigued?, Danny wonders. It's apparent that the three behind the table are not prepared for this unexpected question. They discreetly talk amongst each other, after which the mayor takes the microphone.

'Ladies and gentlemen, we hereby end this press conference and thank you for your attention.' The super trio leaves the scorning arena, followed by the horde of press, who are still firing a bunch of questions which get no answers.

What the fuck, Danny thinks, such commotion. He gets up and goes for a drink. The place that earlier had the bitter coffee, now only offers soda.

'Don't you have anything stronger?' he asks the waiter with the tight pants. The boy looks at him in surprise.

'As a precaution we don't serve alcohol,' he timidly answers.

Out of misery, Danny grabs some apple juice. All they're missing is little straws. As he takes a lap through the worked-up crowd, he sees the man with the notepad. Before he approaches him, he first studies him from head to toe. Danny has a special interest in the man, but he can't really explain why. Is it the intelligent look in his eyes, or his correct appearance? It's something, but what is it? He's never experienced this before, and it makes him feel a bit uncomfortable. It even makes him insecure. Damn, I could really go for a whisky right now, he thinks. The thought makes Danny's mouth all watery. He swallows it down and decides to head over to the mysterious reporter.

'Able to write a nice article?' Danny asks the man.

'I was able to take some notes, yes.'

His voice surprises Danny. He didn't expect a voice like that. You sometimes see someone and picture a voice that goes with him or her. A tough man with a deep voice, a charming woman with a sexy voice, a bald-headed bodybuilder speaking with a thick Amsterdam accent or an Asian lady with a small falsetto voice. You however wouldn't expect a frisky woman in her twenties approaching you at the bar and asks you in a deep, dark whisky voice: *Hey sweetie, come here often?* This is something like that. A tough man, nice appearance, Italian looks, but then… an unexpected, friendly, modest voice.

'I hope the article can contribute to a solution,' Danny somewhat helplessly stammers. The man looks surprised.

'What paper do you work for?' Danny asks.

'Paper? How, what do you mean?' the man asks even more surprised than he looks.

'The article you're writing.'

'Oh,' the man smiles. 'This is something for myself. I take notes for myself. You never know.' Danny nods in understanding, even though he has no clue what he's talking about.

'So why this specific question? About sabotaging archeological research.' The man takes a second to think.

'Ehm, let's just say… pure interest.'

'Ah, ehm sorry… I didn't even introduce myself. De Vries. Danny de Vries. I live here in a house in Loppersum, which is why I'm here.'

'Milan van Donckervoort. Nice to meet you.'

He shakes Danny's hand. The warm handshake feels pleasant and familiar to Danny.

'I have several houses in the area I rent out as an investment. That's why I'm here. But yeah… with these earthquakes I see my empire slowly crumbling,' Milan gently laughs.

'Just kidding,' he adds in modesty.

Not until now, Danny carefully lets go of Milan's hand.

'I understand. The reason why I asked you about your remarkable question, is because I'm an archeologist. I work for the University of Groningen.

'That explains a lot. Do you also do research in the Loppersum area?' Milan asks.

'No, at least not officially?'

'Oh, so you do, off the record?' Milan kindly laughs.

'As an archeologist at heart you naturally can't leave it be if something special comes your way.'

'That's what makes it so thrilling!'

'Exactly, there's for instance this dolmen in the area that occupies my thoughts lately…' Danny thinks about how he doesn't want to say anything else about the topic.

'A dolmen?' Milan is suddenly all ears. 'That's interesting. I have a book by Johan Picardt, who mapped the dolmens. A great piece, first edition from 1660,' Milan proudly assures him. 'But forgive me. I have to go to my next appointment. You know what, here's my card. If you want to know more or need anything, feel free to call me any time.'

After his third apple juice and many thoughts about the meeting with the mysterious Milan, Danny descends the stairs and follows the *toilets* signs. If you drink a lot, you pee a lot. He stands still for a moment at the doors indicating M and F, but eventually takes the appropriate door and walks to the sinks. He turns on the tap, catches some water with his hands and splashes it on his face. What the fuck just happened up there, he thinks, while looking at himself in the mirror. As he stares at himself, he hears two men talking to each other in the other part of the bathroom, which is separated by a thin dry wall. He recognizes one of the voices, but can't yet match the right person with it. Danny can't stop himself from focusing on the conversation.

'You should've admitted more.' an unknown man says.

'Who will pay for that?' the familiar voice says.

'Now, suspicions will rise and people will start digging.'

'No worries, I have everything under control.'

'If you don't handle it the way the boss wants you to, you're in deep shit.'

'It'll be fine. We'll see each other on Lofar.'

Danny almost wets himself. He already really had to go because of all the apple juice, but the floodgates are now really breaking. He freezes in front of the mirror as he sees the CEO of GasCo, Koster, pass by in that same mirror. It takes a while before the second man appears from behind the wall. It's the unknown man that sat beside Koster behind the table. A tall, slender man with straight, grey hair. He has a skinny, sunken face with dark, hollow eyes. The man looks at Danny through the mirror as he passes. Something made him decide to stop and observe Danny in suspicion. Danny's heart is pounding in his throat and he feels the fear extend into his fingertips. What does this dude want?, he thinks. The man takes a look around to see if there are any other people in the bathroom. When he is certain that no one else is present, he approaches Danny and slowly glides his hand into his jacket's inside pocket. Shit, shit, Danny thinks, this creep is going to shoot me right here... I have to do something, I should start screaming, or call for help... or should I break this glass on the sink and cut his throat... Powerless, Danny is frozen to the sink, his entire life passes by. The time he so despises stands still, he's afraid to even move. The man pulls his hand back from under his jacket and slowly takes a pack of cigarettes out of his inner pocket. He takes one out, brings it to his lips, flips open an antique golden lighter in one go and lights the cigarette with the bright blue flame. He takes a long, deep drag. It was only a fraction of a second, but in that second, the man looks at Danny with his hollow eyes. In that one second, Danny sees the man twitches his right eye a bit, such an annoying quirk. People with clogged or hypersensitive tear ducts often do this. The man eventually points his two extended fingers to his own eyes, and then points his index finger to Danny. A clear message. The man turns around and leaves the bathroom. Danny has no time to think about this any further, because he is so close to soiling himself, he rushes to the nearest toilet.

The following day at the university seems to be a day like any other. The freshly made coffee is brewing and splashes from the machine with much buzzing and creaking, into the cardboard cup placed underneath the funnel. Danny calmly waits until the last drop falls into the cup, after which it jumps back up in a leap of happiness. The smell of coffee is doing Danny well. It's been quite hectic lately, and he hasn't slept much. He needs a moment to himself. He carefully takes the cup from the holder and immediately takes a tiny sip. He then turns around with the idea to stroll to his office.

'Mister De Vries.'

Danny bumps into detective Sjoerd as he turns around, but just manages to take his coffee away in order to avoid a disaster.

'Ah, look at that. That's so nice of you.' The young detective takes the coffee cup from Danny, who just stands there, perplexed. The older colleague now approaches.

'Ah Sjoerd, I see you found our friend, mister De Vries.' The grey detective adoringly looks at the cup of coffee.

'Well, if you're already making it, great. I won't say no to a cup of coffee.'

Danny, who is completely overwhelmed, makes another cup of coffee, extra dark.

'Gentlemen, what can I do for you?' Danny asks, annoyed.

'We have some more questions regarding our investigation into the death of professor Dijkstra.'

Danny hands the cup of coffee to detective Houtman.

'Ask away. If I can help you.'

'The professor was researching a certain material.'

Danny nods and guilelessly shrugs his shoulders.

'The professor was regularly doing research on certain materials,' Danny confirms.

'True, but according to our information, you requested that research. That material, we can't find it anywhere.'

'I have no idea. It's possible that my assistant made the request in my name. I will have to look into that.'

'That would be nice.' The detective takes out his notepad and scribbles something in it.

'Do you know Milan van Donckervoort?' the detective asks.

That question spooks Danny. He thinks about how to answer it.

'Yes, I met him at an information evening by GasCo. Because of the earthquakes.' Danny clarifies.

'You were recently seen in the presence of mister Van Donckervoort. What is your relationship?'

What the fuck, Danny thinks. Am I being shadowed?

'Nothing special,' he answers with hesitation. 'We share the same interests, he rents out some houses in the Loppersum area.' Danny gets more annoyed than he already was. 'But if you want to know more about Van Donckervoort, it's best to contact him yourself. I have his phone number right here.'

'Don't trouble yourself, mister De Vries. We know how to reach him.'

The detective again looks at his notepad.

'We have enough for now. Stay available.'

In his goodbye, detective Houtman takes a gulp from the coffee Danny handed to him earlier. He spits the black liquid back into his cup in disgust and stands defeated for a while, with tears in his eyes. With contempt on his face, he gives the cup back to Danny.

'Good luck, mister De Vries.'

15 Fair hearing

It's early in the morning, the sun is already quite strong. It's quiet in Loppersum. A tractor with a leaking slurry tank drives through the street, leaving a trail of liquid hog manure behind. When the tractor hurtles by the De Vries residence, the kitchen table, at which Danny is reading the newspaper, trembles. The coffee cup dances on its dish. 'Even worse than the tremors,' Danny thinks. Anne and the children are still at Aunt Lena, but he decided to pick them up today. He can't stand letting the boys stay under the terrible regime of that old hag. He will free them. He will be the hero, the savior. Danny grabs his phone and calls Anne.

'Good morning. Did you sleep well?' he carefully asks.

'What do you think?' Anne answers from the other side. 'Danny, we made an agreement to not see each other for a while, remember?'

'Yes, not seeing each other. But I can still call you, right?'

'No, also don't call me! Me and the boys need some peace.'

'I know enough. I'll pick you up this afternoon, ok?'

'Danny, you don't have to. We can come home by ourselves.'

'Not a chance! Make sure you're ready around noon.'

The other end is painfully quiet.

'Anne?'

The device says *call ended.*

Danny is embittered and throws the phone onto the table. As he thinks about the boys, the news channel presents a message about the professor that instantly draws Danny's full attention.

'...the remains of professor Dijkstra were found by an employee of the university', the newsreader states from behind her desk. *'Groningen police believes a crime was committed and has put six detectives on the case. The spokesperson of the police states to have different suspects in their sights, but a motive is still unknown. The*

professor was working on research on archeological materials, but whether that is related to the alleged murder is unclear. And then today's stock markets. The Dow Jones got hit hard today...'
Danny sits at the kitchen table, defeated. He still doesn't understand why the professor was murdered. *Suspects in sight?* Is he one of the suspects? The police is right on his tail, so... Danny realizes he has no alibi. According to the two hyenas he was the last one to see the professor alive. And he's on all the university's security cameras. But what if someone visited the professor after him and that person indeed killed the professor. Then this person should also have been captured by the cameras, right? Danny lets out a painful sigh, takes a look at the handless kitchen clock, chugs his weak coffee and decides to go to the office. Hellen probably wants to know what's going on.

Danny steps into his car and reverses down his driveway. He doesn't realize another car approaches at the same time, loudly honking as a result.

'You idiot!' he hears from the other car.

'Yeah, yeah, yeah. Great start of the day', he thinks.
Scared by the accident he almost had, he makes sure he checks all mirrors before he continues. A couple of blocks down, he checks his mirrors again. He gets the impression that a black SUV has been tailing him from the start. He hesitates, but just to be sure he decides to take a different route to find out whether the car is indeed following him. Danny takes a left turn followed by a right.

'Damnit,' he yells to himself, 'there they are again.'
The SUV keeps following Danny from a distance.
Danny takes a full turn, plus another quarter turn at the roundabout.

'Yes!' Danny victoriously clenches his fist. The SUV took a different turn, but he doesn't know whether this was a coincidence or Danny was actually being followed again. He will have to keep his guard up. For the remainder of the drive, Danny keeps looking around in paranoia, but there's no trace of the black SUV.

At the university, he walks through the hallway towards the security gates, past the reception desk. Hey, she's not here, Danny thinks. The annoying receptionist with the red scarf is not behind her desk. Instead, a young man wearing a neat suit and a dark red tie mans the desk. 'Was she fired?', Danny thinks. The young man looks at his monitor and takes some notes. He has a southern appearance, something Italian, with a nice tan. Dark hair and dark eyes. As Danny passes, the young man nods and smiles, showing his bright white teeth. Danny suddenly gets hot. Is it me or did they turn the heat up to 86 degrees, he wonders in agony. He takes off his jacket and unbuttons the collar of his shirt. The liberating beep of the gate makes him realize where he is. He clips his passkey to his pants and walks up the stairs towards his office.

'Good morning Hellen,' Danny says, as he swings the door open. No reaction.

'Hellen?' he calls again. It remains silent.

'Ooohh, we're playing hide and seek?' Danny starts a search through the office.

'Little Helleeeen...?!'

Her bag is under her desk and her computer is on, so she must be here.

'Well, come on now, bitch. It's not funny anymore.'

Tired and defeated, Danny sits down behind his own desk and turns around in his chair. He thinks about the things that happened and gazes out over the campus.

Suddenly, someone bangs on the door.

'You don't have to knock, Hellen!' Danny shouts.

'Police!' the person gruffly responds.

Danny turns around in his chair in horror and sees the two hyenas and two other officers in uniform standing in the doorway. The young detective has a mean smirk on his face and holds a sheet of paper, which he then brings close to Danny's face. So close that Danny can't read a single letter.

'Gentlemen. What is going on?' Danny politely asks while overflowing with adrenaline.

'Mister De Vries, you are hereby arrested under suspicion of the murder of professor Dijkstra.'

'Me?!' Danny asks, confused.

'This here, is an arrest warrant of the District Attorney.' detective Houtman clarifies.

'You have the right to remain silent, and anything you say can be used against you,' the young buck adds.

While those words are being spoken, one of the officers in uniform grabs Danny, turns him around and puts the handcuffs around his wrists. 'This is serious,' Danny thinks.

'We are taking you to the station for further investigation,' the old detective explains.

'But this is a misunderstanding,' Danny stammers. 'I didn't kill the professor!' Or did I?, he thinks to himself.

'At the station you will have all the time in the world to explain everything,' the red dog grins.

The group walks down the stairs, with a downcast Danny handcuffed in the middle. They walk through the hall towards the squad cars parked in front of the door. The young man behind the reception desk looks up in horror. From the corner of his eye, Danny sees the young man look at him in disbelief. He sees that the boy stands up, but eventually remains powerless behind the desk. Danny is deeply ashamed and feels the humiliation as he is dragged away in a police vehicle, like some sort of hardened criminal.

At the police station, Danny is taken to an interrogation room. It's just like in the movies. A poorly lit room with a table and four chairs in the middle of it. One of the walls has a giant mirror. That's one of those one-way mirrors. In his mind he sees that red dude standing on the other side with a big grin on his face. There's a camera in the corner of the room. 'Big brother is watching you,' he thinks. The other wall is dressed with a clock. The second hand moves painfully slow. His forehead starts to cover in sweat. The two detectives enter the interrogation room.

'Before we start the interrogation...' detective Houtman crassly starts, '...I have to remind you of the right to an attorney.'

'Do I need one?' Danny asks.

'We have strong leads and even concrete evidence that you murdered professor Dijkstra.'

'Proof? What kind of proof?' Danny uncomfortably turns around on his chair and looks in the direction of the handless clock.

'The murder weapon has your fingerprints on it.' As the old detective speaks these words, the young buck demonstratively places a transparent plastic bag on the table. A white sticker with big, red letters reads 'police evidence'. Danny looks at it, completely surprised and doesn't understand it at all. A piece of rock.

'Did I...?' A piece of rock from the dolmen, he thinks. Did I use this to kill the professor?

'That's not all,' the young buck continues. 'We also have the camera footage that shows you and the professor together, alone.'
The two detectives hang over the table in order to intimidate Danny and get very close to Danny's comfort zone. So unpleasantly close that he can smell them.

'I think I need a lawyer,' Danny determines, as he starts hyperventilating.

'I'm already here!' someone behind him says.
Both detectives look up to see who's behind Danny...

'Danny, I'm here. Sorry, I was gone for a bit.' Hellen lays her hand on Danny's shoulder. He turns around and sees her standing there.

'Huh? What are you doing here?' he asks, taken aback and bathing in his own sweat.

'Well yeah, I work here... I think.'

Danny slowly comes to his senses and sees Hellen standing in his own office. He stand up, walks through the office and looks around in confusion.

'Did you happen to see the cops here just now?' he asks.

'Cops? Here? No... but damn, you look terrible.'

'Where were you just now?' Danny frantically asks.

'As I said, I was gone for a bit... you know.' Hellen makes a *lady thing* gesture. 'Everything ok?' she asks, worried.

'Yes... ehm, I needed a lawyer and then you were here.'

'Hmmm, mister needs a lawyer...' Hellen canoodles and starts to assume a certain pose in front of Danny, '...for his defense? Should I serve you?' she sexily asks.

'Eh, no Hellen. Let's be serious now. Just let me be.' He waves Hellen away and changes his tone.

'Hellen, I... we have a problem. Professor Dijkstra... You will probably know about it by now.'

'Ehm, yes I do, there's something I have to tell you,' Hellen carefully interrupts him.

'Not now, Hellen,' Danny responds. 'The professor was found dead in the laboratory and the police visited me at home and at the office to investigate and interrogate.'

'Yes, but there's something I have to te-'

'That's not important right now,' Danny assures her. 'The problem is that the professor was working on the research on the gravel I brought from the dolmen. This research is now out in public. Do you understand?' Danny beggingly looks at Hellen.

'If the cops see the results of the research, then... then...'

'Shit hits the fan,' Hellen adds.

'Exactly! Hellen, is there a way to remove the results of the research from the laboratory?'

Hellen thinks.

'I have authorization for the lab. But the question is whether the police sealed the lab. And didn't they already take the information to the police station?'

'We'll just have to see. We have to do something!'

'Ok, I'll do my best. But Danny, there really is something you should know.'

'Not now, Hellen.' Danny naively checks his handless watch and realizes it's time to pick up Anne and the children.

'I have to go to an appointment. Call me when you're ready for us to enter the lab.'

On the way to Loppersum, Danny makes a quick grocery run in a supermarket. He came up with the idea to cook something special for Anne and the kids. Home-made pasta carbonara, something Anne loves. He puts two full grocery bags in the trunk of his car and drives towards Assen, the fortress city of aunt Lena. It's quiet on the road. He really appreciates the peace and space you can find in Drenthe and Groningen. No bustle like in the west, in the busy, overpopulated cities. What's wrong with those people, to want to be packed on top of each other in tiny spaces? He sometimes has to be in Groningen or The Hague for his work. Without noticing it you are dragged into the chaos of all the commotion. Traffic alone: tailgating, not yielding, honking the horn, being in a rush all the time; the thought of this makes Danny appreciate the beautiful landscape of Drenthe even more. The vast farmlands, grazing cows, wooded banks and thatched farms in the distance. The rugged, untouched nature reserves where time stood still, interspersed with freshly green forests that provide plenty of space for deer, does, aardvarks, badgers, owls and even wolves nowadays. Time and miles fly by unnoticed. Danny passes a sign that says *Assen*. He blindly drives to Lena the Terrible's house of horrors. It's a detached house, stately and well-kept, but it has something spooky about it at the same time. The old oak trees surrounding the house place the mansion in a dark light. The ivy that climbs up the walls also creates an overgrown and mysterious atmosphere.

Aunt Lena inherited the crib. She's the only person living in it. But that's for the best, because no one could last very long under the same roof with her. One day with her and I'd be running out of the house, screaming, Danny sniggers. He honks the horn twice as he stands in front of the driveway. Thomas and Benjamin come running out the house, with barking Bor closely behind them. Anne remains in the doorway for a bit and gives Lena a kiss. It gives Danny the shivers. Aunt Lena is exactly the same as he remembers. A skinny woman with long, straight, greying hair. She could've been a member of the Addams Family. Danny opens the window halfway and waves at Lena. He tries to give her a friendly smile, but is struck by spontaneous jaw cramps

'Daddy, daddy.' The boys race to the car.

'Hey, there you are.' Danny steps out to grab the suitcases.

'How was it?'

'Well, we did a scavenger hunt…' Thomas starts.

'There were spiders in our room…' Benjamin follows up.

'We ate goat soup… Bor threw up… Aunt Lena doesn't have Wi-Fi… there was a cat with only three legs… and a giant box in the attic… we weren't allowed to go there…'

'All right, all right, save me the details. You can tell me all about it as we're driving.'

Meanwhile, Anne gets in the car without saying a single word. Danny gives her a questioning look.

'Goat soup?'

Upon arrival at home, everyone starts rushing around. Danny grabs the two grocery bags and heads to the kitchen. He has only one goal, and that's to prepare a delicious *welcome home* meal for Anne.

'Pasta Carbonara!' he yells, and proudly shows her the bag with ingredients. Anne doesn't respond.

'Is there any mail?' she asks.

'Ehm, yes; in the basket.' Despite all the resignation, Danny starts chopping the fresh vegetables and tomatoes.

Anne walks through the hall towards the mail basket. She stops at a big crack in the wall, looks at it and sighs.

Back in the kitchen, Danny is well underway with his pasta sauce. Anne walks to the knife block on the kitchen table, holding a bunch of letters. She pulls one out of the block and thoughtlessly stares at Danny for a while, as she holds the razor-sharp knife. Danny sees his own reflection in the dangerous, shiny blade from the corner of his eye. He carefully dips his finger in the pasta sauce. Completely out of nowhere, Anne cuts open an envelope with a single motion, creating a sharp sound. Danny freezes at the kitchen table, as the red substance slowly seeps over his finger. He tastes it.

'A little bit more salt.' On the wound, he thinks, as he observes Anne's every motion.

'What about that goat soup by the way?' he casually asks.

'Goat's cheese soup,' Anny corrects him with a little, but short smile. 'Disgusting.'

'Well, then this will make up for a lot. Boys, dinner's ready!'

A big pan of pasta carbonara rattles on the table.

Like a couple of starving wolves, Thomas and Benjamin finish the last bits of pasta on their plates. Although it's her favorite meal, Anny only gave herself a small portion, and ended up only eating half of it. Danny and Anne didn't speak to each other the entire meal.

'It wasn't good?' Danny cautiously ends up asking.

'Danny, I don't want anymore.'

'I can see that. Maybe the boys want some more?' He takes Anne's plate and distributes the leftovers across the plates of Thomas and Benjamin.

'No, I mean I don't want to continue,' Anne clarifies.

Danny looks at her in surprise.

'Don't want to continue? Continue what?' he asks.

'With us! I'm quitting us.' As she expresses her emotions, she takes a napkin, cleans her lips with it and then wipes away a tear.

'I can't take it any longer, Danny. You, how busy you are with work, the stuff with the dolmen, the problems with our house here in earthquake land, the… the… death of that professor… Everything!' The emotions overcome her and she starts sobbing.

'And don't think I don't know about your escapades,' she sobbingly adds.

'Escapades???' Danny sanctimoniously exclaims.

Danny had obviously noticed that things weren't going all that great with Anne, but this, this is completely out of left field. He's speechless for a moment.

'I will arrange the divorce papers. You'll be sleeping on the couch for now,' Anne clarifies.

'Anne, isn't this a bit of an exaggeration?' Danny starts to realize the severity of the situation.

'An exaggeration? You call this an exaggeration? The house is about the collapse, and our marriage already collapsed a year ago.'

'Anne, not in front of the boys.'

'Oh, the kids?' Anne emotionally shouts. 'Sure, drag the kids into this again. You didn't do all that much for them anyway. Boys, go to your room. Daddy and mommy are having some grown-up talk. NOW!'

This last command makes Benjamin and Thomas jump out of their chairs and fly upstairs without saying a word.

'All right then, now you can say whatever you want, the boys aren't here!'

'Anne, be reasonable. The house, I can't help it that those shale gas drillings cause earthquakes. It's not fair to blame that on me.'

'But it is your responsibility to fix the damage and to get those GasCo people to stop drilling!'

'Oh, like I can make GasCo stop… me? Danny de Vries?'

His own statement makes him laugh. 'Anne, please.'

'That's not the only thing Danny. It's everything, all of it! I can't do it anymore, I'm worn out. I mean it, Danny. I want a divorce.'
Anne walks away from the table and heads upstairs, leaving Danny behind, defeated.

Danny paces up and down the room. The talk with Anne really got to him. Of course she's right about them clashing now and then, the fact that the butterflies are gone. That happens in the best relationships. And about those escapades… does she know about Hellen? How could she know, he wonders. He trots to the liquor cabinet, pulls a bottle of whisky from the shelf, shakenly pours a good amount into a glass and chugs it in one gulp. He keeps thinking. The thing with Hellen, that's nothing, really… I got dragged into it, Anne has to understand. Danny sighs. What about Thomas and Benjamin. They will be hit the hardest. Moving between houses with their little suitcases, choosing to be with mommy or daddy… It's cozy with daddy, but mommy just nags about what they aren't allowed to do. They do all kinds of fun activities with daddy; play soccer, go to theme parks. Mommy just lets them help with the dishes and do homework. Those are the sort of things that will happen once children have to choose, Danny contemplates. He pours himself another drink, the bottle is empty, the glass half full, and he lets it glide down his throat.

'Children don't even want to choose,' he convinces himself out loud, as he falls into a chair. The liquor is starting to do its job.

'Women are mean… all naggs, allays kno bette, mean nagger witch, yes, shesa witch, wi wit wief hihi.'

The outside door of the De Vries residency loudly slams shut. Danny instantly sits up straight in his chair.

'Huh, what, who?' he confusedly wonders, as he looks around in a daze. He rubs his hands over his head and face and moans so loudly the whole street could hear it. He gets up, or at least he tries to.

'What the fuck was that?'

Danny walks to the kitchen and looks outside through the window. He just sees the back of Anne's car disappear around the corner at the end of the street. He sighs and puts his hands in his pockets like an angry child. He can feel a business card in his right pocket. Disheveled, he takes the card out. *Milan van Donckervoort, entrepreneur – collector.* Danny suddenly starts to feel better. He takes his phone and calls the number on the card.

'Van Donckervoort, good morning,' a pleasant voice answers.
Danny listens as a smile appears on his face.

'Hello, who's there?' Milan asks.

'Oh, I'm sorry. It's De Vries, Danny de Vries. We met in Loppersum, at the GasCo meeting.'

'Ah, the archeologist?'
The response gives Danny a beaming smile from ear to ear, realizing Milan remembers he's an archeologist.

'That's exactly right,' Danny confirms. 'Funny that you remember that, so long ago.'

'Yes of course, memory, the past; that's part of my job.'
Danny tries to draw a picture.

'But ehm, why are you calling me?' Milan asks after some silence.

'Oh yeah...' Why *am* I calling him, Danny wonders. 'Ehm, during our meeting you talked about the book by Johan Picardt. You told me you have a first edition of this title. I'm quite interested in that,' Danny continues and tries to save himself from embarrassment.

'But of course. You're welcome here. When do you want to meet?'
The two check their schedules and make an appointment.
After ending the call, Danny believes it actually wasn't a bad idea to start about Picardt's book. It might give him more information about the dolmen. The fact he now has a meeting with Milan about it, is a nice byproduct, at least that's what he tells himself.

Danny is late for his appointment with Milan. He races across the landscape with incredible speed and again flies over the little bridge of the small river Aa, which shakes on its pillars as he passes. A sudden siren and blue lights give Danny a deja-vu.

'No, not again,' he curses out loud to himself.
The grouchy cop is standing at his car window again, wearing his tight, leather pants.

'I believe I have to explain some stuff to you at the station,' the officer sneers.

'Well, that's not nece-'
Danny is unable to finish his sentence. Before he knows it, his wrist is cuffed.

'Just in case we take off again at great speed, he he.' the officer chuckles.
A while later, Danny sits across from the motorcycle cop at the police station, upset and annoyed. The cop types something on the computer, using his two index fingers.

'Do you have an explanation for your driving behavior?'

'I want to call my lawyer.' Not that he has one, but Danny came up with the idea to mobilize the broad. She is just going to have to get him out of this bizarre situation. Post bail if need be.
Danny is handed a phone, has a conversation and is taken to a depressing, closed room right after. When the cop takes a last inspecting look through the hatch, Danny addresses him.

'You know what's funny? That *we* will be out of here in five minutes. All that work for nothing.' Danny adds a sinister '*Hehe*'.
The cop closes the hatch with a dazzled look in his eyes.
Five minutes later, Danny is out on the street.

Danny drives onto the gravel-covered driveway of the Dickninge estate at mediocre speed. The majestic mansion of the former monastery appears in front of him. The gravel pops underneath the tires, making it absolutely impossible to enter this estate unnoticed. Ones who try will be in for a disappointment. Security cameras are positioned all over, carefully monitoring the entire surroundings. There's probably a control center somewhere in this mansion, where a resident, or maybe even a private security guard, looks at the monitors on a daily basis. Every movement of a leaf, a bird flying by, a bunny that sets off the motion sensors, every wanted or unwanted guest is captures by the camera. Danny's car, crackling across the driveway, also passes through one of the security monitors. The sound of the gravel has been detected by a Labrador that rushes towards the car. The large, sluggish animal manages to make quite an impression with its loud bark and threatening growl. Another reason to not just enter the estate.

'Melchior, here!' A deep male voice calls the dog to stand down. A man in a black suit approaches from the porch. As he gets closer, Danny sees it's not just a suit, but a neat three-piece suit with a traditional tie and pocket square. Danny carefully gets out of the car, to make sure the faithful friend doesn't show his loyalty to his owner and territory by taking a bite from his pants.

'Nice little animal,' Danny says as he points at the dog.

'This *little animal*, with all due respect, is a Newfoundland Labrador, and is a direct descendent of Gordon and St. Johns Flat coated Retrievers family,' the know-it-all snobbishly responds.

'Yes… yes of course, I noticed…' Danny stammers. 'I'm familiar with them. I'm here to see Milan van Donckervoort. And you are?' He extends his hand in order to shake his. The Labrador starts growling again.

'The butler,' the man says. He keeps his hand to himself.

'Oh, of course'. That explains a lot, Danny thinks.

'Is mister Van Donckervoort present?'

'Who can I tell him is here for him?'

'De Vries, Danny de Vries. I have an appointment.'

'Follow me.'

The butler walks into the house, with the Labrador obediently by his side. Danny follows him over the beautiful, marble floor that leads to the large, central hall.

'Please wait here. I will notify mister Van Donckervoort of your presence.'

He disappears behind one of the many doors of the hall.

'*I will notify mister…*' Danny quietly imitates the butler who reminds him of a penguin. As he waits for what's to come, he takes a good look around the hall. Various paintings of landscapes and portraits of insignificant people hang on the walls. A large dresser supports some vases and pots. There's a thirteenth century baptismal font made of Bentheimer sandstone in the corner. Definitely Made in China, he thinks to himself. With curiosity he walks towards the dresser and picks up a ceramic pot to give it a closer look. A fine piece. He bring the pot a bit closer to his face to check out the details. He's left dumbfounded.

'About seven thousand years old,' he suddenly hears a voice behind him say. On the other side of the hall, near the door through which the butler disappeared, there's a totally different caliber of penguin. Above a black suit with a sharp cut and a characteristic bowtie, the friendly face of Milan, clean-shaven, with dark, short-cut hair. That's definitely a *mister*, Danny thinks. He swallows his dumbfoundedness and starts an awkward apology.

'Yes, from one of the northern Funnel beaker peoples. I haven't seen a piece this nice before. I first thought…'

'It was one of those cheap, Chinese knockoffs,' Milan adds. He takes the valuable ceramic piece from Danny's hands and carefully places it back on the dresser.

'My apologies. De Vries. Danny de Vries. We met at the GasCo party.'

'Yeah, that was definitely a party that caused some turmoil,' Milan laughs. Another intimate handshake follows.

'Milan van Donckervoort, call me Milan.'

The two look straight into each other's eyes for a moment. Milan has confident, bright blue eyes. Danny hasn't seen eyes like this before. A remarkable combination with the dark hair. He has an overall intelligent appearance.

'Could I offer you a drink?' Milan asks.

'A beer would be nice.'

'Follow me. We can sit in the lounge, by the lit fireplace.'

They enter the rustic space. A large, standing clock with roman numerals and majestic arms instantly draws Danny's attention. It makes him uncomfortable.

'You have a beautiful house. Do you live here alone?' he asks.

Milan detects Danny's behavior and reassures him.

'No, I live here with Harry.'

'Harry?' With a Harry, Danny wonders in surprise.

'Yes, you just met him. The butler. He's actually everything, guard, gardener, chef, driver. I prefer to not call him butler, and call him personal assistant instead. It's convenient that he resides here in the house.'

Damn, such decadence, Danny thinks as he nods in agreement.

'I have this one. A Peatdigger.' Milan shows Danny a dark bottle of beer with a historic label. 'An excellent beer, if I say so myself. It's brewed here somewhere in Drenthe. You know what, I'll have one as well.'

The lounge is a light, attractive space with a large, white couch, comfortable chairs and a robust, oak coffee table on top of a shaggy woolen carpet. The smell of smoldering wood in the fireplace gives it a homely atmosphere. There's some classical music playing in the background. Mozart? Bach? Danny recognizes the music, but is unable to link it to its composer. He's not that fond of classical music. He is able to appreciate it at times and it calms him down.

Milan pours the Peatdigger into a tall, slim beer glass. Exactly right with two fingers of foam on top.

'It tastes great this way, here you go.' He hands Danny the glass.

'Thank you.' Danny thinks about how he will turn this conversation.

'Let's get to it. You mentioned that you are in the possession of a copy of Picardt's book.' Danny has to think about the correct title.

'Korte Beschryvinge Van...'

'Eenige Vergetene En Verborgene Antiquiteiten,' Milan adds with a smile. 'I know the book, a hell of a title. No pompous literature, but it is an icon from the era it was written in. But I have to correct you. I don't know if it's an *original copy*. I never really focused on that, you know.'

'Can I see it?' Danny asks.

'Of course, let me go get it.' Milan puts his beer on the table and walks to a large bookcase, one you find in traditional libraries, with a sliding ladder in front of it. He moves the ladder to the side, to the *K* department and climbs two steps up.

Danny closely watches how Milan glides his finger over the back of the books.

'Ah, here it is. Picardt.' Milan descends the stairs and gives the book to Danny. Danny instantly checks the inside of the cover. '*Nieuw-Amsterdam Publishers, 2nd Edition, 1870'*. He closes the book in disappointment.

'Second edition,' he sighs. 'This is not what I'm looking for. You mentioned the first edition, from 1660.'

Milan throws a questioning look at Danny.

'This is what I have,' Milan assures him. 'But why are you specifically looking for an original copy?'

Danny takes a moment to think about how to answer this. He doesn't want to say too much about his search to just anyone.

'According to my information, the original copy contains additional notes about the dolmens Picardt mapped.'

'So, what is so interesting about those additional notes?' Milan curiously asks. 'After all, we already know everything about the dolmens, right?'

'Apparently not everything.' Danny gives him back the book. When Milan takes the book, they stare into each other's eyes for a moment. Danny experiences an unusual feeling. Something that happened to him before, and doesn't know what to do with. He guilelessly checks his handless watch.

'I have to get going,' he nervously stammers. 'Thank you for your hospitality and the beer.'

He walks towards the door, assuming it leads to the central hall, opens it and walks straight into a supply closet. He looks around in confusion, trying to find his way.

'This way,' Milan laughs as he shows Danny the way to go.

'Sorry. It's been a long day. Thanks again and goodbye.'

'Goodbye.' They briefly shake hands.

Danny walks down the porch stairs to his car and nearly slips on one of the steps. He skittishly looks over his shoulder to make sure Milan didn't see it. Luckily he already went inside. Danny clumsily puts on his safety belt and starts the car. At least he tries. Again. What is this, he thinks, as a helpless and lost feeling overcome him. He breaks out into a sweat.

'Come on, come on!' he rants.

After the third try, the engine starts. Let's get out of here, he thinks, as he floors it. When Danny leaves the estate via the driveway, he checks the rearview mirror and catches a glimpse of Milan standing behind a window.

17   The letters

Danny's phone rings.
Unknown number.
  'Danny de Vries here, good afternoon,' he formally responds. After all, you never know who's on the other side.
  'It's Milan.'
It's quiet on both sides.
  'Milan van Donckervoort... from the Picardt book... Second edition.'
Milan wants to jolt Danny's memory, but that's unnecessary. Those blue eyes underneath that pitch-black hair. He gets the same sweats as when he left Milan's estate.
Danny gets his act together.
  'Milan! Of course I know who you are, ha-ha.' Danny laughs as if he's reciting the script of a comedy play.
  'How are you?' he asks, because he can't think of anything else to say.
  'Fine.'
  'Good, good.'
  'Sure, sure.'
  '...'
The conversation is going smoothly.
Milan then gets to the point.
  'Danny, I called to ask you over for dinner at my place.'
Dinner? At Milan's place? Danny's adrenaline is flowing at hyper speed after this unexpected invitation.
  'When do you have time?' Milan asks.
  'Ehm, I'm fine whenever. I always have time.' Danny says as he checks his watch.

'I have something you might be interested in.'
Danny frowns. What the fuck? What does he have for me? Is it about
the earthquakes and the developments surrounding the compensation
of damages by GasCo, or about Picardt's book. Does he have the first
edition after all, or the original manuscript? Or is it something else?

'Is tomorrow night ok for you?'

'Tomorrow night is fine. I'll be there.'

'Six thirty. See you then!'

He forgot he was going to go out to dinner with Anne tomorrow
night. A reconciliation attempt. Fuck!

It's late at night when Danny and Milan are having dessert, a
champagne mousse with fresh forest fruits.

'This is delicious,' Danny says, as he scrapes the last bits off his plate.
'Yes, Harry has outdone himself once again. And the great thing about
it all is that he has fun doing it. Cooking was spoon-fed to him.' A big
smile appears on Milan's face as he speaks these words.

Danny thinks about Anne. She also loves to cook. Her mother taught
her at an early age. He feels bad about the thought of cancelling the
meeting with Anne. *For work. I have to finalize some research*, he
said. Not even a lie, really.

'I can cook too! And boil stuff.' Danny suddenly exclaims. 'Boil some
water, cook an egg!'

Milan laughs.

'And I'm also good at boiling over! And I'm into cookies as well!'
Danny rattles on. Milan is cracking up. The red wine is starting to pay
off. There's four empty bottles on the table already.

'Shall I pour some more?' Harry asks, standing by the dinner table
like a chameleon to clear the table.

'Thank you, Harry.'

'I... I... I also some more.'

Milan and Danny almost die laughing, like two adolescent best friends
in their college days.

'Would you look at us, we look like a newlywed cooking couple.'

'Cook? What about coke? Want some?' Milan sniffs.

Harry leaves the scene, shaking his head.

'Oh, Harry from Expedia, I'd like to go on vacation with you to a tropical cooking island,' Danny rambles.

After the two somewhat come back to their senses and wipe the tears of laughter off their faces with a napkin, Milan takes a deep breath and puts on a serious face.

'Danny, I invited you here tonight, because I want to show you something.' Milan gets up. 'Come, walk with me.'

Upon arrival in the library, Milan carefully moves aside a painting of a dark portrait of an unknown man. The man has such a dark look on his face, that it seems like he is warning everyone who comes too close. Danny, quite tipsy, watches the whole ordeal unfold. The man in the painting comes threateningly close to him, increasingly closer. He turns his dark, hollow eyes. It makes Danny a bit nauseous.

'Whos htat dude?' he hiccups. 'E a friend of you?'

Milan doesn't answer and opens the painting like a window, revealing a large, grey steel vault door with a combination lock. Milan gives it a few spins, clockwise and counter-clockwise, after which the door opens with a click. He takes out a cardboard folder with a stack of old papers and hands it to Danny.

'This is something you might be interested in.'

'Whas dis?' Danny staggers as he takes the folder.

When he opens the folder, a large number of handwritten notes, letters and documents appear. He initially doesn't realize what exactly he's holding. But as he focuses and reads some lines, his breath is taken away.

'But these are... these are...' Danny is suddenly very sharp again.

'Maybe you should take a seat,' Milan suggests.

'These are letters by Van Gogh!'

'The original ones!' Milan adds.

'And his memoirs about his stay in Nieuw-Amsterdam.' Danny is completely befuddled as he looks through the documents.

'The great unknown letters by Van Gogh. The letters that were never sent by mail. No one knows their content and people doubt their existence. How did you get these?' He asks, surprised and stunned. Milan hesitates.

'Sometimes, things are better left untold. It's also not wise to always know everything. People won't understand it anyway.'

'Are they stolen?' Danny asks, taken aback.

'No, no,' Milan laughs. 'To the contrary, they're originals and obtained legitimately! Maybe you will learn about it some time, maybe not. But that's not important now, Danny. What's important is that this is valuable to your research. Correct?'

'Absolutely! I, I...'

'If you want, you can read them here. You can't take them with you! Do you want anything else to drink?'

'A cup of strong coffee would be nice right now.'

'I'll go get it!'

Danny quickly scans all letters and notes to gain insight into their content, and tries to come up with an order and a structure. He even finds some sort of bill for a week's stay at the Guesthouse Hendrik Scholte. Three guilders? Does that include tourist taxes, he wonders. He then starts reading a letter.

Dear Theo,

That must be written to his brother, Danny thinks.

I've been here for almost three days now, in this godforsaken place. There's nothing to do here, unless you like peat! Peat here, peat there. Flat bottoms full of the stuff come and go over the canals. It's crap.

You can't even roll a cigarette with that dry stuff. I wonder what those Amsterdam merchants saw in this stuffy hole. And to call it Nieuw-Amsterdam... there's not a decent canal house or bar along the water here, just sod houses. But oh well, who knows, maybe it will change and it indeed becomes a second Amsterdam in the North. Besides that, Drenthe is however really peaceful, and the nature is beautiful. I'm working on a painting of the drawbridge, here in Nieuw-Amsterdam. Don't expect too much of it, because the bridge over the river Amstel looks better.

'Stand still, Gertie.'

'Owww... but my calves are cramping up, Vince!'

'Yes, that's why you have to stay relaxed, my little puppet.'

'Yes, that's how I feel! Like a puppet! And why do I have to wear these ridiculous clothes? And those clogs? They hurt my little feet. Viihiiiince!'

'Everyone here walks around in these dresses. I want to keep the drawing authentic.'

'Old and sick you mean!'

'A bit longer, Gertie. Then I'll be done.'

Gertrude resists some more, but bravely remains standing in order to keep Vincent satisfied. And also because she's a bit vain and wants to be on a masterpiece by Vincent. It strokes her ego. Her beauty and her appearance will indelibly be on the canvas for eternity, she thinks.

On the banks of the Verlengde Hoogeveensevaart at the drawbridge of Nieuw-Amsterdam, Vincent van Gogh sits behind his easel, painting. He almost finished his piece *the drawbridge in Nieuw-Amsterdam*. In order to make it all seem less lifeless, he asked his female companion Gertrude to pose in front of the bridge, wearing traditional clothing from Drenthe. She wasn't up for it at first, but when Vincent told her she'd be the center of the painting, she agreed.

'All right. Done!'

'Owww, I can't stand on these damn clogs for another second!'

'Gertie!'

'Yeah, sorry. Can I see?' Gertrude jumps out of her clogs and rushes towards Vincent like a whirlwind.

'Easy! Don't fly around so much! The paint still has to dry.'
Somewhat restrained, Gertrude approaches and walks around the easel on her bare feet, in order to admire the beautiful, promising portrait of her.

'WHAT???' she yells.
Vincent starts laughing out loud.

'Vihiiince????! What is this? Where am I?'
The pen drawing *Drawbridge in Nieuw-Amsterdam* has become a masterpiece, with the epic bridge connects the northern and southern banks of the Verlengde Hoogeveensevaart to each other. On the other side of the bridge, two thatched rural farms arise, enriched with trees. And on this side of the bridge... we see a small, insignificant little person standing on the sandy path, completely unrecognizable.

'This is not funny, Vince! I'm going to the inn.'

'Gertie! Isn't it beautiful?' Vincent laughs, as she walks away.
As he sees the dust cloud leave for Hendrik Scholte's inn, Simon the stable boy suddenly, from behind Vincent, rides towards him on a brown horse. He stops a couple of yards away from Vincent.

'Mister Van Gogh?'

'Yes, what is it, Simon?'

'I have a letter for you.'

'A letter? For me? Who sent it?'
The boy says nothing and hands him the white, sealed envelope. Before Vincent can even open the letter or ask any more questions, the boys has disappeared.
There's no sender on the envelope. Vincent unfolds the sealed letter. The first thing he sees is the diocese sign of the reformed church of Coevorden and the name underneath the letter; *Picardt.*

'See, now we're getting somewhere,' Danny says, as he finished the last bit of coffee.

'Would you like some more?' Milan asks. Danny nods.

'I think we will now finally find out what that Picardt knows about the dolmen.' Danny sounds euphoric, while Milan shows a smile, but has an otherwise resignedly response, as he checks his watch. It's already 1:30 at night.

Danny continues to read.

I have to tell you something, dear Theo. I received a letter by that preacher from Coevorden, the one I told you about at some point. He asked me to come visit him. I did, in the church of Sweeloo. That's where he would be. Well, he wasn't. I didn't see that Picardt guy at all there. I received another letter from him today, inviting me again. But this time he reveals why he wants to speak with me. He believes something is going on with a dolmen in the north. Something he can't put on paper. That's why he wants to speak to me in person. 'A dolmen!' my dear Theo. Why would I care about a godforsaken dolmen?! Those piles of rocks have been collecting dust for 5,000 years or longer. They'll still be here 30,000 years from now.

I wouldn't even take the effort to paint those things. Waste of my expensive paint and canvas! Ha. Who would want a sad pile of rocks hanging from their wall? Would you?

Anyway, my dear, I decided to hear what this Picardt wants, or has to say. Tomorrow, Gertrude and I will go to Coevorden. I will drop her off at the small businesses, so she can take her time picking a nice dress, or a leather bag, or have a drink at the local tea house, if they have one of those over there, hah. But this stays between us, my dear! I will write you again after I speak to Picardt.

The clouds of dust fan out from under the wooden wheels that bounce on the cart track. The carriage is pulled by a black stallion, which can barely be kept in check by the coachman.

'Hoooo! Easy now, Bonzo! Hooooo.' The coachman tries to somewhat tighten the reins. The horse is uneasy and swarms from left to right like a man who drank too much. It's unclear what causes this distress in the animal. There's no other traffic on the cart track to Coevorden. It's however quite serious, because the animal is foaming at the mouth.

'Huuuu Bonzo.' The good man's forehead is covered in sweat.

'Who calls his horse Bonzo, Vince?' Gertrude asks. She clings on to the carriage and is visibly concerned about this little ride. Vincent shrugs.

'What are they feeding this horse, Vince? Dog food? It'll start barking soon.'

'Driver, could you slow it down a bit?' Vincent urges. '… We have nothing but time,' he adds, to get the driver to slow the horse down a bit.

'Yeah, coachie, put on the brakes! What's with this animal?' Gertrude yells in a panic.

'We're almost there Gertie. Look, there's the church tower of Coevorden.'

A small, pointy tower emerges in the blue sky, in line with the cart track. It tries to skewer all the floating clouds. The woolly shapes barely escape the tip and continue their path. The cart track, with oaks and birches on both sides, typical for the landscape in Drenthe, heads straight towards the fortified city. Excavators and construction workers are carrying out a monstrous job in the distance; they're digging the new Stieltjes canal. Another new sailing route through the Amsterdam Field for merchants with peat, manure and merchandise. Coevorden was an important fortified city. Many garrisons and battalions of the Dutch forces battled the advancing French invasion, led by Napoleon, and later the German annexation of Bismarck here. But not much is left of the *fortified* part. All walls and gates were torn down around 1870. Sad. The destruction of Coevorden as a historic fortified city has been irreversibly initiated. As the rudderless carriage passes the city's borders, it comes across some desolate stacks of remnants of the once proud city wall. Coevorden is working on innovation and progress, heading into the twentieth century. The old city wall doesn't fit the vision of the new city officials and honorable notables, such as Slingenberg and Dommers. The carriage blows past the castle of those same city destroyers. The castle, with its illustrious rich history dates back to the eleventh century. Because of its strategic location along an important trade route through the marshlands between hanseatic cities in the Netherlands and Germany, the castle was plundered, destroyed during battles, and again rebuilt many times. Famous rulers such as bishop Frederick of Blankenheim and Charles II, Duke of Guelders, used to live in this castle. As the driver manages to guide his horse past the harbor along the arsenal at the trading dock, they eventually reach their destination; the market square where merchants and traders are situated. The driver tries to get Bonzo to stop.

'Hooo! Huuuu! Bonzo! Hooooo! I really don't know what's the matter with my horse today,' the coachman apologizes.

'It's okay, keep the change,' Vincent says. He pays fifty cents to the coachman.

'Okay? OKAY??? Gertrude rambles. 'Not at all okay!'
Gertrude seems a bit drunk and nauseous from the ride. Vincent reaches out his hand to help Gertrude get out of the carriage.

'We're here now, Gertie, unharm-'
Before Vincent can finish his sentence, Gertrude steps out the carriage like a wobbling duck, but forgets there's a step.

'Viihhhhoeoe…ince!'
She falls on the ground with a dull thump. Vincent comes to the rescue.

'Unharmed?' he asks.

'Do I look unharmed?' She brushes the dust off her clothes.

'It's all because of… of… Bonzo here.' The horse starts to sniff and reacts agitated as Gertrude walks by.

'I even smell like horse!' She takes a bottle of perfume from her purse and sprays some on both sides of her neck. As if it were hit by a bullet, the horse prances and flies off, carriage and all, while loudly whinnying. Gertrude is left in shock, still holding the bottle of perfume. Vincent takes the bottle out of her hand, looks at it, smells it and gives her a look of disapproval. He shakes his head, laughs and gracefully throws the bottle in a trashcan.

'Vince!!!'

Vincent keeps walking without looking back, raises his hand and urges her to follow him.

Gertrude enjoys a cup of tea and the warm rays of sunshine on the terrace of a picturesque cafe on the Market Square.

'See, it's much better here than in dusty Amsterdam.'

'Nieuw-Amsterdam,' Vincent corrects her.

'What's so *new* about it? There's nothing to do there! Can't you just paint something here, Vince?'

'I prefer rural areas more, you know that.'

'So what about Paris?'

'Yes, Paris... that's a completely different story. That's a metropolis!' Gertrude looks at Vincent and nods, showing him she understands.

'I have no other business here, Gertie. I'll just paint some landscapes, farms, churches. Speaking of churches... I have to get to my appointment. You'll enjoy yourself on the market? There are some merchants selling draperies, some sell trinkets, and there's a blacksmith. There's even a perfumer here with *real* perfumes!'

'Hm, Vince, do you have some money for me?'

'Here's five guilders. That should be enough, right? I'll see you in two hours, here on the terrace.'

Van Gogh stands in front of the large door of the Reformed Church. He pushes it, but it won't move. Locked. He walks to a side door and pulls up the handle. It opens. Van Gogh enters the church via a dark portal that lets in little light through a stained-glass window. There's no one in the church. The building in its current state dates back to

1645. It was originally built around 1500, but it was destroyed and rebuilt five or six times. Van Gogh is always intrigued by churches, but not this time; this building is boring, cold and austere.

'Hello? Is anybody here?' His voice echoing through the galleries startles him. He takes a lap and looks at the pulpit, the altar, the choir and takes a seat on a wooden bench. Not another one of these jokes, like in Zweeloo, Van Gogh thinks.

'I'm glad you're here,' a voice suddenly sounds behind him.
Van Gogh jumps up. An older man, dressed in a black robe stands behind him in the aisle. He's wearing a heavy, silver necklace with a little silver cross around his neck.

'Picardt?' Van Gogh asks.

'My dear. May I call you Vincent?'

'Of course! Reverend.'

'I'm happy you received my letter and came over here!'

'Naturally. It was quite the journey, but you caught my attention. I'm very curious to find out how I can be of service to you.'
Picardt nods, takes a deep breath and sighs.

'You know, Vincent, wars and violence took place throughout all ages. That won't ever change. It's a time of anger, and it's all about power, land, money... faith. Are you religious, Vincent?'

'As you may know, Reverend, my father was a preacher in the past, and faith interests me.'

'But do you believe in more? In the afterlife? In myths and sagas? Do you believe in giants, trolls and witte wieven?' Picardt starts making emotional gestures. 'The devil, Sodom and Gomorra?'

'Eh...' Van Gogh is overwhelmed. 'What does all of this have to do with dolmens?'

'Exactly!' Picardt stands in front of the altar, quickly makes a sign of the cross and pulls open de door of the tabernacle.

'Bishop's wine?' he asks. Vincent nods in surprise.
Picardt takes the wine carafe and two chalices, fills them, hands one to Van Gogh and drinks the other in one go.

While Vincent takes a sip, Picardt fills his chalice once more. He puts the carafe back in the tabernacle.

'Walk with me to the rectory. I want to show you something.'
Vincent and Picardt exit the church through a small door and enter a dark hallway. The hallway has cold tiles and is connected to the rectory next to the church. Upon arrival, Picardt takes a book from a large wooden bookcase.

'You're familiar with this book?' he asks Van Gogh.
Vincent looks at the book. *Korte Beschryvinge Van Eenige Vergetene En Verborgene Antiquiteiten. Johan Picardt.*

'I know it. This was written by your great-grandfather. In 1660 if I'm not mistaken.'

'Correct! A historic book. Renowned, revolutionary for its time. He described the history of Drenthe and the North, include the biblical Flood story. A masterpiece!'

'Well...' Van Gogh disputes. 'I haven't read it yet, but I know what it's about, yes.'

'My great-grandfather was intrigued by the stone megalithic crypts, the dolmens. He researched, numbered and completely mapped them.'

'I'm familiar with the reports, yes.' Vincent confirms. 'But why did you ask me to come here?'

'There's something strange going on with one of the dolmens. I don't know exactly what it is, but my great-grandfather was on to something. Look, there are some notes on the last page of Johan's book that I've been thinking about for a while now. See this, for instance; *The curved time ticks on through wisps lighters... between stoned piles... under the blue rigid starry nights...* Does this sound familiar?'
Van Gogh reads the notes one more time. He initially doesn't realize, but then his face freezes. He looks at Picardt in disbelief.

'But... time... wisps... stoned piles... starry night... that's the triptych I painted!' he yells, totally perplexed.

'Correct! Now I ask you, my dear, did you paint this triptych based on this passage?'

'No, I haven't even read the book.' Vincent scratches behind his ear and looks at Picardt in surprise.

'Do you understand this? Picardt asks. 'Is this a coincidence, or are there other forces at play? But then there's this. Johan writes; *the stoned pile is the key to the time, found at the back of the middle of three.'*

Van Gogh is stunned.

'Your great-grandfather speaks in riddles.'

'Yes, not to mention the numbers and codes he described. What to do with those? Do you now understand why I asked you to come here, Vincent? I'm very curious about the middle of the triptych… and the key my great-grandfather speaks of.'

'But that will be difficult. The middle painting, the dolmen underneath the starry night, or *the stoned pile* as Johan Picardt called it, I don't have it anymore. I sold it during an exhibition in a gallery last year. An unknown merchant was hugely impressed by it. He made me an offer I would've sold all three pieces for. But no, he was only interested in *The dolmen underneath the starry night*. He also wanted to take it with him right away. He paid… and he was gone.'

'Do you remember who it was, where he came from?' Picardt asks, befuddled.

'No, I'm sorry.'

'The devil is messing with us.' Picardt says a little prayer. 'Now we still don't know what it's about and what's going on.'

'I might be able to find out who it was by asking the gallery owner and checking the guest list, but...'

'Yes, do that, Vincent! Please! This is something I've had my mind set on for years. I'd like to get some answers.'

'I understand. It's strange, and I would also like to know what's going on. Could I borrow the manuscript from you?'

'No, I'd rather keep it myself, but you can take the last page with the notes for now.'

Picardt rips the page from the book, hands it to Van Gogh, but firmly holds on to it for a bit, while intensely looking at Vincent.

'My dear Vincent... I would like to get it back.'

He then gives Vincent a firm handshake and disappears as abruptly as he entered.

Van Gogh walks back to the market square. Gertrude is waiting for him, and clumsily stumbles around holding three large bags of merchandise. On the way back she proudly shows Vincent all the items she purchased. Vincent just stares straight ahead. The key, he thinks.

'The starry night' Danny shouts.

Milan looks at him, not understanding what he means.

'The middle of a triptych? It's always been a mystery of whether or not a triptych existed. Some letters and notes by Van Gogh talk about a lamplighter, dolmen and little town under the starry night, but other than the Starry Night, no one has ever seen the other two alleged paintings. This confirms their existence!' Danny sounds excited, while Milan rubs his eyes.

'Shall we continue this tomorrow?' Milan asks. 'It's the middle of night. You could stay the night if you want.'

Danny looks at him.

'If that's not too much trouble.'

'No problem whatsoever! The guest room is always ready for unexpected, but definitely not unwanted visitors,' Milan assures him with a smile. 'Come, I'll show you the way,' and he taps Danny on the shoulder.

Several months later, Van Gogh returns to the Reformed Church in Coevorden to tell Picardt the big news. Through the gallery he was able to trace a nobleman who bought the middle painting of the triptych Starry Night. He hasn't found him yet, but he hopes to find him with the help of Picardt. Van Gogh also brought the last page with him. He would return it, as promised. It's a quick visit this time, without Gertrude. The relationship ended, they weren't that great of a match. Gertrude returned to The Hague.

The carriage stops in front of the entrance of the church. The big front doors are open, the service just ended. The last churchgoers, dressed in traditional black attire, exit the building. Van Gogh is euphoric because of the important news and can't wait to share it with Picardt. In his excitement he accidentally bumps into churchgoers a couple of times.

'Excuse me! I'm sorry. Apologies!'

He asks a passer-by where the pastor is.

The hunched man points behind him.

'Thank you.' Van Gogh walks to the rectory. That's where the pastor stands; dressed in black, with a purple band around his waist, facing the other way.

'Picardt!' Van Gogh shouts.

The pastor stands still, looks up to Him and makes a cross.

'Picardt?!' Van Gogh yells again.

The pastor turns around. Van Gogh freezes. It's not Picardt.

'Oh, I'm sorry. I thought you were pastor Picardt.' The pastor gives him a surprised and questioning look.

'You mean Johan Picardt?' he asks.

'No, ehh… his great-grandson.'

'My dear man, I don't know who you are and what's wrong with you, but pastor Picardt died in 1670. God rest his soul.' He makes another cross. 'I don't know anything about a great-grandson.'

'But the pastor who was here a couple of months ago…'

'I've been a pastor here for six years, no one else!'
Van Gogh is completely rattled and can't say anything that makes sense. For the record he returns the last page to the pastor, for it to rejoin the rest of the manuscript. He then leaves for Arles in southern France, in great confusion. Upon arrival he lights the painting *Lamplighter* on fire out of anger and frustration. The flames coming from the lantern create a bright blue glow. In his devastation he also wants to burn the *Starry Night*, but he fails. In disappointment and complete damnation, he cuts off his own ear.

Danny, still sleepy, walks through the library. He's in the same spot he read Van Gogh's memoires and notes with Milan until the middle of the night. He's excited about the information he read in the letters and notes. He just has to get some things confirmed; a different source, or evidence. If I manage to do that and take it public, it will cause a complete disruption of the worlds of art, culture, religion and politics. But what about *the key...* it all keeps running through Danny's head.

He continues to browse through the large, high cases that hold many rows of books. While he pulls the book *Ik, Jan Cremer* by the author with the same name from the bookcase and leafs through it, the butler stands behind him, unnoticed, like a sniper.

'Good morning. Would you like a cup of coffee, sir?'

'I'd like that. Black please.'

'That's an excellent choice!' the butler assures him.

Danny doesn't really understand why black coffee is an excellent choice, but gives him a polite response:

'It sure is, helps me to wake up.'

'The book,' the butler clarifies. 'A fine piece of literature that... how should I say this... detaches you from the madness of day-to-day reality for a bit.'

Danny nods politely. He reads a random passage, until the butler stands next to him holding a silver platter, carrying a mug of black coffee.

'Enjoy!'

'Yes, it's literature you really have to wrestle through,' Danny says.

'The coffee,' the butler responds, as he walks away again.

'Touché,' Danny whispers and holds the mug up to the butler as if to say 'cheers'.

He takes a sip of coffee.

'Hm, strong.' The butler I mean, Danny thinks.

He puts the book by Jan back in the case. He's not really interested in it at all, but he is however intrigued by the huge collection.

Danny walks around the library a bit more and takes his time checking everything out, including the beautiful paintings of landscapes and portraits of unknown masters. He thinks the vases, chandeliers and porcelain are cute, but not really interesting. He stops for a second at an abstract tapestry. He is excited by the combination of colors and shapes. Danny is drawn by the tapestry, because there's also something he can't really explain. A strange line pattern, highly illogical. He takes a step back to get the complete picture, and then takes a step forward to check out some details. It's as if something's not right about this, he thinks. It's as if the tapestry consists of two parts. Danny tries to unravel it by running his fingers over de tapestry in order to feel something, discover something. To his shock, his intuition didn't abandon him. There's indeed a connection in the tapestry. Why? he thinks. He follows the line and ends up at a little red square box that almost invisibly sticks out of the tapestry a bit. With his nose against the tapestry, he carefully pushes the square box. Surprised, because of the fact the red box can be pushed at all, Danny stands still as he holds his breath. He waits to see if something will happen, like you sometimes see in adventure movies. After waiting for several seconds, nothing happens and he backs off.

'I watch too many movies,' he sighs.

Right after Danny turns around, he hears a sound, a dull thump, like a heavy handle being lifted off a wooden door. He looks back at the tapestry and sees an opening. While the hinges squeak and grind, the opening slowly increases in size. Danny looks around to make sure he's alone, and walks towards the opening. It turns out to be an entrance door. But an entrance to what, he thinks. He hesitantly looks through the opening, but as he already expected, there's nothing to see. It's pitch dark.

'A lamp! Where can I quickly find a lamp?' he whispers to himself. He looks around and sees a chandelier with candles. Such a cliché, he thinks, and he looks around to make sure he's not getting pranked. What a prank that would be. Danny takes a silver lighter from the dresser and lights the candles. With the chandelier held in front of him, he walks through the opening into the other area. First through a narrow hallway with walls on both side, made of coarse rocks. The hallway slowly, but noticeably descends. Danny then approaches a vaulted gate that leads to a larger area. It smells musty and stuffy, but it's not moist, like one would expect of a basement. It feels cool, but dry. The chandelier provides too little light to see the entire room. Danny walks to the side to see whether he can perhaps find a light switch. The candlelight reveals indefinable things, such as an unfamiliar face, a skeleton, a stuffed animal. It's like Disneyland, only without the fun. Danny holds the chandelier with clammy hands. He quickly finds something that resembles a switch. He pulls it, and some lights go on instantly. When he looks around, he's completely baffled.

'What the fuck...' is the first reaction he's able to utter.

A huge basement room with vaults, gates and a marble floor reveals itself. The soft light from the lamps light up a variety of macabre objects, stuffed animals from a species Danny has never seen before. A bird with a wingspan of twenty feet hangs from the ceiling, an armored knight, holding swords and spears. Danny keeps walking and comes across something that looks extraterrestrial. Next to it stands a caveman wearing a bearskin and holding a club, looking very lifelike. The man might as well have stepped out of the wax museum. A space- and caveman face each other and are almost touching hands. In short, a bizarre scene that seems to have no end. When Danny passes through a gate, he enters an adjacent basement room, with a desk with a computer and two monitors. There are also some drawings and designs on the desk, one of which immediately draws his attention. It's the design of some sort of jet fighter, one of those stealth models.

The design depicts measurements and notes he doesn't understand at all, such as; *wingspan; 56 miles, material shield; Zefka C4, propulsion; 6x paralax O-drin* and more terms like that, whatever they are. The computer is running.

'Of course it's password protected,' Danny criticizes himself after giving it a try.

He continues to look around and sees a huge collection of paintings hanging from the walls. Not just any paintings, but recognizable masterpieces. Danny recognizes the *Unconscious Patient* by Rembrandt, *The man with bowtie* by Picasso, and...

'Holy shit!' he yells out loud.

Danny stands face to face with two paintings by Van Gogh. *The Starry Night* and another one, in the identical, characteristic style, with lots of rocks in the landscape. *The dolmen underneath the starry night.* His heart is pounding in his chest.

'What is this?' he rambles to himself out loud. 'No, no... These must be replicas. They must be. Damn good replicas, I must say.'

He takes a closer look at the two paintings, carefully runs his fingers over the paint, swallows in excitement and continues to stare at the paintings like a zombie. The two parts of the alleged triptych both have the identical characteristic features of the master. The strokes of the brush, the contours of the round, woolly stars, the opal blue color of the thickly applied paint, the smell of the oil. They're authentic, he thinks. But how is that possible, he wonders. *The Starry Night* hangs in the Museum Of Modern Art in New York...

Then the light suddenly cuts out. It's pitch dark.

'Shit, Shit!' Danny rants, as he attempts to slowly shuffle to where the light switch should be. He kicks and bumps into everything that crosses his path.

'I hope you're treating my collection with some respect!' a voice echoes.

'Collection?' Danny yells. 'Man, this is… this is…' Danny can't finish his sentence, because he stumbles over something, making a lot of noise.

'Bizarre?' the voice adds. The lights come back on. Milan enters the basement and sees Danny with his arms hanging around a terrified ET.

'Sorry I left you in the dark for a bit. I had no idea you were here and I thought I had left the lights on.'

'Hottie!' Danny climbs up and tries to put the ET from space back into position. Danny tries to apologize for his spontaneous *Hottie* outburst.

'Eh, I mean…' and he points to ET.
Milan smiles and extends his hand.

'Welcome in the wondrous world of…' Milan hesitates about how to finish the sentence. He then continues '… the Huns.'

'The Huns?' Danny asks surprised.

'The Huns!' Milan confirms. 'A lifeform from ten thousands of years back in time… or perhaps forward in time…'

'Who or what are the Huns?'

'Let's say they're explorers, visionaries who are far ahead of their time, with their origin here on Earth dating back about five thousand years. They built the dolmens. They control time and space. The lonely few of this planet possess knowledge and power. In fact; the Huns are time and space, they know how to move through multiple dimensions.

'Explorers? Time and space?'

'Yeah, I don't really know where to start, Dan.'

'How about five thousand years ago?' Danny jokes.

'Yes the world looked a bit differently five thousand years ago.'

'The world? Or the people?' Danny cynically asks.

'Both. The people in the northern land were mostly hunters and farmers, and lived in little villages as tribes. The landscape was rugged and rough and consisted mainly of primeval forests and heathers. But the peaceful life quickly came to an end. Other forces entered in the north. Dark forces.'

'Dark forces? Do you mean demons and witches?'

'Danny, Danny, Danny…' Milan shakes his head. 'Those are earthly fantasies, made up by people. That's nothing compared to the forces I'm talking about.'

'Be a bit more concrete then.' Danny is getting impatient. 'And how did you get your hands on *The Starry Night* by Van Gogh? Or is this a fake? Of is the painting in New York fake? That would be a good joke.'

'Yes,' Milan laughs, 'Do you really believe I would want those Yanks to have this masterpiece by Van Gogh? Their President is fake enough already, so indeed, the painting in the MOMA is a replica, a damn good one, if I may say so myself. I really fooled that curator.'
Danny is completely disillusioned and sees Milan cherish *The Starry Night* with his fingers.

'And *The dolmen underneath the starry sky*, is that one real? Does the back contain any clues?' he asks.

'I'd love to tell you all about it, my dear Danny… but I can't!' As Milan completes this sentence with convincing seriousness, he slowly takes a gun from the inner pocket of his jacket and aims it at Danny.

'HO HO!' Danny exclaims in fear, and takes a step back. 'What is the meaning of this?!' he nervously asks.

'There are certain things I can't tell you. First of all, you won't understand, and secondly, I'm forced to keep my identity a secret.'

'Identity? So you're not who you say you are?'

'Not completely. I am Milan van Donckervoort, but… let me say I also go by several other names.'

'Such as?'

'Tssss, don't be so naive, Danny.'

'I thought we were friends.'

'Were?? We're still friends in my book!' Milan sneakily smiles.

'But don't worry, Danny, I won't harm you, as long as you do what I tell you. For now, I have to secure my own interests.'

Milan loses his focus a little at this point in this conversation. Danny doesn't hesitate for a second and smacks the gun out of Milan's hand and makes a run for it. Milan barely manages to grab his arm, and they start fighting. Both fighters take some hard punches. Danny manages to bring Milan to the ground and knock him out. Danny gasps for air and gets back on his feet. He leaves Milan on the ground and runs towards the exit through the dark hallway. Barely realizing what just happened, he sprints outside, to his car. He gets in and hurriedly tries to get the key in the ignition. His hands shake like those of an addict. Let's get out of here, is the only thing on his mind. Murphy's Law however kicks in, and Danny's car again won't start.

'Come on, fucking car!' he screams as he punches the steering wheel. Meanwhile, Milan emerges from the house and walks towards the car. He's wobbling and waving his arm, holding the gun in his hand. He aims and shoots. At that exact moment the car roars and screams. Danny puts it in gear, floors the gas pedal and races to the exit across the gravel road. The gravel flies up from under the tires. He hears three more shots being fired from behind him. The back-window shatters and he feels a sting in his shoulder. He doesn't feel the pain because of the adrenaline rushing through his body. He keeps on driving, away from that moron, whoever he is.

A gentle breeze blows through the open window of Hellen's apartment. The dulled sound of the passing traffic rides the wave of the wind into the room. It's a minimalistic apartment with a sober design. Two meaningless paintings hang from the white walls. The furniture is simple. If one were to yell out the name of a large Swedish superstore, everything would fall apart. There's a picture of Hellen on vacation in Corfu on a cabinet. On the coffee table there's another picture of Hellen on skis in the Austrian snow. A retro frame is located on the wall, under the clock, again showing only Hellen. This time she's proudly sitting on a horse, with the ocean in the background, somewhere along the Turkish coast. I wonder if there are any other people in Hellen's life, Danny thinks. He sits on an Ekenäset from the aforementioned superstore, looking grim.

'Ouuch… easy, Hellen,' he says as he grinds his teeth.

'Yes, don't be such a baby. I have to clean the wound, right? Otherwise it will become infected.'

'I don't understand. Why did Milan shoot me?'

'Just be glad he's not a good shot. A few inches down and you wouldn't have been sitting here.'

'This is some shady stuff, Hellen. All those historic objects in his secret basement, Picardt's book, the unknown letters by Van Gogh… How did he obtain all these?'

Hellen shrugs and her face tells him she's completely clueless.

'This will sting a little.' She sprinkles some iodine on the wound.

'Ouch, fuck.'

'Danny, come one, it only grazed you.'

'What do you know about this? Have you ever been shot?'

Hellen applies a clean bandage to the wound and nods in confirmation.

'There, that will do. Come on, I'll get you a strong drink. For the pain, all right cutie?'

Hellen pours two drinks. Danny doesn't hesitate for one second and gulps the numbing liquid down, puts the empty glass back down and looks at Hellen with a look that speaks volumes. Hellen meekly pours him another one.

'Maybe Milan is afraid you already know too much?' she asks.

'I know too much???' Danny looks surprised.

'What do I know too much about?' he wonders out loud, as he stares out the open window to broaden his view. As he stares outside, he lets the second shot of whisky pass his throat. Hellen stands behind him with her hands by his sides. She slowly moves her hands up over his shoulders.

'Ouch, gently. I don't know anything. Actually, I know a lot but it's going nowhere yet. They're individual pieces to a puzzle.'

'Hmm, shall we continue making the puzzle then?' Hellen rhetorically asks as she unbuttons Danny's shirt. 'I love solving puzzles, tying all loose ends together...'
Danny walks to the coffee table that supports the bottle of whisky, and completely fills his glass this time, takes a sip and starts pacing through the room. Hellen tiptoes after him and sensually takes off her shoes.

'Shall we figure some stuff out, hm? Find some clues?' She stands in front of Danny, puts her sexy, red lips on his and starts passionately kissing him. Danny shows some resistance at first, but he quickly lets himself go in the fiery battle with her. His hands lustfully run through Hellen's hair and descend to her full, round breasts. Danny and Hellen's pieces of clothing leave their bodies one by one and both naked bodies wriggle in and through each other. They're longing and begging for more, from head to toe. Not a single corner of the room is safe anymore. A wild spectacle, like a tornado, unfolds through the apartment, in which curtains, the coffee table with a lamp, the Ekenäset, the picture frames and a painting on the wall take a beating. The tornado ends up in the king-size Oppland in the bedroom, without any signs of calming down. They moan and groan until deep in the night and eventually lie down, exhausted.

Danny tries to see the world with one eye pinched, although his world is limited to Hellen's bedroom. When he realizes where he is, he jumps up. Half asleep and still in a daze, he first looks besides him, but that side of the bed is deserted. When he extends his view, he sees a battlefield of pieces of clothing, furniture on its side, empty glasses and bottles on the floor. He throws the duvet off him, jumps off the bed and feels for his pants.

'Hellen?' he yells loudly.

'Yoo-hoo cutie pie,' she responds from the bathroom.
When Danny walks towards the yoo-hoo, he sees a naked Hellen, causing him to instantly turn around in shame.

'Ehm sorry, I didn't know...'

'That I was naked?'

'No, I mean... What happened?'

'You don't remember, pumpkin?'

Danny sighs and firmly presses his hands against his forehead. He starts rubbing it and tries to remember what happened the night before.

'Argh, that whisky,' he sighs and moans.

'Yes, the bottle is completely empty. All the way,' Hellen assures him as she holds the bottle upside down.

Danny looks around in confusion and sees the bed that's been slept in.

'Did we...?'

'Yep,' Hellen nods.

'That's impossible... how... what?' Danny sounds downcast.

'Hellen, promise me one thing. Don't talk to anyone about this. This didn't happen, ok?'

'Ehh... ok.' She runs her fingers over her lips, locks them with an imaginary key and throws it over her shoulder.

'Milan!' Danny yells. 'Milan shot me! I have to know why.' Hellen carefully nods, because something else is bothering her, which she hasn't yet discussed with Danny.

'Ehm Danny,' she starts. Danny looks at her.

'There's something else you need to know.'

'No, no time for that now.' Danny hastily puts on his clothes.

'There is, you will make time for this,' Hellen assures him. 'Sit down! There's something I wanted to tell you much sooner. Regarding professor Dijkstra.'

'Professor Dijkstra?' Danny asks, confused.

Hellen nods, takes a deep breath and starts talking.

'Do you remember that time you asked me to seduce the professor? To charm him in order to convince him to examine that gravel of yours?'

'Eh yes, that's right. I remember.'

'Well... that kind of worked.' Hellen says, a bit ashamed.

'Oh? But what are you trying to say?'

Hellen starts sauntering around and thinks about how to tell him.

'Well, I went to him and stuff... and then... it wasn't easy... but eh... the good news is that I managed to seduce him. So that's one part.'

Danny gives her a surprised and confused look.

'And the other part?' he asks.

'Thawagrampalastrick,' Hellen quietly mumbles.

'What?'

'Thawagrampalastrick,' she repeats.

'Hellen, I have no time for this.' Danny checks his handless watch, visibly annoyed.

'That was grandpa's last trick.' Hellen clarifies.

'What?'

'His last trick...' Hellen looks at the ground, defeated.

'Do you mean...'

'Yes. He died right on the spot.'

'After you and him...?' Danny still has to process the information.

'Oh my god,' he exclaims, not knowing whether to laugh or cry. 'So the professor wasn't murdered?'

'No, at least that's some good news,' Hellen confirms in relief, finally being able to tell Danny her secret.

'But why didn't you tell me this much sooner?'

'Well, duh... I tried, but you wouldn't listen. You were too busy with yourself and your research!' Hellen yells, outraged

'Ok ok! Time for a new strategy!'

19 Unknown territory

Danny drives onto the university's parking lot. His plan for today is to do some more research in the library. There are still many ambiguities and loose ends. It's crowded, so he has to make a few of laps to find a spot. He finally sees an empty spot. But right before he can park his car, a red Mini Cooper with tinted windows pops up. The Mini cuts him off and slides into the open spot. Danny barely manages to slam the brakes in time to prevent colliding with the reckless driver.

'What the fuck,' Danny yells angrily. He gets out, walks towards the red Mini and starts yelling

'Hey, asshole! What the hell are you doing, man? Idiot. Douchebag!' The door of the Mini clicks and slowly opens. A leg appears from the doorway and somewhat clumsily exits the car. Danny looks at the leg and to his surprise sees a high heel. That can only mean one thing. Just what I need, he thinks. A woman driver.

'Ehm, sorry miss. I didn't know that...' Danny seizes his apology when he sees the owner of the high-heeled leg in her entirety. In front of him stands the lady with the red scarf from reception, of all people.

'Oh would you look at that,' the woman cheerfully yaps. 'Mister Dijkstra. That's convenient, because you could help me with my bag. It's quite heavy, you see.'

As she rambles on, she awkwardly pulls a heavy red bag from the backseat that ends up on the street with a dull thump.

'Ehm miss, I'm not mister Dij...' Danny changes his mind.

'Sorry, I don't have time for this. Have a nice day.'

He leaves the confused and helpless lady from reception and her red bag behind, and gets back in his car to continue his search for an empty parking spot. After two more laps, Danny starts to get quite cranky. He drives around the building to the back, to the reserved parking spots for the Board and suppliers. Right when he turns around the corner he sees a black Chevrolet. That's that fucking SUV, he thinks, and immediately stops. The large car is completely tinted, which is quite unusual on the Dutch roads. Danny looks at the license plate. Foreign, but he can't figure out in which country the car is registered. Two men, dressed in dark clothes, enter the passenger's side of the car, after which the car sprints off. Danny doesn't hesitate for a second and follows them. He follows the black Chevy at a safe distance to the exit of the parking lot. He passes the woman from the reception desk. From the rearview mirror he sees how she struggles to drag the heavy, red bag with her.

'What the hell am I doing?' Danny wonders out loud, as he follows the Chevy onto the road.

After about thirty minutes of steering and peering, the city is left far behind. Danny, who now drives through Drenthe's landscapes, is still behind the black Chevrolet, at a safe distance. He notices a road sign in the direction they're going. *Exloo 2 km*, it says. The SUV makes a turn onto a gravel road, through a wooded area. To avoid being noticed, Danny takes his foot off the gas and lets himself fall behind a bit more. He's able to follow the SUV for a while through the trees. When the car is out of sight, Danny slowly enters the gravel road. After about a hundred yards he sees a building in the distance, with the black Chevy parked next to it. Since it's already getting dark, he decides to park his car a bit farther into the woods. At least I can find a parking spot here, he thinks.

He sneaks through the bushes towards the building and passes an entrance gate with a wooden sign that says L.O.F... Netherlands. There's something else written behind the F, but the splashed-up mud makes it illegible. L.o.f, L.o.f... No idea what this is, Danny thinks. As he carefully continues to sneak around, he observes the area. The building is relatively small and is located on a large site filled with little poles with wires strung in between. There are clusters that seem to be solar panels. A bit further, some strange, white objects sit on a pedestal. He manages to hide behind a power box, about 60 feet from the building. Just in time, because the two men, dressed in black, just exited the building and are walking towards the car. They're talking to each other. Danny hears they're probably Americans. This is insane. I have to call someone to let them know where I am, Danny thinks. He looks for Hellen's phone number and tries to get a call through.

'Fuck!' Danny hisses to himself. The only thing he hears on his phone is white noise and cracking. 'No service in this area.'
The Americans look up, because they believe they heard something.

'Did you hear something?' one guy asks the other.

'I don't know for sure. Let's have a look.'

'This way,' the other says. He throws his cigarette on the ground, steps on it, clicks on his flashlight and walks towards the power box. Danny almost wets himself.

'Did you see something?'

'No. Probably a bird or a rabbit, hè hè.'

'Or an alien. ET phone home whaha,' the other roars.
Phone home? I wish I could, Danny thinks. He looks around the corner to the American who's only a couple yards away from him. He sees that the man in black keeps his hand close to his waist. Danny sees a holster attached to his belt. Shit, they're armed, Danny thinks.

'Let's call the boss that all is clear.' The American lights a cigarette, takes out his phone and mumbles something to the other end of the line. What? Danny thinks. How are they able to make a call?

'Okay, let's go to the car. The boss is coming.'
The two Americans walk to the SUV and stay vigilant. Danny's attention is drawn to the woods, when two headlights emerge, and another big black Chevrolet enters the site. The SUV parks behind the other one. No one gets out. Nothing happens. The two guards don't move an inch. Suddenly, the door of the building opens with a dull thump and a tall man in a dark suit steps out. With an upright posture, he swiftly walks to the second SUV. Since he's walking so upright, Danny sees he's very slender. The man stops halfway, as if he realizes

he'd forgotten something. He looks back to the building. Danny is now able to take a proper look at the man. It's as if they're almost looking each other straight in the eyes. Danny starts sweating. He holds his breath and freezes once he recognizes the man. It's the assistant of GasCo's CEO. That creep he saw during the press conference about those earthquakes. That weirdo that was acting all shady in the bathroom and gave him a clear message. Danny is certain, it's him. The tall man continues his walk to the SUV that just arrived with confidence. The front door opens and a fourth man slowly gets out and walks to the creep.

'What the fuck...' Danny has to deal with shock after shock. He squints his eyes to get a closer look of the fourth man. It's Milan.
Milan walks to the creep and shakes his hand and pats him on the shoulder. The discuss something and get in the SUVs. The creep in the front one and Milan in the other, followed by the two guards. Danny sees how both cars storm off the site and is left disillusioned.

A while back

20   The hidden city

Eight feet quickly follow each other over the soft moss and the crackling leaves. Dead twigs succumb under the weight of the large, animal-skin covered feet and break the icy silence of the forest. A familiar scene takes place at the bank of a small river.

'If I'm correct, we should follow this river east and we'll end up at the first Eksloo,' Hunze argues. He waves at the others, telling them to follow him.

'Finally, I can't wait to take a hot bath,' Ems moans. He's in last place.

'Like that's going to help,' Havelt chuckles.

As the four hunters wade through the water, they sing a song. Battle songs are an important part of the Funnel beakers' way of life. Singing creates brotherhood and increases the energy. It also keeps evil spirits and wild animals away. After having walked for several hours, with the singing reduced to some humming, Hunze suddenly stops and raises his arm to tell his followers to stop and be quiet.

'What is it?' a startled Havelt asks.

'Quiet!' Hunze hisses. 'Do you hear that?'

Ems is so scared he lets out a fart. 'Sorry.'

'Yes, I hear it now too...' Jor laughs. '... and now I smell it too.'

'Do you mean that?' Havelt asks surprised. 'Nice joke, Hunze.'

'No, just listen, you douchebags!'

'Why are you whispering, Hunze?' Ems asks.

'I'm hearing voices!'

'I knew it! I knew it!' Havelt says with a big grin on his face, as he makes a circling motion with his finger near his head.

'This is all very confusing to me,' Ems complains.

Hunze is getting annoyed with all the chatting and presses his hand against Ems' mouth, who can't utter more than a hmmmhmmm.

Havelt suddenly jumps up and points his ears.

'Holy funnel beakers, I hear it too. Voices!'

'Hmwwwwwhooooo?' Ems mumbles from behind Hunze's hand.

'It's coming from that direction.' Havelt points to a forest up ahead. The voices are unintelligible at first, but as they get closer, they're able to listen in on the conversation.

'*That old dude is getting quite annoying.*'

'*You know what to do when he can no longer be handled.*'

'*I understand, Lofar. But what's in it for me?*'

'*We'll work it out. I can recommend you to the Council and give you a leading role with a great salary.*'

The intense conversation is coming from two men walking along the path towards the forest. They're both heavy and are wearing dark robes and capes over their heads. They walk in a steady pace and gesture wildly. Hunze recognizes them instantly.

'They're Huns!' he whispers.

Hunze, Ems, Havelt and Jor carefully sneak towards the two men, but remain invisible in the dense bushes.

'Can you understand what they're saying?' Havelt asks.

'Yes, I can get some of it, but I don't always understand. But we have to be quiet,' Hunze whispers.

The two men head farther into the forest. Once they're out of sight, Hunze decides to follow them.

'Come, let's see where they're going.'

'Are you insane?!' Ems yells. 'Just let them be!'

'But this is a great opportunity to find out where they live!'

'Over my dead body! I'm not going after those giants!'

'Ems is right. We have to go to Eksloo,' Havelt cautiously interrupts.

'Whose side are you on?' Hunze asks, surprised.

'I think th-'

'No, I decide! We're going!'

Before the others can argue against it, Hunze takes up his spear and decisively walks towards the forest that devoured the two men. He sneakily looks back over his shoulder, and smiles a little when he sees the others are following him.

Hunze quickly has his eye on the mysterious Huns again. They're standing by a great oak tree, when a third person joins them. Hunze wants to get closer, in order to listen in on their conversation. Havelt stays at a close distance. Ems and Jor are behind Havelt. Like a chameleon, Hunze sneaks from tree to tree in order to stay unnoticed, but fate strikes. He steps on a fragile branch, alerting the Huns. One of the men instantly looks in the direction of the crackling. Hunze barely manages to hide behind a tree and holds his breath. He very carefully looks around the tree to the Huns and sees only two men near the big oak tree. He thinks about what to do.

'HUNZE!' Havelt's voice shouts through the forest.

'HUNZE!!!!'

When Hunze looks around in shock, he sees something that will stay with him forever. Havelt's fearful eyes break his heart. The third Hun wearing a black cape jumps towards the four unsuspecting warriors from the dark and in a blink of an eye grabs Havelt, who doesn't stand a chance. Hunze faces their large, brute assailant, but freezes. He sees a skinny, grey face with hollow eyes underneath the dark cape. It's the devil himself, Hunze thinks as his blood starts to boil.

'That's what you get!' A raspy, dark voice comes from under the cape. 'Your curiosity is going to cost you.'

'Take him to the Ballerpit!' one of the two other Huns shouts.

Before Hunze can say anything, the devilish Hun disappears, holding Havelt in his arms.

Ems and Jor come running, distraught.

'What do we do, Hunze?' Ems is out of breath.

'Go after them!' Hunze exclaims with determination.

'That's suicide!'

'What then? Give up Havelt? NEVER!!'

Hunze takes the lead, without awaiting further response. He chooses the path the Hun before him took, straight through bushes and undergrowth, with Ems and Jor closely behind. The Hun has quite a big lead, so they have to pick up their pace. Hunze puts his nose in the wind, like a wolf following its prey. He smells the Hun who's ahead of them, that unmistakable stench of rotten meat and manure. He also smells something else, the air of burnt wood. He sees a fire emerge between the trees in the distance. Although Hunze is furious and races on like a mad dog, he's now vigilant and waves at Ems and Jor to stop.

'What is it?' Ems pants.

'Let's first take a look at the situation and see where Havelt is,' Hunze whispers.

Slowly and carefully, they walk towards the fire. They now hear voices of multiple men.

When they get close, they can hide behind a small hill, and have a good view of what's going on in front of them. Hunze whispers with fear in his voice:

'It's the Ballerpit! We're in Hunsingo... the hidden city.'

Three crackling fires rage in the middle of a large, round, open spot, with flames as high as the tallest trees. The open spot is a bit lower than the surrounding area. The large pit is surrounded by a bank, with flat ledges at different levels. About ten men wearing dark robes sit on these ledges. They're busy talking and gesturing. Hunze recognizes the event. He's seen these men at the dolmen before, with the fireflies.

The Hun who calls himself Lofar stands in the open spot in the Ballerpit, with Havelt in his hands.

'Men!' Lofar roars, and gets the attention of the group. 'See here, a heathen creature. A puny dwarf from the Funnel beakers that want to make our lives, the Hun people, miserable with their weapons and potions.'

The listeners mumble in confirmation.

'But they won't succeed.' Lofar continues. We are stronger and smarter. Those Funnel beakers won't do us any harm! We will exterminate those dwarves, wipe them off the face of this earth!'
The Huns start cheering and stomp the ground with their feet.

'And we will start with this pesky rodent, this monster!' Lofar holds Havelt up in the light of the fires.

'Rodent? Monster? How dare this piece of rotten meat!' Ems hisses, all worked up. 'I will... I will...'

'You will nothing!' Hunze pulls Ems back. 'There's nothing we can do.' Hunze whispers in disappointment.

'Men!' Lofar raises his voice. 'Here in our democratic Ballerpit we will make a judgement on this dwarf. Will it be fire or will it be blue?'

'Fire, fire fire!' it sounds in unison. The men throw their fists in the air and stomp the ground even harder with their bare feet.

'Fire it shall be!' Lofar relentlessly throws the young Havelt on the middle fire.

Hunze, Ems and Jor are completely frozen and terrified, as they see the fire light up with a twinkling blue glow. A hopeless Havelt can be seen through the sea of flames. But he's soon gone, with only a large, blue fire that remains.

'Let this be a warning to anyone who stands in the way of the brotherhood of the Huns!' As Lofar overwhelms everyone with these ominous words, he turns around to the three Funnel beakers, as if he knows they're hiding behind the hill.

'We have to get out of here!' Hunze doesn't hesitate for a second. Ems and Jor follow suit.

The three Funnel beakers stop at a quiet place in the forest, far from the Ballerpit. The moist fog dances its way through the trees. The only sound the wind carries comes from some chirping wagtails and an owl that calls every so often. Hunze drops down against a breadfruit tree in exhaustion. His face still clearly shows the memory of the horrible event that took place earlier at the Ballerpit. Ems and Jor squat next to him and pant. They look at each other in disbelief. A big tear runs down Hunze's face.

'Holy Funnel beakers!' Ems rants, as he shoots up and wildly swings his fists around. 'I will... I will... that black devil... that schmuck... with his fires... I'll chop him up!'

'How could it happen... poor sweet Havelt.' Hunze starts crying. 'How could I have been so stupid to give him up?'

'It's not your fault.' Jor tries to ease Hunze's sadness, and places his hand on Hunze's shoulder. 'No one is a match for those terrible Huns. Havelt went down as a brave warrior. We will keep him in our hearts and give him an honorable memorial.'

'I agree with that!' Ems confirms, and with his spear in the air, he feistily yells; 'Our Havelt!'

'Our Havelt!' Jor brotherly crosses his spear with Ems'. Hunze gets up and pulls himself together. He puts on his hat as properly as he can. He then pulls a questionable face and addresses Ems.

'What did that Hun mean when he said *blue*?'

'Yes. Blue. *In the fire or in the blue...* what's that blue?'
Ems shrugs and looks at Jor. But Jor also doesn't have an answer.

'Let's go back to Borg,' Hunze says with confidence. 'There's nothing we can do here. Too much blood has been shed already.'
With another long, dangerous journey ahead of them, the three Funnel beakers return home, defeated, to share the loss of Havelt with the village.

Here and now

21 A mission

It's a quiet day on the campus of the university. Danny sits behind his desk, thinking about the previous day; all the things that happened, it's like a movie. The phone rings and he starts a conversation.

'So we can start our first excavations in Witteveen in three weeks?' The confirming nods by Danny indicate that the person on the other end approved. As the conversation continues, Hellen enters the office. Danny waves at her, showing her to wait a minute.

'Good. Then I will see the permit as quickly as possible. Thank you for your cooperation. Goodbye.' Danny puts the phone down.

'We can start in Witteveen in three weeks!'

'Well done,' Hellen excitedly responds. 'I will start the preparations. Another thing... did you know the publisher of the book by Picardt sold the original manuscript and the rights to it a number of years ago?'

Danny gets up and looks at Hellen. He's surprised and looks like he has many questions.

'You'll never guess to whom,' she continues.

Danny's asking eyes grow bigger, and he tries to show Hellen through his facial expressions that she should reveal the answer.

'To the Vatican!' she euphorically shrieks.

'The Vatican???' Danny responds, totally befuddled.

'Yes, the Vatican, Rome, the Pope!' Hellen confirms.

Danny falls into his chair and nervously spins around a bit.

'What does the Vatican want with the book?' he wonders out loud.

'Isn't it hilarious?' Hellen yells. 'But do you know what that means?' she continues to Danny. She answers her own question without waiting. 'This is the opportunity to see the original manuscript. If you're right, this manuscript contains the last handwritten page that can decipher the secret of the dolmen. You have to go to Rome!'

It's insanely busy at the airport in Rome. Thousands of people with suitcases and bags swarm like ants in a nest. The speakers of the central hall make announcements in Italian and English. Danny makes a quick phone call to Hellen.

'I arrived safely. Could you keep Milan and the cops at a distance?' He awkwardly makes his way towards customs. A strict looking man with a thick moustache and eyebrows sits behind the desk in a black-green uniform. He's short, but he still oozes authority because of his uniform and cap. Danny puts his passport on the desk. The man opens the document, scans the information, glances at Danny, checks the passport again, and takes another look at Danny.

'Whate is the purpus of yur visit?' he asks in broken English, with an Italian accent. 'Busnis or 'olidee?'

'Bu.. ehm holiday.' Danny instantly corrects himself. He prepared this trip with Hellen, and all information showed it's better to come to Rome as a holidaymaker than a business man. In that case you'll get fewer questions. The custom's official takes another look at Danny and the passport and eventually gives it a firm stamp.

'Ave a neis stee.'
Danny follows a herd of people to the exit of the airport.

'Taxi!'
He hands the driver a note with the hotel's address on it.
As Danny takes in the city during the drive, he thinks about tomorrow, the day he will go to the Vatican. It's no audience with the Pope, but it's close. Hellen used the university to get approval for Danny to visit the Vatican's library for thirty minutes. That's where Picardt's manuscript is supposed to be. He has an appointment with the library's secretary, monsignor Salvatori. They're all called Salvatori, Ginori, Armani or Albelli in Italy, as long as it ends with an *i*. Danni di Vrisi. Definitely possible.

Normally it's not that easy for a tourist to enter the Vatican, let alone the library. But Hellen did a good job. There was still an open appointment regarding an exchange program between the University of Groningen and the one in Rome. The Italians still owed Groningen, so it was a good deal. Thirty minutes was a compromise however. But Danny knows what to look for, and so does secretary Salvatori, so the visit could possibly contribute to the research. The taxi stops in front of the entrance of the hotel. *Hotel Helini.* Typical.

The following morning, Danny sets foot on St. Peter's Square, as the pigeons fly by him, left and right. He instantly thinks of the legendary words by astronaut Neil Armstrong; *It's a small step for man.* Danny feels insignificant next to the colossal building of St. Peter's Church, which surrounds the square. The columns and statues are overwhelming. So are the people walking around the square, from all walks of life and different nationalities. He checks the letter and invitation from the Vatican to see where he has to be exactly. *Go to the main entrance and follow the signs that say Bibliotheca*, Hellen wrote. It's like a scavenger hunt, Danny thinks. Just have to answer some questions and complete several assignments, he smiles. Upon arrival in the large, central dome, he sees lots of men wearing black and white robes, and some of them purple. Danny is not part of a church, and he's not religious, but this spectacle is impressive. He looks around and lets the large paintings on the walls and the medieval frescoes in the dome impress him. He also recognizes the marvelous works by Leonardo da Vinci. The middle of the hall has signage with indeed *Bibliotheca* on it. It's to the left. He follows the signs that take him through endless hallways, and eventually to where he needs to be.

Upon arrival at a desk he keeps his distance and observes the scene. A dark, heavy oak wood desk with a monitor on top. Behind it stands a young man in a neat suit with a red tie. His hair is cut short and he has a jolly cowlick. A typical model boy picked straight out of a magazine by the Vatican's top dogs. Danny is intrigued as he looks at the boy and tries to find out what's not right about this picture, but he can't find anything. The young man looks up and yells:

'Scusi, forse posso aiutarti con qualcosa?'

Danny doesn't understand the words, but he gets what he means. The boy has a very friendly voice, combined with the Latin singing coming from a nearby building. Danny could listen to this for hours.

'Scusi signore?' the boy asks again.

Danny awakes.

'Sorry, can you help me in English?' he asks politely.

'Of course. What can I do for you?'

'I have an appointment with the librarian, monsignor Salvatori.' Danny hands over the invitation.

'One moment, please. I will notify the monsignor about your arrival.' The young man picks up the phone and starts speaking Italian.

'The monsignor is on his way.'

Danny nods politely and waits patiently.

Several minutes later, a little man comes walking in a hurry. The young man behind the desk points to Danny. The man has a balding forehead and meets the stereotype of a clergymen. Some droplets of sweat dance on his shiny forehead, which he swiftly and skillfully wipes off with a white handkerchief. He has a cord around his neck, with a pair of horn-rim glasses dangling from it. After the dwarf put his handkerchief away, he extends his hand to Danny.

'Mister de Vries?'

'Monsignor. I would like to thank you for this opportunity you're giving me to view the manuscript.' Danny sure knows how to blow smoke up someone's ass.

'You can thank Him.'

'Who?'

The little man looks at Danny in surprise, and starts to laugh after three painful seconds that seem to last hours. Danny doesn't really know how to respond to this at first, but decides to join in with a fake laugh, just to keep the peace. He's surprised about how in god's name it's possible for a dwarf to produce such a roaring laugh.

After opening a number of doors with passes, pin codes and beeps, Danny and the monsignor arrive in the library of all libraries. An enormous space, with dark, oak shelves along the walls of different stories, filled with books, books and more books. There are long tables with reading lamps with faint green-lit lampshades. Several people are sat at the table, reading, browsing or researching. Most of them are dressed in white, black, or purple robes, with one exception. Three tables away from Danny, a man in a regular black suit sits at a table. He sneakily looks up at Danny and then quickly hides behind his book. Danny also notices the silence and the conditioned air with the right humidity and temperature to keep the books in optimal condition.

'Follow me, please. The manuscript is in de P department, right this way.'

'Picardt,' Danny wisely adds. He lets his eyes glide over the shelves that have signs every so many feet; *D...E...* Still a bit of a walk, he thinks.

'We're here,' the monsignor sighs, a bit apologetically. Indeed, above his head, the *P* sign can be seen. He takes his white handkerchief, gives it two good snaps, and wipes the piece of cotton along his forehead.

'I have to work on my stamina,' he laughs. Danny laughs along. The dwarf puts on his horn-rim glasses and runs his fingers along the books. As he does this, he mumbles *PA...PE...*

'PI! Here!' The man victoriously grins and continues. 'Pia... Piblo... Pide... Pide???' His finger glides back along the books. His face is now pressed against the back of the books.

'Pide... Piblo???' The dwarf sounds confused.

'Is something wrong?' Danny asks

'Is something wrong? Is something wrong???' the dwarf repeats, all worked up. 'This is where Picardt's manuscript should be! This is a disaster.' The white handkerchief comes out again.

'Couldn't it be in a different spot? Or that someone already borrowed the manuscript?' Danny tries to put the monsignor's mind at ease.

'Mister de Vries, I know exactly what's where, who has what. I manage the library, I AM the library.'
An invasive 'shh' comes from the area.

'Of course.' Danny looks around, shy and ashamed. He feels the eyes like daggers in his back.
The man wearing the suit looks at him. Is it possible that this guy has the manuscript, and took it right from under his nose? As Danny thinks this, the man gets up from his chair and takes a hesitant step in Danny's direction.

'Momento da prici confermo mama mia...' The monsignor is rambling on in tempered Latin, and wildly gestures. Hail Marys and crosses all over the place. A cardinal with a pink hat rushes to the scene and tells the monsignor to calm down. They whisper some things to each other. This seems to help, because the dwarf takes a step back, looks at the cardinal over his horn-rim glasses in a daze, shrugs his shoulders in defeat and shakes his head. He gestures at Danny to follow him to the gallery, to a couch.

'Mister de Vries, could you wait here for a moment, please?'

'Of course. But, is there something wrong?'

'I don't know. The manuscript isn't where it should be. Mama mia, cara lucifer di domino mi casa.'
That doesn't sound good, Danny thinks.

'Mister de Vries. Please have a seat. I have to speak with someone. I will be right back. I'll have someone bring you a cup of coffee. Espresso?' The monsignor is completely taken aback.

'Espresso.' Danny confirms. 'Thank you.'

The monsignor leaves as quickly as he came, rubbing his forehead with his white handkerchief.

Danny sits down on the couch, but gets right back up, takes his phone and starts calling.

'This is the voicemail of Hellen...' the speaker says.

'Damnit.' Danny tries again.

'This is the voi-'

'Yeah, yeah. Damnit Hellen, pick up!'

A black figure emerges from the other side of the gallery. Fuck, it's that guy in the black suit, Danny thinks. What does this guy want from me? The figure brings a strange rattling along with him. As the figure gets threateningly close, the sound becomes more invasive and louder. Danny anxiously looks around to see whether other people walk around the gallery as well, or if he's all alone. What if they're here to come and get me?, he thinks. They of course want to prevent me from unravelling the secret. Their secret. Or is it someone from secret services who is here to arrest me. Should I walk away now? Or should I resist arrest? If they take me for questioning, I'm not saying a word. My name is Danny de Vries from the Netherlands. The man is now only ten feet away from Danny. The cowlick with the red tie from behind the desk majestically walks behind a silver trolley, the wheels of which rattle on the uneven tile floor.

'Your espresso, sir.'

The young man gracefully takes the cup from the trolley and hands it to Danny.

'Milk? Sugar?' he asks politely, as he refers to two little, silver pots with his hand.

He quickly leaves again and leaves Danny alone with the trolley. With a pounding heart and shaky fingers, Danny follows the boy until he's out of sight. He chugs the coffee in one gulp.

'Wow.' What happened to me, he thinks.

After this coffee break, Danny pulls himself together and in a frantic attempt tries to reach Hellen again.

'HEEEY PUMPKIN!'

'Hellen, listen! Something is going on here.'

'Where is here?' she asks.

'I'm still in the Vatican.'

'Eh? Still? I thought you only had thirty minutes?'

'The manuscript is gone!'

'…'

'Hellen?'

'I'm listening. But what do you mean, gone? Gone, like gone?'

'Yes, it's not where it should be. The monsignor is completely losing it. This isn't good, Hellen!'

'So where could it be?' she asks surprised.

'How do I know? Maybe it's stolen. But I can sense that something is going on here, Hellen. I'm being watched.'

'Huh? By whom?'

'Men in black suits. I don't know who they are.'

'Danny…' Hellen laughs.

'No, really. They're here. I think they snatched the manuscript from under my nose. Or maybe it's the Pope himself.'

'The Pope???' This is getting a bit too much for Hellen.

'Yes. Think about it, Hellen. Who knew I was here to see the manuscript? Who else knows about the secret? The Pope is trying to hinder my research and gave the order to get rid of it. That must be it!'

Danny is all bouncing around.

'… and what now?' Hellen asks with worry in her voice.

'I'm coming back to Groningen. There's nothing left for me to search here.'

Danny puts the phone in his pocket and looks at the Vatican's courtyard from the gallery. Here you are, in Rome, he thinks. You take a whole trip to fucking Italy just to see the fucking manuscript by that fucking Picardt… you get there and it's gone! And it's only about that fucking last page. Why didn't he just put it online?!

22 The blessed key

Danny didn't await the return of the monsignor. He's totally done with it. He walks back to the library's desk and returns his pass. The cowlick with the red tie isn't there. Such a deception, he thinks. Went all the way to fucking Rome for nothing. Going back empty-handed.

'Signore de Vries. Signore de Vries!'

Danny sees two guards of the Vatican in full uniform approach him. The historic uniforms impress him. Danny has no idea what's in store for him this time. Was he right all along? Is he being arrested?

'Are you mister de Vries?' one of the guards asks.

'That's me, yes.

'Would you follow us? This way.'

'Can I ask why?'

'Unfortunately I am unable to say, sir.'

Danny thinks for a second and checks his handless watch.

'Then I am sorry, but I won't come with you. I have to catch my flight.'

Danny turns around to walk away, but the other gatekeeper stands right in front of him and prevents a free passage. Danny frowns.

'Seriously?'

'It's not a request, but an instruction.'

Danny nods and sighs.

'Should I call my lawyer?'

Highly irritated, Danny walks back to the library, in between the two gatekeepers. It feels as if everyone is watching him. Like people are whispering to each other and pointing at him. He drags the wooden cross along and feels it weighing on his shoulders. I'm seriously going to get crucified here in the Vatican of all places, he thinks. The walk seems to last for hours.

One of the guards knocks three times on a large, solid wooden door.

'Entre,' the other side responds.

The heavy door slowly opens, accompanied by lots of cracking and moaning. One of the guards stands in the opening, firmly taps the floor with his staff and makes the announcement.

'Signore de Vries!'

Danny hesitates, but steps into a large area that resembles an office, but with a stylish, classical design. A thick carpet covers the floor, large medieval paintings and a gothic clock cover the walls. What the fuck, Danny thinks, no hands. There's a dark oak desk in the office, the size of a dining table an entire family could dine at. The desk supports a green table lamp and a computer. Behind it sits an old man with a pink robe on a huge, leather swivel chair. A cardinal, Danny thinks. The man gets up, walks over to Danny and extends his hand.

'Mister de Vries. My apologies for all the inconvenience and delay. This is highly unusual.'

'That's an understatement,' Danny grins.

As the cardinal speaks these words, another door opens on the side, with the dwarf rushing out in a hurry, heavily panting.

'Monsignor?' Danny is surprised.

'Forgive me that it took a bit longer. I'm happy I found you. This is unusual.'

'Oh well, I was still hanging about, so.'

'Good.'

The monsignor discreetly addresses the cardinal.

'D'ora in poi prenderò quell folle olandese al guinzaglio, grazi.'

And then addresses Danny.

'May I ask you to follow me?' The dwarf dribbles to an adjacent room. He walks to a glass display case, sticks a key in the lock, turns it around a whopping three times and slowly lifts the lid of the case with a grinding sound. It looks as if the dwarf takes out his handkerchief again, but this time it's white gloves he acrobatically puts on. He cautiously takes a parchment book from the display case. *Korte beschryvinge van eenige vergetene verborgene antiquiteten*. He victoriously shows Danny the book, as if he just won first prize at a major event.

'There. Picardt's manuscript, original, 1670.'
Danny is dumbfounded. He's seen many historic objects, but never an old parchment book. The monsignor continues his apology.

'The reason it wasn't in its right place in the library, is because it is currently being processed for a small revision by the cardinal. I wasn't aware of it.'

'Revision?' It's a strange story to Danny's ears.

'Yes, you see, the back is starting to let loose.'
The monsignor shows the side of the book with his white little gloves. Nothing special can be seen.

'Ah, so it works out in the end,' Danny says, relieved.

'Definitely. This valuable document must be properly preserved.'

'So I can still see the book, which is what I came for,' Danny laughs. The monsignor laughs along with him and shows Danny to a workplace.

'You may take a seat here. No more than thirty minutes,' the monsignor emphasizes as he checks his gold watch.

'And please put on these gloves. You understand.'

'I understand. No problem,' Danny assures him.
It's now or never, Danny thinks. He puts on the white gloves and starts browsing through the manuscript. He already knows what he's looking for. The last page, the addendum. He opens the book towards the end, with his heart pounding. And there it is, right in front of him, the handwritten addendum, the final page in all its glory. Danny can't believe it. The addendum indeed shows some clues regarding Van Gogh's triptych, just like he read in his letters. It says the back of the middle one, *the stoned pile*, holds the key to the clues. The handwritten addendum also describes some other matters. He tries to decipher what Picardt is trying to say with this, but it's more difficult

than he had hoped. They're questions including a referral to a page and line number.

'What the fu...' The cursing out loud startles Danny, as he looks around to make sure no one else is in the room. He then looks at the handless clock.
'How much time do I have left?'
In a crazy hurry, he tries to decipher some of the clues and collects some letters from the referred pages. This is going to take far too long. I won't get this done in time, he feverishly thinks. Why did I even get only thirty minutes? There's no way in hell I can sneak this book home, past security, past the Papal guards. What should I do, Danny thinks. He gets up and paces through the room, with sweat dripping from his forehead. He looks around to see if anyone's around and to make sure there are no cameras around. He then decides to do something that will curse him. Black smoke will ascend from the Vatican's chimney. So much black smoke the entire city of Rome will go on smog code red. Pope Pius X and Pontius Pilate would turn in their graves. Danny stands near the edge of the table where Picardt's book is laid out. The book in which the great secret of the Huns is hermetically hidden. Danny can hear the Vatican's church bells in his head, louder and louder. Now, he thinks. He resolutely rips the final page from the book and puts it in his inner pocket.

'Signore de Vries.'
The dwarf enters the room with big steps.
Danny immediately closes the book and anxiously looks at the librarian.
'Monsignor.' he stammers, as his heart skips a beat.
'Did you find what you're looking for?' the dwarf asks.
'Ehm no, yes.. Ehh, partly.'
The monsignor walks towards the table the book is on and carefully examines it without touching it.

'You see, we don't want to expose the book to daylight too much. The ink is very sensitive to light.' The dwarf suddenly has a very serious look on his face. He annoyingly taps the table with his fingers. He checks his oversized gold watch.

'You have five more minutes. I will go get the Papal guard to get you on your way.'

The dwarf exits the room. Danny blows out all the breath he held during the past minute. He opens the book one last time to get a final impression. As he does this, a little brown tip sticks out the book. He carefully takes it out. It's a brown envelope with a seal of the Vatican on it. Danny can't control his curiosity and opens the envelope. In fucking Italian again, he thinks. He however manages to find out it comes from the Dutch cardinal, addressed to the Pope and... Dated July 20, 1671. Jesus, things shouldn't get much crazier, he thinks. Since he's already going down the criminal path, he decides to put this letter in his inside pocket as well. At that moment, the monsignor and a colorful guard come in.

'Signore de Vries, your time is up.'

'I understand. I know enough for now.' Danny takes off the white gloves and carefully places them on the table. His hands are cold and clammy.

'Good. Then I will show you the way out. Please let me know if you want to research something in the future.'

'I will. Please convey my personal gratitude to His Eminence for his hospitality.' Danny can't believe the words coming from his mouth.

The monsignor shows Danny the door, where the guard walks him to the exit. Danny puts his clammy hand in his inside pocket. During the walk to the exit he anxiously looks around to make sure he doesn't see any men in black suits. I'm not caught, am I?, he thinks. Once he smells the fresh air and feels the sun on his face, his confidence returns. Yes, I did it!

After a tiring trip, Danny is back at the office and calls a number from his phone.

'Hellen. I'm back.'

'...'

'Do you have a moment to come to the office? I will tell you everything.'

Not ten minutes later, she comes flying into the office.

'Danny, I'm so happy to see you. Did you see Picardt's manuscript?'

'Yes. And then some.' He takes the torn-out page from his folder and victoriously shows it to her.

Hellen puts on a pair of red hexagonal reading glasses. Danny looks at the gaudy design in surprise. He wants to say something about it, but wisely keeps his mouth shut. Hellen carefully examines the page and instantly frowns.

'Is this what I think it is?' she asks in total disbelief.

'Yes,' Danny assures her.

'No way?!'

'Yes, really.' Danny sheepishly laughs.

'No fucking way! Danny, did you...'

'Tear it from the manuscript? Yes.'

Hellen stares at Danny with astonishment.

'And this is not all.' Danny takes out the brown envelope and shows her the letter with the Papal seal.

'Danny! You can go to jail for life for this!' Hellen furiously screams.

'Shhh!' Danny urges. 'This is our secret, and... Ehm, I'll take it back one day,' he says without actually meaning it. He then goes on to tell her the entire story, including all details.

'Hellen, you speak Latin right?'

'En pico,' she laughs.

'Try to translate this letter, please. I'm curious.'

Hellen puts on her reading glasses again and mumbles each sentence in Italian.

'Yes, I still don't understand a word of it,' Danny exclaims, visibly irritated.

'Ok, take it easy,' Hellen responds. 'I have to warm up a bit. It's ancient Roman, all right?' She carefully starts translating.

'The cardinal writes he's not happy with Picardt's practices. He has read the book and demonizes Picardt's views and ideas. Practices with witte wieven, giants and his theories about the dolmens. The cardinal believes Picardt should be called to account, and that the book should be burnt. He has summoned his follower, a preacher from the county Bentheim who is responsible for Drenthe. He wants to discuss with him how this mischief can be averted.' Hellen reads on.

Rome, February 8, 1670. It's peacefully quiet in the Vatican's galleries. Nervous footsteps sound from one of the hallways. A door opens and an old man with a red kippah sits on a chair, staring out the window. Alfonso Giovanni is acting cardinal of the Bishopric of Utrecht and resides in Rome, because practicing Catholicism and faith in the Netherlands was prohibited by the States of Utrecht in 1580. When the door of his place opens, the cardinal gets up, turns around and looks into the eyes of a tall, timid man who nervously steps around the marble floor, wearing a black cloak and cape. The cape deadens the daylight and conceals his face.

'Calm down,' the cardinal commands. 'Do they know of your coming?'

'No. I rushed here upon your request.'

'Listen carefully, my dear Marnix. I want to discuss an utmost delicate matter with you, and I need not just your loyalty, but also your discretion.'

'Definitely.' The follower humbly replies.

The cardinal gives him an intrusive look, until he's convinced the follower is being sincere. He walks around his large worktable, opens a drawer, takes a book out and throws it on the table with a dull thump.

'This will kick up some dust!' the cardinal assures him with a powerful voice. The follower coughs and looks at the book in surprise. He doesn't know it. *Korte Beschryvinge van eenige Vergetene en Verborgene Antiquiteten* can be read on the cover.

'A book about antiquities?' the follower asks surprised.

'Antiquities??? God, save me,' the cardinal mocks him, as he looks up and draws a quick cross. 'This is a devilish work! Heresy of our faith, our origin, our history, the norms and values we stand for, what we have built in this fine country. This book describes things that cannot see the light of day, Marnix!' The cardinal emphasizes his name to make sure he is aware of the great severity of this matter.

'Yes, I believe I understand,' the follower stammers.

'You understand nothing yet,' the Cardinal roars.

'Oh no... Sorry.' The follower humbly bows his head.

'If this book is read by the believers, our loyal churchgoers, and... and...' the cardinal starts hyperventilating, '... if they value this and start to preach this book, it will be the end of the Catholic Church and everything He stands for.' The cardinal looks up again, draws another quick cross and continues preaching.

'We have to prevent that! He gave me the assignment to stop this devilish work.'

'How do you want to do that, reverend?'

'That's where you come in, Marnix!' The cardinal places his hand on the narrow shoulder of the skinny man and nods.

'Do you know Johan Picardt? Preacher, as he calls himself, in Drenthe.'
The follower thinks for a bit and then shakes his head.

'Picardt is the creator of this devilish pact... 'Antiquities'... yes, one could call it that, but kitsch.' The cardinal shows a big smile.

'Listen Marnix, what it comes down to is that we have to make sure that these words are not spread. I will ensure this book will disappear, deep in the Vatican's basements, in a very dusty archive.' The cardinal squints his eyes. 'And you, my dear Marnix, you have to make sure Picardt never preaches again. Do you understand?!'

'I believe I understand, Reverend.'

'Do whatever is necessary. I don't want to know the details, just make it stop!'
The follower nods in confirmation, makes a little bow, draws a cross and turns around to face the door.

'Oh... and Marnix... this conversation never took place. You were never here.'

A crow soars through the dark skies of Coevorden en makes a fluttering landing on a branch of a tree. The silence of the evening of May 20, 1670 is disrupted by its screeching. A man in a dark robe pushes the heavy oak door of the Reformed Church open and silently enters. He walks towards the pulpit across the marble floor. As he gets there, he timidly looks around. Once he's certain no one is watching him, he kneels near a marked stone in the floor and wipes the dust off it.

'Hello, my dearest,' he quietly whispers.
The stone is engraved and reads *Rocha Picardt – May 20, 1666.*
The man says a quick prayer and draws a cross. He gets up and wipes a tear off his face.

'I miss you. We'll meet again.'
Once outside, he pulls the cape over his head and follows his own shadow, with the moon behind him.
The last wisps, coming from the oil lamps of thatched farms and sod houses in the landscape, form a beacon for the civilized world, which slowly disappears behind his footsteps. Not until he's out of sight of the civilized world, he lights a torch and calmly carries on along the cart track. Johan Picardt is sixty years old at this point, so walking at a fast pace is no longer an option. During the walk, he thinks back to his youth. How his father, Johan Picardt Sr., destroyed Calvinism as a preacher, in service of the Earl of Bentheim.

He thinks about how he finished his theology studies in 1623 and became a preacher in Egmond aan Zee himself. How he also ran a medical practice and fixed up some commoners every now and then. How he met his love Rocha and how they moved to Drenthe, to that beautiful farm in Lhee. How he upset the believers in Rolde. Picardt laughs about how he fooled the churchgoers with his preaching. He knew better. Everything became clear to him when he researched the history of Drenthe and the North.

'Ha-ha, those fools!'

His own loud laughter startles Picardt. He looks back, because he feels like someone is following him. He scours the dark landscape, but he can't see anything or anyone. Ah, the night, he thinks in disgust. The night like a negro. Picardt knew that his positive views on negroes and slavery weren't appreciated by everyone. Such nonsense. It's even written in the story of Ham. If he had had the chance, he would've also taken one of those black helpers in. Perhaps Rocha would still be alive then. As Picardt ponders, he hears the breaking of a twig behind him. He turns around and uses his torch to illuminate the area.

'Hello? Who's there?'

It remains quiet.

I'm sure I heard something, Picardt thinks. He unsuspectingly continues to walk over the sandy path, while a dark figure follows in his footsteps. Picardt is almost at his destination. Take a right at this old oak tree, then another quarter mile or so and I'm there, he thinks. And that's a good thing, because his legs are starting to resist. He holds the torch in front of him. The sparkly light of the fire reflects against the large, stacked rocks. The dolmen, finally, I made it, Picardt sighs. He takes a lap around it.

About thirty feet away, the dark figure observes how Picardt walks around the dolmen. At least, he sees how the torch moves around the dolmen. What's this Picardt guy doing at this dolmen in the middle of the night, Marnix wonders. Cardinal Alfonso Giovanni's follower has been keeping an eye on Picardt from Coevorden. He makes a plan to silence him, but he has no idea how. His idea is to first observe Picardt's actions in order to determine the right moment. Time and place are important, the follower thinks. I have to find something that puts pressure on Picardt, something to blackmail him with, and use it to force him to cease his devilish preaching. Silence him once and for all. The cardinal will be pleased with me. As the follower daydreams about it all, he sees how the torch disappears between the stones of the dolmen. A faint glow can still be seen between the caverns of the rocks, but this quickly dissipates as well. Darkness completely took control. After a full minute, Marnix grows tired of waiting. Just as he takes a step towards the dolmen, a blue glow emerges from between the rocks; very faint at first, but it grows increasingly brighter, the light is so bright, he's unable to look right at it. He holds his hands in front of his face. After several seconds, it's gone.

He cautiously walks towards the dolmen in a daze, walks around and tries to look inside. It's too dark.

He decides to make his presence known.

   'Hello? Picardt? I'm friendly.'

An icy silence follows.

   'Picardt?'

It stays quiet. The follower lights his torch and walks through the rocks. Nothing.

Nothing???, He thinks, disillusioned. He looks everywhere, but there's no trace of Picardt. He again checks all corners. He then sees Picardt's extinguished torch.

   'Et circumduxit per lumen hyacintho bona tempore,' the cardinal's follower quietly whispers, as he draws a cross.

Danny throws Hellen a questioning look.

   'What does that mean?' he asks.

   'It's difficult to translate,' Hellen answers. 'The cardinal gave his second the order to keep an eye on Picardt. This got out of hand. The mercenary followed Picardt to the dolmen. Picardt disappeared there in the blue.

'In the blue?' Danny asks surprised.

'Yes, that's literally what it says. Also something with time...'

'Time?' Danny doesn't understand any of this.

'Time... getting lost... hm, something else. Because it was known that the church had an aversion against Picardt and it would be inexplicable for him to disappear into nothing, the cardinal ordered his mercenary to kill a random drifter and bury this body as the dead Picardt. So there's someone else in Picardt's grave. The real Picardt was never found.'

'And the pope sealed this secretive act and stored it in the Vatican's basements forever,' Danny adds.

'Yes, until now,' Hellen cautiously concludes her interpretation of the letter. She takes of her red reading glasses.

Danny stares into space, motionlessly.

'Danny?' Hellen sounds worried.

'Yes... I...ehm,' Danny stammers and gets up.

'Hellen, if this is true...'

'Signed by the cardinal...' Hellen confirms again, as she waves the Papal letter.

They look at each other in silence. Danny breaks it.

'There's something else I need to do,' he says.

'Danny, you've gotten into enough trouble. If this sees the light of day, they'll nail you to the cross.'

'No, I have to decipher the puzzle on the last page. I'm going to do that now.'

Hellen checks her watch and sighs.

'It's ten in the evening, Danny, tomorrow's another day. Come, let's go to my place. You need to relax now.' Hellen gently presses her body against Danny's.

'No, I'm going to do this now,' he decisively responds, and pushes Hellen away from him.

'Is there anything I can do to help?'

'Just go home. I'll see you tomorrow.'

Danny gets a cup of coffee and prepares for a long night at the office. He sits behind his desk with a reprint of Picardt's book, the last page and the cardinal's letter, and starts putting the pieces of the puzzle together. He has no idea of what he will discover, but he takes the unexplainable and impossible into account. Once I unravel the mystery, I have to take action, he thinks with determination.

22   On a trip

It's super crowded at the police station in Groningen. An officer in uniform sitting behind a desk is writing up a report from a man whose car was stolen. Two officers enter the station, with a detainee between them. He allegedly committed a robbery. A young cop enters, holding a stack of papers, and walks straight to the desk of detective Sjoerd van Oranje.

'Sjoerd! I have the login information of all security cameras of the university, just like you asked.'

'That's great, dude. Thanks.'

'You and the sack are on that case, right?' the officer asks.

'Correct. But I'll have a look at it first, and I'll discuss it with him if the tapes show something suspicious.'

'Hm, the sack still owes me a bottle of whisky from a bet he lost,' the cop continues.

'Ha, well, you won't ever see that coming your way. Dick really hates losing,' the young detective laughs. 'But eh,... if you don't mind?' He gestures the cop to leave, he turns on his computer and starts typing. The cop moves along and takes out his frustration on his colleagues.

Detective Van Oranje sits behind his computer and looks at all the security camera footage. He and Dick are convinced that Danny has something to do with the death of professor Dijkstra. They're also convinced that it's murder. After all, there are motives, such as the strange substance. All clues for the murder point towards Danny, but they still have to prove it. Now, with access to the different footage from right before and right after the murder, detective Van Oranje hopes to find the missing pieces to the puzzle.

After a number of hours of checking tapes, the young detective's eyes open wide. He found it. The last footage with professor Dijkstra and Danny de Vries on it. He euphorically shuts down his computer and runs to the sack.

Detective Dick van Houten lingers in the courtyard of the station, also called the smoker's den by the people who don't smoke, and lights a fat, Cuban cigar.

'Dick!' Van Oranje euphorically exclaims. I checked the footage from the UMG. Guess what?'

'Bloody?' the old detective puffs, as he blows several clouds of smoke into the air.

'Bloody???' the young detective asks.

'Yes. Bloody surgeries and such...'

'No. The Dijkstra case. Danny de Vries. I think we got something.'

'Think? Think? Sjoerd boy, how many times do I have to tell you? Leave thinking to a horse.'

'We have something. You won't believe it.'

'All right, show me then.'

The old detective gently pushes his Cuban on the ashtray, carefully turns it around and extinguishes it with a sizzling sound, making sure not too much of the valuable product is lost.

'Go!' he waves at Sjoerd.

At the office, both detective sit behind the monitor. The faint light gives their faces a secretive bright blue glow, making it seem they're from another planet. The old detective closely watches the footage. Sjoerd tensely looks at the sack. Both are astonished.

'And?' Sjoerd curiously asks.

'This is bizarre, but it's surely looks like something.' the old detective confirms. 'Ok Sjoerd, get an AT to remain standby. Let's get on De Vries' tail. And his assistant as well!' he nearly yells.

While Sjoerd arranges an AT via his walkie, the two quickly walk to the parking lot and get into a civilian car. The sack struggles to get behind the wheel. Right when both doors close, the tires spin on the asphalt, creating a bunch of smoke. On their way to the university, Sjoerd gets a report from a surveillance car on his walkie that Danny has been spotted there. The civilian car inconspicuously enters the parking lot of the complex, after which the duo take several laps.

'Look, that's De Vries' car,' Sjoerd says.

'Good, then I'll park it a bit farther down and we'll keep an eye on it,' Dick says. He puts the car in reverse and parks it between two other cars.

'Why don't we go straight to him?' Sjoerd asks.

'The legal evidence against De Vries is rather thin. I want to know more about his comings and goings. And those of his assistant.'

'Of course, I understand,' Sjoerd says in a eureka moment. 'The motive! That's what it's about, of course,' he continues. 'But well, it could also have been an accident...'
The old detective looks at him in surprise, shakes his head and sighs.

'This might take a while.' He pushes the window button, causing it to slowly glide down, accompanied by lots of squeaking. A breeze of fresh air blows on the old face. He takes a red tube from his inner pocket and takes out the brown Cuban. He rolls it between his fingers and slowly slides it across his upper lip. The old detective deeply inhales the scent of the fat cigar and intensely enjoys the wonderful aroma. He gets in a comfortable position, cuts a small tip off the cigar, ritually puts it between his lips, takes a lighter from his jacket pocket and lights it near the other end of the cigar. The yellow-blue flame makes the tobacco glow. The sack takes a big drag and inhales.

'Look, there he is!' Sjoerd yells.
It shocks the old detective. He coughs and chokes on his Cuban.

'Damnit Sjoerd!' he fumes. 'Just chill out, man!'

'Yes, but–'
'Yes but, yes but what? I can see him, moron,' the old guy firmly interrupts him. 'There's no reason to panic. He won't just disappear into thin air.' Having said that, he sees Danny's car drive towards the

exit. Detective Van Houten starts the car and races off the parking lot with spinning tires.

'He took a right there,' Sjoerd yells.

'I see him,' the old man confirms.

Right before Dick wants to turn the wheel to the right to chase after Danny, a black SUV shows up from the left and blocks his path.

'God damnit,' the old guy rants as he slams the brakes.

'What is this? Idiot!' Sjoerd flips.

Barely recovered from the shock, a black SUV races by.

The two detectives look at each other in surprise.

'Drive, Dick!' Sjoerd yells.

No need to tell the sack twice.

'Try to see the license plate of that hearse.'

'Yes, just get a bit closer.'

'Even closer? I'll be in his trunk,' the old guy steams.

'Damnit.'

'What?'

'It's a foreign plate.'

'Foreign?' The old guy doesn't understand. 'What are you babbling about?'

'Looks like American plates.'

It's still early and quiet at the university. Danny stands in front of the window of his office and looks outside in silence. He worked all night to try and unravel Picardt's secret. He looks tired and his hair has that out-of-bed look. Hellen enters.

'Good morning,' she carefully says. Danny remains silent.

Hellen sees the chaos of papers and books on the desk.

'Did you work it out?'

Danny turns around to face Hellen and nods in confirmation.

'It's even crazier than I expected.'

Hellen gives Danny a questioning look.

'Hellen, I have to arrange something. Here's the book with the last page, the letter and all my notes. Store it in a safe place!'

'What are you going to do?'

'I'm going to make something right. I don't know when I'll be back.'

'But...' Hellen doesn't get a chance to say her piece. Danny gives her a big kiss on her mouth.

'You've been a great assistant, Hellen. I love you... for who you are,' he casually adds.

'Take good care of yourself.'

He leaves a disconcerted and perplexed Hellen in his office and walks to the parking lot, to his car. He calls Milan from his car.

'Milan, it's Danny. I know everything.'

'...'

'No, listen, I'm on my way to the dolmen now. I'm going back.'

'...'

'You can't stop me, Milan. So long.'

Danny ends the call and is determined to race to the dolmen at full speed. Where it all started, where he hit his head some time ago.

He sees two black SUVs in his rearview mirror. Fuckers, I first have to get rid of them, he thinks. Danny is convinced these are American cops. He's tired of going in circles. After all, he has to move on, he has a mission, he has to get to the dolmen, but without any Yankees tailing him. He makes an unexpected left turn, without yielding, and floors it, right before a pedestrian crossing.

'Idiot!' he hears a pedestrian yell. He sees a man with his fist in the air in the rearview mirror, and the Americans right behind him.

Danny decides to enter a narrow alley, in the hopes the Americans will stop the chase. He takes a sharp right turn and enters the alley. He's too close to the wall, so the right sideview mirror falls off.

'Shit!' Danny yells out loud. Not because of the sideview mirror, but because it's a dead end... Two red-white posts block the end of the alley. He checks his rearview mirror to see if he can reverse.

'Shit, shit, shit!' The bright blue lights of the American car emerge in his mirror. He floors it and hits one of the posts, which flies over the car, into the air. Before Danny even realizes it, he's driving into a pedestrian area and speeds onto a busy church square. Pedestrians jump to the sides in a panic. Danny honks his horn a number of times to warn the unsuspecting people. A little vegetable stall pops up out of nowhere... he can't evade it anymore. Tons of green goods fly all over the place, including apples and tomatoes. The Americans turn these into mush.

Danny exits the church square, but notices his driving skills are starting to show their shortcomings. He also hears sirens, indicating the local cops have entered the Wild West scene. He has to do something to get rid of the Americans. He drives towards a busy crossing, where many people are waiting for the light to turn green. He has a good idea of how to get rid of his attackers. Right before the crossing, he does something that would cause envy among the world's best stunt men. While going fifty miles an hour, he throws the car into neutral and opens the door. He jumps out without thinking. He rolls over a couple of times because of the high speed, but actually manages to get on his feet. Like a chameleon he joins the people who observed the scene with astonishment.

'Would you like to have my hat?' a broad-shouldered, yet perplexed man asks. Danny gives him a friendly nod and puts it on. He pulls the black hat a bit more over his ears and disappears in the crowd, like a ghost. The broad-shouldered man remains behind, with a subtle, little smile.

The Americans were fooled. They're still chasing Danny's empty car to the crossing, where it slows down. The get out and walk towards the empty vehicle with their pistols drawn. In the meantime, notified police cars show up at the scene from two sides. The detectives also join the party. The cops get out without hesitation.

'Stand still and put your hands up,' the officers yell. A between both authorities arises. They point their guns at each other in total confusion. The person they're after is however long gone.

A couple blocks away, Danny walks at a steady pace. He walks around like a ghost, with the collar of his jacket pulled up high and his well-deserved hat far over his ears. Once he's certain he lost his tail, he pulls another stunt. He no longer cares, after everything he's been through. He stands in the middle of the road, brings his hands forward and forces an approaching car to stop.

'Police! Get out! Quickly!' he orders the unsuspecting driver. He shows his ID as if it were a police badge. Danny gets into the car, hits the gas and leaves the driver behind in bewilderment.

After several miles and an impossible drive across narrow forest trails, he reaches his destination. He slams the brakes, creating an enormous cloud of dust that conceals the entire area. As the dust slowly settles, the ancient dolmen emerges. It's exactly the same as it was a number of weeks ago. Exactly the same as five thousand years ago.

Danny looks at it through the windshield of the car for a while. He then hesitantly gets out and beholds the megalithic structure. With some reservation, he walks towards the dolmen. Now or never, he thinks. He believes he sees the shepherd and his flock of sheep in the distance. The shepherd nods at Danny in approval.

'Danny!'

Danny turns around and sees Milan. Fuck, how did he get here so quickly, Danny thinks.

'Don't do it, Danny.'

'I have to, Milan. I have to set some things straight.'

'You can't change history, Danny, you know that. That won't end well.'

As Milan says this, he takes a pistol from his jacket pocket and initially aims it at the ground.

Oh no, not again, Danny thinks. The gun is making him nervous again, but he's determined. Instead of continuing to the dolmen, he walks towards Milan and stops several yards in front of him. He looks Milan straight in the eyes and sighs.

'You're a special man, Milan. I respect you for the way you are.' Danny thinks of what other things he can say to him, and how he will phrase it.

'You've unlocked something in me. Something I can't explain.' Danny walks towards Milan as he says these words, somewhat befuddling him.

'So did you, Danny. I want to remem-'
Milan can't finish his sentence. Completely unexpected, Danny throws his arms around Milan and holds him tight. After several seconds he carefully lets go and glides his hands over Milan's shoulder. A smile appears on Danny's face.

'The future has already changed. I just have to do it.'
Danny turns around and walks towards the dolmen. He turns around again once he's halfway there.

'I'm sure we'll see each other again, Milan,' Danny assures him.
At that moment, the black SUVs appear, approaching with high speeds and kicking up big dust clouds. Two men exit the first vehicle near Milan, wearing dark sunglasses and long, black coats. Milan raises his hand and aims his gun at Danny. His gut tells him not to shoot. How could he ever justify this to himself? The two black suits don't make a move and wait for what's going to happen. During the few seconds that pass, the two detectives enter the site. They see the ominous scene and exit the car with their guns drawn. Everything seems to take place in slow motion. The icy silence of the Drenthe landscape is entirely disrupted when a shot is fired that presses against the walls of the trees like a big bang, from left to right and back again. Black crows flutter into all directions out of fear. A blue glow appears from the caverns of the dolmen.

The ancient oaks filter the bright sunlight. Strange noises fill up the forest. An aardvark, the ones that roamed these woods thousands of years ago, peacefully scavenges between the leaves and the soft moss. The animal leaves his lunch be, lifts its head and looks straight into the eyes of a man that crosses its path out of nowhere. Danny checks his phone. The display reads *Out of Range.* This is no use to me anymore, he thinks, and carelessly throws it over his shoulder. Decisively and combatively he walks into the ancient primeval forest.